RUNAWAY SKIES

Simon Doyle

RUNAWAY SKIES

RUNAWAY BAY BOOK 2

SD Press
A division of Nightsgale Books

1 3 5 7 9 10 8 6 4 2

Copyright © Simon Doyle, 2023

The right of Simon Doyle to be identified as the author of this Work
has been asserted by him in accordance with the Copyright, Designs
and Patents Act 1988

First published in 2023 by
SD Press, a division of Nightsgale Books,
Suite 97320, PO Box 1213, Belfast, BT1 9JY

Paperback ISBN 978 1 7397276 5 9
Hardcover ISBN 978 1 7397276 4 2

Cover by SD Press

A CIP catalogue record of this book
is available from the British Library and the
Library of Trinity College Dublin

Typeset in Caslon Pro by SD Press

For everyone who ever had a secret.

And for all those who were brave enough
to confide in it.

ALSO BY SIMON DOYLE

Runaway Train

1.

KAI

"Terrorist," someone spat.

Kai had been in the airport for less than five minutes when he heard the woman say the word. As a Parisian of Algerian descent, he lowered his gaze and turned away—he'd heard it all before—but she hadn't directed the insult at him. A tall man with a turban and a thick beard was walking by and when the woman called him a terrorist he smiled at her and bowed.

"Praise Jesus," he said in perfect French.

He winked at Kai as he passed.

Kaiser Kateb took a deep breath. Unless you counted his trip to Algeria when he was eight months old, he'd never flown before. His parents took him over to see his grandparents for a week, and though he had no recollection of it, there was a framed photograph hanging on the wall above the kitchen table where he was perched on his grandfather's knee. Kai couldn't tell if the lines on the old man's face were wrinkles or watermarks from a burst pipe that marred the image when he was six.

He'd never seen his grandparents again.

He looked at the ticket on his phone screen. He was booked on the 17:30 from Charles de Gaulle to Dublin and was already running behind schedule. He checked in his luggage and joined the queue that snaked through airport security. The smell of fresh coffee permeated the open area and masked the undertones of greasy fast food. And the queue inched forward.

Today was the start of Kai's new life. He was clawing his way out from under his father's shadow—a carpenter who had been reduced to fitting shelving units in a new shopping mall south of Paris just to make ends meet—and he was on his way to freedom. Trinity College Dublin.

But like any great escape, his journey was marked by fear. He was scared of flying. So terrified, in fact, that he could feel the sweat that bled down his spine beneath a thin cotton T-shirt and his heavy winter jacket because Ireland was always freezing, his mother told him. Not that she'd ever been.

He kept the jacket zipped up because he'd dripped ketchup on his T-shirt in the food court twenty minutes ago. And the straps of his backpack cut into his shoulders with the weight of his life.

He knew he was giving off terrorism vibes, his eyes circled in anxiety and his upper lip slick with sweat where the fine downy hairs of adulthood stained his appearance. And as his body overheated and flushed his cheeks, the dark freckles that blotched his pale brown face shone like a glow-in-the-dark star chart. Don't look nervous, he thought, switching his phone from one hand to the other and wiping his wet palms on his jeans.

Don't look nervous.

"Boarding pass, please."

The woman in front of him ushered her brood of kids forward and handed over their paper tickets. The security officer inspected them, nodded, and pointed at one of the walk-in scanners.

Kai stepped forward.

"You've been selected for a random search. Can you step out of line, please?"

"What've I done?" Kai asked. A bead of sweat rolled off his lashes.

"It's just a random check. We're calling out every tenth person. Step out of line, please."

"This way," another officer said. "Follow me, please."

Kai looked around. The people in the queue behind him had heard the exchange and one of them was counting the heads in front of him, probably to see if he was the next tenth person.

"Please," the officer said again.

Kai followed, his feet shuffling over the cheap grey carpet tiles, head bowed to avoid the attention of the other passengers. It felt like his death march, like they'd accuse him of war crimes, strap him down in an electrified chair, and flick the switch before dinner.

He was led into a small, brightly-lit room with a table and three chairs, none of which looked electrified. "Boarding pass and passport," the man behind the table said.

Kai handed over his phone and his French passport. He'd only had the document for three weeks and it looked pristine and new. "I have an Irish residency card, too," he said, sliding it across the table.

"Sit."

He did.

He couldn't look at either of the two officers directly.

"You've been selected for a random search. This means we have the right to inspect your hand luggage and to search your body. Do you understand?"

"I'm not a terrorist," Kai said. He had visions of being stripped naked and asked to bend over.

"Nobody is accusing you of anything, young man. Please stand on the cross."

Two lines of yellow tape marked the floor. "Raise your arms," the second officer said.

"I'm just a nervous flyer," Kai said. "I mean, I'm not a nervous flyer; I've not flown since I was a baby. But I'm really nervous."

"Unzip your jacket, please."

He felt embarrassed as the man patted him down, large hands gliding over his arms, chest, back and legs. They were hairy hands, he noticed, sharp knuckles coated in black fur, and he wanted them to linger on him.

He blushed.

"Name, please," the first officer said.

"Kai. Kaiser Kateb."

"What is that—Arabic?"

"Algerian. My parents are originally from there. But I'm a French national."

"What is the nature of your flight today?"

"University. I'm going to Dublin. To study."

"Oh, yeah? What are you studying?"

Kai lowered his arms when the officer finished touching him. He wanted to zip his jacket up again, but they hadn't mentioned the ketchup stain on his shirt, and he was glad of the cool breeze from the air conditioning unit.

"Classic Literature. Pre-1900s."

"French universities aren't good enough for you?" the man asked.

Kai's nervousness made his throat close. "I want to experience the world."

The man pulled on a pair of blue latex gloves and laughed. "Place your bag on the table, please. Open the zip. Are there any sharp objects or anything in here that is on this list?" He pointed to a poster on the wall that gave a list of banned substances.

"No, sir." He tried to remember what was in the bag. A clean pair of underwear because Mum had said, "Just in case," and his toiletry bag. A Frank Herbert novel that he'd been reading for six months and still hadn't finished. His laptop and a tablet that he forgot to charge before leaving. And a note from his sister; the last thing she ever wrote.

The officer rooted through the bag as the other man picked up Kai's passport and inspected it. "You look nervous."

"Sorry."

"I mean in the picture."

"I hate having my photo taken."

"Rabbit in the headlights," the man said. "What did you say you were studying?"

"Classic Lit."

"How long will you be in Ireland?"

"It's a three-year course."

"You don't intend to come back for three years?"

"No. I mean, it's a three-year course but I'll be back in December for Christmas break. Probably."

"Probably?"

Kai looked at the clock on the wall. "Depends if I make my flight or not."

"Are you being funny?"

"No, sir."

"What is the address where you are staying in Ireland?"

"It's on the back of my residency card." When he applied to stay at Trinity College Dublin's halls of residence, they told him he was too late. His mum helped him find a family to stay with for the first semester, after which he could reapply for student accommodation.

"Don't you know the address?"

Kai puffed up his cheeks in thought and he could feel the sweat drying on his forehead. "28 Channing Street? Charing Street?"

"Chancel Street," the man said.

"Yeah."

The other officer had finished rooting through his backpack. "How will you be supporting yourself while abroad? Do you have a job?"

"I've been awarded a maintenance grant."

"You have proof of this?"

Kai's eyes widened. He hadn't brought his SUSI letter

indicating his award. "I can show you my bank account? The deposit went in two days ago."

"That won't be necessary. Everything seems in order here. You can continue to your gate. Have a good flight."

Kai could have cried. "So that's that?" he said, glancing at the clock and stuffing his possessions back into his bag.

"Is that not enough?"

One of the officers walked him back down the corridor and let him out into the main concourse where, through the large sheet windows, he saw a plane power its way down the runway and whip into the sky. It seemed to struggle against the wind, its wings tilting before righting itself, and then the plane rose like it was on a collision course with heaven.

He should have taken the Eurostar to London and then a train to the coast where he'd catch a ferry to Ireland. But the cheaper—and faster—option was a direct flight. And as he was packing last night, Mum had said, "Why do you fear flying?"

"I don't. It's the crashing part I don't like."

"You have a better chance of getting hit by a bus while you sleep in a bathtub."

"That doesn't make sense."

"Neither does a fear of flying."

And maybe that did make sense after all, but it didn't stop the anxiety that curled like a fist in his chest at the prospect of strapping himself into a tin can and hurtling through the air at eight hundred kilometres an hour.

He tapped his pockets. Passport, phone, residency card; he still had them. But he checked again two minutes later. Just to make sure.

This morning, when he was getting ready to leave, Mum took a photograph of him standing by his luggage, and Dad shook his hand.

Mum said, "If only Fatima could see you now."

Dad cursed and went back to his chair at the kitchen table. "Why'd you have to say her name?"

Kai said, "I'm going to be late."

Mum hugged him. "She's watching over you from heaven. She'd be so proud of her little brother."

"I'm not little," Kai said. What he didn't add was that Fatima wasn't in heaven.

Mum was one of the very few Christians in Algeria, and when Dad fell in love with her, they fled the country. "Why I had to marry the only Christian girl in a hundred miles, I don't know," he'd say, sliding up behind her at the breakfast table and kissing the back of her neck.

"Because I was the prettiest girl in all the world. You told me so."

"And don't ever forget it."

Kai would pretend to retch but, in truth, theirs was a love he longed to experience. Dad had given up his religion for her, his country. His life.

They moved to Paris and had two children, four years apart. And when Fatima died at the age of seventeen, their parents' relationship fell apart with it. They were still together, still in love as far as Kai could tell, but now they hardly spoke to each other, as though doing so opened fresh wounds every time. And sometimes, in the middle of the night, with car horns and sirens framing the bleakness, he could hear his mum crying and Dad soothing her with whispers.

Fatima, Kai was told, had accidentally fallen into the Seine. Her jacket and one shoe were found, its lace still tied in a double knot, but her body was never recovered.

Kai had to cry like he meant it. Like he was devastated by her loss.

But she hadn't accidentally fallen into the river. And he was the only one who knew the truth.

2.
CALEB

Caleb Burke's heart wasn't beating. It hadn't been for four years, but that didn't stop him from enjoying life.

Sitting in the hospital waiting room, he stared at the noticeboard where a poster said, *Have a heart! (Or a lung. Or a kidney.) Join the donor register today*, and he wondered if it was possible to donate a donated organ. He'd have to ask Dr Hughes.

"Stop jiggling your leg," Mum said. She came to all his hospital appointments like he was a five-year-old who couldn't cross the street on his own.

"Stop biting your nails," he countered.

He remembered the first time he sat here, four years ago, waiting for his name to be called and feeling a pain in his chest where the donated heart felt like it didn't belong. And even though it had been in there for five months, doing its thing, the scar on his chest still looked raw and angry.

"We'll increase your immunosuppressants," Dr Hughes had said. "The heart is doing well. There's no cause for alarm."

"But what about the other thing?" Caleb asked. At sixteen, he already had a flair for the dramatics. "The thoughts and the anger."

"Are you having some negative thoughts?"

"It's like I'm being taken over, Doc. By this rage inside me that isn't mine. I feel torn. Part of me wants to shut down and go into hiding. But part of me wants to lash out. Is that normal?"

"You've been through an ordeal, Caleb. It's okay to feel irrational at times."

"But it's not that, Doc. It's like this heart, this thing beating inside me, it wants me to do things." He lowered his voice, finding it hard to hide the smirk from his face. "I hear it calling to me at night. Whispering. It wants me to kill people."

"You're telling me the donor heart is turning you into a serial killer?"

"Can I use that as a defence in court? It wasn't me; it was my heart."

Dr Hughes turned to his desk, adjusting the glasses over his nose. "This is very serious. I'm going to have to prescribe a new course of tablets, Caleb." He scribbled on a piece of paper, folded it, and pressed it into Caleb's hand. "You come right back and see me if you experience any side effects, won't you?"

"Yes, Doc." He unfolded the paper on his way through the door. *Take one funny pill twice daily.*

Four years later and neither his heart nor his humour had

been rejected.

Mum put her hand on his knee to stop him from jiggling it. He had a build-up of nervous energy and most of the time he didn't even realise he was doing it. Next week, he was starting a new training course, and the days were ticking by so slowly that he felt mired in quicksand, watching the minutes eke out every last drop of sunlight from the day. Patience was not one of his virtues.

"Caleb Burke," a nurse called.

Mum stood but Caleb told her to sit. "You can hold my hand while we cross the road, but you gotta let me do some things on my own." He went into Dr Hughes' office and closed the door. Twenty-year-olds do not need their mummy. At least not all the time.

"Murdered anyone yet?" Dr Hughes asked.

"If I told you, I'd have to kill you."

"You're going to need a bigger patio."

They discussed his life since his last visit a few months ago. Four and a half years after the transplant, Dr Hughes was more concerned with Caleb's social life than he was with the function of the heart, but Caleb knew it was all just small talk while he ran his tests.

As he took off his shirt, he said, "I'm thinking of getting a tattoo."

"Your scar is beautiful, Caleb. You don't need to cover it up."

"It's not about covering it up, it's about owning it. I think I'll get a tattoo like an x-ray, showing my ribs and lungs, and a black empty hole where my heart should be."

"I hope you're joking."

"Kind of."

Dr Hughes attached half a dozen electrodes to his chest, side and back, and Caleb started a walking pace on the treadmill in the corner.

After a minute, Hughes said, "Step it up, please."

Caleb tapped the screen on the treadmill to increase the speed. In two minutes, he was jogging. He watched his heart rate spike across the doctor's monitor.

"How's she looking, Doc?"

They hadn't told him who his donor was, so when he lay in the hospital during his recovery after surgery, he'd made up a profile. It had belonged, he decided, to a girl called Alice who would be around his age. She would have died in a car crash. Her boyfriend was going to propose to her that evening, and as their car tumbled off the road, in her dying breath, she said, "Yes."

"You have the heart of a girl," he told his reflection in the hospital room's mirror that day. His stitches itched like the needles of a cactus, and he told himself this was why he liked boys. Because his heart belonged to a girl. It was a ruse, of course. He'd liked boys since he was nine and wanted to kiss Johnny Appleby behind the school gym. But now he had an excuse.

"Step it up," Dr Hughes said.

Caleb was running now, clinging to the treadmill's handlebar and feeling his chest burn.

Hughes watched his monitor for a minute before saying, "And stop." He typed some notes.

When he caught his breath and Hughes removed the electrodes, he asked him to stand on the weighing scales and then take a seat.

The scar on his chest was white where the skin had grafted shut, and it ran in a jagged line from his collarbone to below the base of his sternum. Dr Hughes had called it beautiful, but Caleb thought of it as beautifully ugly.

Hughes took two vials of blood from his arm. "You haven't taken up any new sports? No scuba diving or hang gliding?"

"Not this week, Doc. I start my flight training next week, though. Soaring through the skies, not a care in the world."

"You're going to run out of steam one of these days."

"No chance. I've got my energy as well as Alice's."

Dr Hughes' finger was cold when he tapped Caleb's chest. "Don't come crying to me if Alice ends your relationship."

Hughes had already cleared him for training. "Just keep it under Mach one, okay?"

For the last four years, Caleb had done everything he could to prove that being a heart transplant recipient would not degrade his lifestyle. Before the operation, he'd been an athlete. He played football and basketball, and he was on the track team, too. His bedroom was filled with old Sports Day medals. The excess energy his body contained needed many outlets.

That was how they'd discovered his hypertrophic cardiomyopathy. His heart was getting thicker and couldn't pump his blood fast enough. He'd collapsed on the football pitch right before taking a shot at the goal.

He'd been on the recipient list for less than a month when a match was found. Dad called it a miracle. Mum wept for six days without taking a breath. And Caleb's younger brother, who'd been six at the time, said, "If Caleb takes his heart out, will he forget how to love me?"

That made Mum cry even harder. And they were all there in his hospital room when he woke up. Charlie was sitting on the edge of the bed and when Caleb opened his eyes, he held out a small hand that gripped a superhero action figure, and he'd said, "You can keep this if you still love me."

Caleb had been too weak to make fun of his little brother. He took the figurine and smiled.

"Mum's taking on some foreign exchange student or something," he told Dr Hughes now. "He arrives tonight, and she still hasn't cleared out the spare room for him."

"Didn't she do the same thing last year?"

"Yeah. And Yang Xui took my room while I had to bunk in with Charlie for a week. That was not a pretty week. Boys stink."

"I'm sure you didn't smell any better at his age." Dr Hughes took his stethoscope and held it against Caleb's back. "Breathe in, please. And out. Any new symptoms? Any pain or discomfort?"

"My left hand was tingling the other day, but I probably just slept on it funny, or something."

"Deep breath. It's not tingling anymore?"

"No. It was only for half an hour or so."

"And breathe out. Let's keep an eye on it, but I don't think it's cause for concern. How's your breathing? Any problems?"

"Do you think my HCM is coming back?"

"Stop jumping to conclusions, Caleb."

For weeks before he collapsed on the football pitch, he'd been getting a shortness of breath. Running suicide laps across the pitch was always strenuous, but he'd been doing fewer laps and feeling the burn a lot quicker. And once, in the privacy of his own room, doing that thing that boys do, he couldn't catch his breath after he'd spent himself. He panicked, afraid he'd have to call out for his parents, and he cleaned himself up even as he struggled to breathe.

"My breathing has been fine. I could run a marathon and still feel good."

"I'm surprised you haven't tried that already."

"It's on my bucket list."

"I don't know where you get your energy from."

"I told you," Caleb said, tapping his chest before putting his shirt back on. "It's from Alice."

"Alice is a bad influence," Dr Hughes said.

He gave Caleb a clean bill of health and, as he showed him out of the office, he shook Mrs Burke's hand. "Your son's like an ox. Just make sure he slows down once in a while. He'll run out of new activities to try at this rate."

On the way home, they stopped for ice cream. It had become a tradition that Caleb let her keep. Sometimes she treated him like a little kid, and other times she spoke to him like they were confidantes. When Dad moved out two years ago, Caleb figured it was his fault, but Mum bought him a bottle of prosecco on his eighteenth birthday—as if that was the first time he'd ever had a drink—and after two glasses, she huddled into him on the sofa and said, "I don't think he ever truly loved me. There was always another woman."

"Even when I was sick?"

"For months he stayed at your side, watching over you. But I guess the pull of adventure was too strong. Don't you ever do that, okay? Don't leave a string of broken hearts behind you. You're a better man than your father. Find the right boy and stick with him not because you need to but because you want to."

They'd never discussed his sexuality before. "Find the right boy?" he asked, sliding his prosecco glass closer.

"Am I wrong?"

"No."

"Okay, then."

"Well. That was easy." As far as coming out went, he couldn't have imagined it going any better. And then Mum cried against his shoulder for the rest of the night and Caleb prised the glass out of her hand. "That's enough booze for you."

She slapped his leg. "I'm not drunk, I'm emotional."

"Is there a difference?"

"Happy birthday," she said.

When they'd finished their ice cream, Mum wanted to stop off at the market and pick up some French baguettes to help the foreign student feel at home.

"You know we're not living in a nineteen-sixties *Carry On* film, right? Why don't we get a string of garlic to drape around his neck and wear berets while we're at it?"

"And a carton of those peach yoghurts your brother likes," Mum said, her mind already on other things.

When they got home, Charlie was in the lounge, screaming into his headset as a team of animated soldiers spread out across the TV screen. He pulled the earpiece aside when Caleb came in and said, "All good?" He'd turned eleven last week and was about to start secondary school.

Caleb slapped the back of his head. "On your right, dipshit."

Charlie turned back to his game just as a zombie chomped down on his character's face.

Caleb could hear his friends screaming through the headset.

Upstairs, he looked into the spare room that Dad had used as a home office before he moved out. Mum put a bed in it a week after he left, but because it wasn't in use, it had become a junk room, stacked high with boxes and old toys that Charlie had outgrown. When Yang Xui stayed with them last year, she was there for only one semester. For a week, she slept in Caleb's room and he'd been forced in with Charlie. He spent every evening in the spare room, digging through stacks of boxes to help create some semblance of order in there so that Xui could move in and he'd get his room back.

When she moved into halls of residence in time for the new semester, Mum said, "Never again," even as she stacked new boxes into the room.

And now here they were, knee-deep in organised chaos because Mum worked full time, and no one had the energy to sort the room out before their new guest arrived.

"Damn it," Mum said from behind him. "He'll have to sleep in your room until we get this mess sorted."

"He'd better not smell," Caleb said. "Oh, and Mum?"

"Yeah?"

"Don't tell him about my scar, okay?"

3.

KAI

He was almost positive he wasn't having a panic attack. He'd had one of those the night Fatima disappeared, and this felt different. This was further down in his chest than the ball of fear had been that night.

Kai's vision tunnelled up the steps towards the plane, where a flight attendant beckoned him like a siren. He put a foot on the metal casing and felt the steps shudder, and he gripped the railing as he climbed. A crosswind rattled through his hair.

The attendant checked his boarding pass and pointed down the plane as if he had any other way to go. Like maybe they would confuse him for the pilot. He felt the sweat on the back of his neck being chilled by an overhead breeze that unnerved him as he shuffled along the narrow aisle.

"*Pardon. Excusez-moi.*"

A baby was crying somewhere further back and a short woman was swearing as she tried to hoist her suitcase into the overhead locker above her. He smiled and nudged it into place for her. Somebody was talking through the speakers, and no one was paying any attention.

Kai found 14B and buckled his seatbelt, glad of the security, but had to unlatch it to stand up and let a woman into 14A. She smiled and apologised in French, but her accent was foreign.

He adjusted his belt again and made sure it was snug. He took a breath, staring through the window beyond the woman's face, watching more passengers queue up the steps from the concourse to the plane.

It was packed. And warm. And he had no elbow room. And the air from the nozzle above his head was like a dead man's breath.

The dull hum that resounded through the cabin was incessant, and all other sounds were muffled because of it. He gripped his paperback, but he was sure he wouldn't be able to concentrate on reading during the flight.

"Ladies and gentlemen," a soothing voice issued from the speakers. "I'd like to welcome you onboard this Airbus A320 direct flight to Dublin Airport, arriving at 18:10 local time. We will be taking off shortly and I'd like to advise all passengers to ensure their luggage is stowed securely in the overhead lockers or beneath the seat in front of you. For your safety and security, please pay attention to the following in-flight safety briefing."

Kai watched the flight attendants as they demonstrated how to fasten and unfasten his seatbelt, and what would happen in the event of a loss in cabin pressure. He looked over his shoulder when advised to check if his nearest exit was behind him, and he discovered that nobody else was watching the attendants. The woman beside him was typing on her phone, and the man who took the seat at his other side had his eyes closed and his hands clasped loosely in his lap as though he was already asleep.

The baby behind him continued to cry and Kai knew how it felt.

The engines whined to life. "Shit," he whispered and gripped the armrests with tight fists.

The plane didn't explode.

It backed away from the building and turned, and Kai watched as the world disappeared outside.

It was an eternity as they manoeuvred into place before they charged down the runway. Kai held his breath. He felt the blood sink from his face into his feet. He didn't know if closing his eyes would make it any better, but when he did, he felt dizzy. He opened them again just as the nose of the plane tilted towards the heavens. His stomach lurched like it wanted to stay on the ground without him, and the back of his head hit the headrest. He kept it there until the plane levelled out above an ocean of white clouds. The knot in his chest burned hotter than it had done the night Fatima went missing.

They'd argued that night before she left the house, and the slam of the front door echoed in his head still. He'd called her stupid. Said she didn't know what she was doing.

She was drunk.

She had knotted her wild curls at the base of her neck and flipped the coat's hood up over her head, and then she was gone.

"I'll call you later. When you've calmed down," she'd said,

with a flatness in her voice that matched the tired look in her hollow eyes. He went to the window and watched as she ran down the street.

He was thirteen. And that was the last time he'd seen her.

He told his mum he wasn't feeling well and curled under a blanket on the couch beside her. She felt his forehead and then rubbed his feet as they watched TV.

Mum made him hot chocolate and tucked the blanket around him, and dad sat at the kitchen table, sanding down a piece of wood that was destined to become a clock or a table leg or a joist for something bigger. It didn't matter. Three hours later, the wood would be forgotten about.

He had fallen asleep to the soft sounds of sandpaper, and he woke when Mum nudged him, sweat flattening his hair to the side of his head, and his eyes went wide when he saw Mum's face.

"Check your phone. Have you heard from Fatima?"

Kai reached for his phone but there'd been no calls or messages.

"It's almost midnight. Where could she be?"

He shrugged because his voice wouldn't work. The panic was already itching across his chest and into his throat.

He sent her a text. *Come home, Tima. Mum's frantic.*

But she didn't respond. She hated when he called her Tima, anyway.

At twelve-thirty, Dad called Zameer, Fatima's fiancé. It had been arranged before she was thirteen by their grandparents. Dad apologised for the late call, but Zameer hadn't heard from her. Born in Paris but from a strict Muslim family, he offered to check the local bars and parks.

Dad said, "Fatima is a good girl. She would not go to the bars alone." He hung up the phone and reached for his overcoat. "Come, Kaiser. We will find her." He kissed his wife and went outside.

Kai sat in the backseat of the car with a padded coat zipped up to the neck as the heaters tried to warm the space, and he watched the rain lash against the windows as the wipers pumped on full power. The headlights cut through the night like lasers.

He didn't even know when the storm had rolled in.

"She'll get herself killed," Dad said, turning the car at a dead end to go back the way he came.

The plane banked to the left and Kai opened his eyes.

He hadn't realised he'd been grinding his teeth and now he loosened his mouth, flexing his jaw muscles and twisting his neck to ease the tension. There'd been no meal option for the flight on the booking website, not that he thought he'd be able to eat anyway, but his stomach rumbled. The woman beside him was eating a chocolate bar that she'd brought with her and the man at his other side was still asleep.

Kai checked his watch. They'd only been in the air for fifteen minutes. But so far, the plane was still in one piece, so that was a good sign. He glanced out of the window and saw nothing. Everything was grey. They could have been flying upside down and he wouldn't know it.

The plane shook.

Kai put his hands on the back of the chair in front of him as the seatbelt lights came on. On the monitors, they were still over northern France. His ears had swollen shut with the lack of pressure and he didn't know how to pop them. And the plane lurched again. One of the overhead lockers popped open and a flight attendant was quick to close it.

"Seatbelts, please," she said.

Kai checked his belt. He hadn't opened it, but he tightened it just the same.

The baby in the back was screaming now.

Outside the plane, the world had disappeared. He tried to take a breath, but it caught in his throat and there was a fuzz of pinkness around the edges of his vision as it darkened. The plane shuddered and it felt like they dropped a few feet before levelling out. He could almost feel his feet rising off the floor for a second as though they were weightless.

And Kai felt a hand on his arm.

"First time flying?" The woman spoke in English and her voice was soft and controlled.

He nodded. And the plane walls rattled.

"You're doing fine. It's just a bit of turbulence. It'll be over in a minute."

He hoped the face he made resembled something like a smile and not a baby evacuating its bowels.

She nodded at the man in the aisle seat. "I wish I could sleep like that."

When she took her hand off his arm, Kai felt the fear flood back in, but given how rational she sounded, he wanted to believe that whatever was making the plane judder would really be over in a minute like she'd said. He jiggled his finger at his ears. He could hear very little.

"Yawn," she told him. "It'll help pop your ears." She demonstrated and, because yawning was contagious, he copied her.

His left ear popped before the right one, and there was a sudden rush of loud air that flooded through his brain.

He smiled again.

And in a few minutes, the plane settled down and the seatbelt lights went out.

The woman didn't say anything else. He was glad that she'd been there to soothe him before he went into a blind panic, but he was happy when she returned her attention to the magazine she'd been leafing through. Smalltalk with strangers was one of those social norms he didn't like.

Fatima had been the sociable one. When he was a little kid, she used to dress him up in their mother's clothes and walk him down the street to her friend's house where they'd play Hide and Seek. Kai would stumble around the house in a pair of oversized heels, tripping over Mum's dress in a desperate bid to find his sister last. And when he found her under the kitchen table or tucked into a closet, she'd hold her finger to her lips, and he'd move on in search of the others. Nobody ever questioned why she was so good at hiding.

The night she disappeared, Kai thought of it as a giant game of Hide and Seek. He knew where she'd gone and who she was with, but it was up to Dad to find her before she went too far.

Ready or not.

Avery Truffaut lived four blocks from theirs, but she was never at home and Kai wasn't sure if Mum and Dad knew she even existed. Fatima had become distant over the last few months. And he only knew she'd been out because she'd climbed up to the garage roof and in through Kai's bedroom window. He wasn't sure how to tell Dad about Avery, so he kept quiet as the wiper blades fought against the rain outside.

"Where have you been?" he'd asked her once when she'd slipped in through his window and woke him as she tripped over a tennis racquet. Her clothes were wet, her hair was knotted, and she had the dark remnants of black lipstick at the corner of her mouth and the faint scent of a perfume he didn't recognise.

"Not now, Kai. I'm tired."

He stood in front of his bedroom door. "Tell me where you were, or I'll tell Mum."

"I was with Avery Truffaut."

"Who's that?"

"She's my girlfriend."

"Girlfriend?"

"You wouldn't understand."

But he was twelve at the time. Of course he understood. He opened the bedroom door and looked across the corridor before letting her out.

Fatima kissed his cheek and winked, just like the night she disappeared. Even though they'd argued, she still kissed him and winked. She'd ruffled his hair and said she'd call him later. And then she was gone.

In the back of Dad's car, Kai typed another text to her. *Where are you? Dad's mad and Mum's going mental.* The delivery notification spun in a circle before telling him it had failed.

They drove across the Seine and back, along eight different bridges, and then Dad sighed and turned the car for home.

And as they drove up the street, two Police Nationale cars were parked outside their house and their blue lights swirled a thick panic in the air.

Even the neighbours had come out to see what was going on.

4.

CALEB

C aleb put the lid back on a box and shoved it aside. He'd promised his mum that he'd help move some of the junk from the spare room but looking at the stacks of boxes and papers made his eyes bleed. "We'll never get this cleared in time," he said, feeling his phone vibrate in his jeans pocket.

Charlie said, "It's not my loss. You're the one that will have to share. Mum's not going to put an adult in with me."

"She could force me in beside you and let this bloody French guy have my room by himself." He checked his messages. It was from the hospital. *Jayne's feeling under the weather today. Any chance you can be here?*

"Not after last time," Charlie said. "You farted every night and stank my room out."

"I have to go. Look. I'll give you ten Euros if you clear some of this stuff. Just stack it in the garage, okay?"

Charlie scoffed. "Ten? Wow, I'll be super rich."

"Don't be a dick, Charlie. I've got to go and see Jayne."

"Make it twenty."

"I don't have time for this. Fine. Twenty." He pulled a crumpled banknote from his pocket and waved it in front of Charlie's face. "But there needs to be a clear path to the bed by the time Mum gets home. Deal?"

Charlie snatched the money. "Fine."

Caleb rolled his moped out of the garage and keyed the ignition. It was a 50cc model with a top speed of fifty kilometres per hour, but Mum refused to let him get anything bigger. She begged him to get a car instead, but he liked the freedom of zipping around town on the moped. And as long as he lived under her roof, she said, her word was gospel.

By the time he got to the hospital, a wall of leaden rainclouds had amassed over the city, and he made a dash for the building with his helmet on. The security guard inside made him take it off when he went in, and Caleb said, "Don't you have a home to go to, Darren?"

"Fourteen-hour shifts," the guard said. "I practically live here."

"I know the feeling." He took the stairs to the third floor and as he entered the transplant unit, Abigail, the ward manager, offered her fist to him.

He bumped it.

"She's not too bad right now, but she was vomiting a lot earlier."

"Is she awake?" Caleb asked.

"Go on in. Steve's in there with her."

He entered Jayne's room just as Steve was pinning another badge to her baseball cap. He adjusted the pillows behind her and nodded at Caleb before leaving. Steve was the resident shrink whose sole responsibility was to keep the kids smiling. He had a knack for pulling funny faces at the worst possible times.

"I hear you've been making a nuisance of yourself," Caleb said. He hopped onto the edge of Jayne's bed.

She was thirteen and had been on the transplant list for four months. They'd had a hopeful donor come in last month, but it turned out the heart wasn't viable, and Jayne's spirits degraded along with the organ.

"I was just throwing a fit so you would have to come and play with me," she smiled.

She had congenital heart disease that couldn't be fixed with reparative surgery, and Caleb had never seen her looking so grey. Since his own successful transplant, he'd been volunteering at the unit as often as he could. It was his way of giving back what he owed to the staff here at the Dedicated Transplant Centre at St. Aloysius' Hospital.

He nudged the blanket where her knee was. "What does your new badge say?"

Jayne took her cap off and handed it to him. Her hair was lank and thin and looked as ashen as her face.

The front of the cap was crowded with buttons and badges filled with funny slogans or silly pictures. The one that Steve pinned there this evening read, *I'm not lazy. I'm in energy-saving mode.*

With the right level of humour, there is no joke off limits, even for a child.

Jayne coughed and rubbed her chest. "You should take me dancing."

"You should have a brain transplant instead of a heart. I can't dance for toffee."

"So, get a foot transplant. Then you can take me to my prom."

"You've been watching too many teen movies."

Jayne coughed again and it took her a minute to catch her breath. When he first met her, she'd looked ill but vibrant. She was a girl with her path marked out, and a vision of the future. But as the weeks rolled into months and they still hadn't found a donor, her mind became as fragile as her body.

"I'm going to die," she told him once. She could barely lift her head off the pillows that day.

"No, you're not," he'd said. But he couldn't make it a promise. He was grateful every day for being so lucky. He knew not everyone had that chance.

Now, Jayne said, "You'll have to learn the Waltz. That's all. And maybe the tango."

"You're thirteen, Jayne. You're years away from thinking about prom."

"It's never too early to be prepared. Besides, one day you're going to meet somebody and forget all about me."

"Never."

"Anyway, how's Alice?"

Caleb tapped his heart. "Ticking away just nicely."

"And how many tablets do you have to take a day? I forget."

She asked him this every time as if the number of immunosuppressants he needed would change overnight. "As well as the standard dozen, there's three pink ones, a green-and-white one, and a blue one the size of a horse tranquiliser." The idea of having to take a series of pills every day for the rest of his life—or his new heart could be rejected—had been a daunting prospect at the time, but it became second nature to him. Even so, he often had to think about whether he took them that day or not. He never wanted to feel like an old man, but he'd been given a dosette box that was labelled with each day of the week, and it really helped.

"Not long now," he said, "and we can be pill buddies."

"Promise?"

Caleb smiled. He was always careful not to fall into these traps with the other patients. "I promise that when you're taking immunosuppressants, I'll be calling you up every morning so we can take them at the same time." He skipped over the fact that that promise was dependent on her successful transplant surgery first. He'd already been heartbroken last year when James Tanner passed away before getting his new heart. James' mother had hugged Caleb so tight that he could still remember the feel of her arms around his neck. A picture of the nine-year-old hung on the wall behind reception, along with all the other kids they'd lost over the years. It was a memorial that Caleb found hard to look at. He preferred the opposite wall. The one with the success pictures.

He fetched a wheelchair from reception and helped Jayne into it, attaching her drip to the upright pole. He didn't really know where he was taking her, but he always felt better when he was on the move rather than being stuck in a hospital bed, and Jayne loved the attention from the other patients and their families as he wheeled her around.

"What happens if I wake up during surgery?" she asked him.

"You won't."

"But what if I do?"

"You mean, what if you wake up after they've removed your heart but before they put the new one in?"

"Like a zombie," she said.

"It's a good job zombies only eat brains and not hearts because you'd probably rip the new heart out of the surgeon's hands and stuff it in your mouth."

"What if I eat the doctor's brains and he can't perform the surgery anymore?"

Caleb wheeled her into the family room where there was a wall of vending machines. She had a love for chocolate M&Ms that outweighed a zombie's love for brains.

"They always have a spare surgeon, but I think that's a risk you're just going to have to take."

"What if they do the surgery and leave a scalpel inside me?"

"Why do none of your what-if scenarios ever have a happy ending?"

"Because happy endings are for fairy tales," Jayne said.

Caleb paid for the M&Ms and watched as they spat into the tray at the bottom of the vending machine. He tore the packet open and handed them over, then sat on a chair opposite her. "Happy endings are for everyone, Jayne. There's a Prince Charming out there for all of us."

"Even you?"

"Especially me."

"With that face, he'd have to be blind," she said, stuffing a fistful of candy into her mouth to hide her grin.

Caleb snatched the packet from her and said, "No more of these until you can be nice. Besides, he can be blind as long as he's attractive."

He wheeled her back to her room.

"I hope you're feeling better now."

"Don't forget to come back soon," she said.

"I'll come by at the weekend and then I've got flight training."

"Will you take me up in a plane one day?"

"If you promise not to throw up all over the place."

"I promise."

Caleb bumped his forehead against hers after he'd helped her into bed. "Be good."

"Be evil," she said.

And he rode home. His visit didn't feel like much, but sometimes just being there was enough for the patients. And the kids always took to him quite well, much more so than the adults—some of them could be as grumpy as sin.

He knew not to think about Jayne's future—not after losing James Tanner last year—and he tried not to think about his own future, either. Next week was as far as he could see. Beyond that, his life—or death—was anyone's guess.

When he pulled his moped into the garage, Mum's car was parked outside. That meant the French kid was here. He knew his mum needed the extra help that the student's accommodation fees brought in, but he'd had a hard time letting Yang Xui into his life last year and putting up with her hogging the bathroom in the mornings. The new student's English was probably as bad as Xui's had been and they'd have nothing in common. Caleb had little in common with anyone. He'd never been to France, and the extent of his interest in French things was a love of Jean Reno from the *Léon* movie. He was one of those old guys whose arms would likely feel comforting around you.

The new kid would be in the spare room, and they wouldn't have to speak much during the semester until he moved out.

Caleb opened the connecting door from the garage to the kitchen and found Mum staring into the fridge like it held the answers to the universe.

"Earth to Mum."

"We should go out for dinner."

"Are you asking me out on a date? Because that's sick."

She kissed his cheek. "Go in and say hello to Kaiser. Charlie's got him playing his games."

"I'm sure Charlie's got it covered."

"Tell them to be ready in five minutes; we're going to eat out."

He pulled a bottle of water from the fridge and unscrewed the lid as he walked into the living room.

"Get him, get him," Charlie was screaming, and the new guy was pounding on the controller from the couch in front of the TV.

Behind them, Caleb said, "All right? Mum says we're going out for dinner."

Kaiser paused the game and turned his head, a wide smile showing his teeth.

And Caleb felt his cheeks flush. Kaiser's skin was the colour of stained teak, and even in the soft glow from the table lamp, Caleb could see the dark rash of freckles that blotched his cheeks like an artist had flicked a paintbrush around in a frenzied attack.

But mostly, all he could see were those amber eyes, almost yellow, that stared at him with a frank earnestness that he didn't know how to take. It was probably a trick of the light, but they glowed brighter than the lamp.

"Hi," the young man said, and Caleb had already forgotten his own name.

"There's that new restaurant on Heaney Avenue," Mum said from the doorway, and she broke the hold Kaiser's gaze had over him.

Caleb held out his hand. "Nice to meet you."

Charlie said, "Kai found the golden sickle in the third dungeon and now he's a level four mage."

"Kai?"

"Kaiser," the guy said as he stood up. "Everyone calls me Kai."

As they got in the car, Caleb was annoyed that Charlie hadn't called shotgun like he normally would. Caleb had to sit in the front while his little brother jumped in the back beside Kai. But at least at the restaurant, they were sitting opposite each other. Not that Caleb could bring himself to look into those amber eyes for long.

Kai's smile was infectious, and when he looked around the restaurant, Caleb took the opportunity to check out his face, his thin neck that was swallowed by an oversized T-shirt with the picture of a band on it that Caleb didn't recognise. He saw how slender Kai's arms appeared and how long his fingers were as they gripped his steak knife. Red meat was usually off the menu for Caleb, given the tenuous connection he had to his heart, but tonight he'd happily feast on all the meat if Kai was feeding it to him.

"Caleb," Mum said, snapping him from his thoughts. "Kaiser asked you a question."

Caleb blushed.

"You don't go to university?" Kai asked.

"No, I start flight school next week."

"What is flight school?"

"I'm learning to fly a light aircraft."

"You are not afraid of dying?"

Caleb narrowed his eyes. "I'm always afraid of dying."

"I don't understand," Kai said.

Caleb twisted some more alfredo onto his fork. "Just because you fear death, doesn't mean you have to run from it."

When Mum paid the bill, Charlie whispered something to Kai, and as they walked through the door towards the car, Kai said, "Shotgun?"

Charlie laughed.

In the back seat, Caleb made sure he was sitting behind the driver's seat so that he could stare at Kai's profile in the passenger side. And Charlie was regaling them about some game he'd been begging Mum to buy all week.

As they pulled into the driveway, Charlie reached into his pocket and handed something to Caleb. "This is for you."

"What is it?" He unfolded the crumpled banknote. "Wait.

Why are you giving it back? You earned it. Didn't you?"

Charlie's grin was huge. "About that."

"Oh," Mum said. "We still have to clear out the spare room. I'm sorry, Kaiser. I hope you don't mind bunking in with Caleb for a night or two."

"I don't mind, Mrs Burke," Kai said. His voice was soft and buttery.

"Please, call me Charlotte."

"Can I call you Charlotte?" Charlie asked as he clambered out of the car.

"The day I let you call me Charlotte is the day your grand-mother turns in her grave."

Kai said, "What does this mean? Turn in her grave?"

"It's an expression," Caleb said. "Come on, I'll show you to our room."

Between them, they managed to drag the mattress out of the spare room and drop it on the floor of Caleb's tidy space, and Caleb told Kai he could have the bed. Giving up his own bed wasn't something he'd offered lightly, but knowing that Kai had slept in it, even once, was a thought that thrilled him.

"I'll take the mattress," he said. "It's only for a couple of nights."

"No, we can swap," Kai said. His English was pretty good, but his accent was making Caleb's chest hurt. He rubbed the area where his scar was.

In bed, that night, lying on the mattress on the floor with the lights out and Kai asleep in his bed, Caleb listened to the sound of the young Frenchman's soft breathing. And he wondered how easy it would be to slip under the duvet beside him.

He pinched the skin at his wrist to stop himself from spiralling.

There was a man in his bed.

And he wasn't in there with him.

5.

KAI

When Kai woke in Caleb's bed, it took him a second to remember that he wasn't at home. The pillows smelled of orange blossom even though the room had that underlying muskiness of man that he inhaled with ardour. Even the air smelled different when he stepped off the plane, weak-kneed and dizzy, as though Ireland was earthier than France.

He reached for his phone. It was a little after seven and he'd already had a text message from his mum. *Morning sweetheart. Call me. Miss you.* On the floor, the mattress that Caleb had slept on was empty, the sheets crumpled and kicked aside.

Caleb. When Kai and his mum had found Mrs Burke on the university's approved list of off-campus room shares, her listing hadn't mentioned anything about having children, let alone someone similar to Kai's age. And attractive.

Kai looked around the bedroom. There was sports memorabilia everywhere, trophies on top of cabinets, medals hanging from the wardrobe door handle, framed certificates, and a collage of photos on one wall. He rolled out of bed to investigate. The photos were of Caleb, some in a football kit, some in a basketball shirt and shorts, and one of him crouched on the starting line of a running track, head up, staring straight into the camera as though he was looking out at Kai. He must have been around fifteen in the photo. None of the pictures had images of him any older than fifteen or sixteen.

From the photos, and from their short time together last night, Kai couldn't tell what colour Caleb's eyes were. At first, he was convinced they'd been blue, but when he looked again they were grey and then green, like they couldn't decide what they wanted to be.

He tripped over the mattress on the floor as he pulled on yesterday's jeans—he'd have to buy some shorts if he was going to be sharing the room for a while; he couldn't walk around the house in his boxers and the last thing he wanted was for Caleb to catch him half naked in the mornings.

Or maybe that was the first thing he wanted.

He pulled back the curtains and opened the window, wondering where Caleb had gone so early, and the room was flooded with sunlight and birdsong. He felt like he was in an aviary, surrounded by a million birds. And he was convinced he heard the bleating of sheep somewhere in the distance.

Pulling on a T-shirt, he went to the landing and took a second to orientate himself. Bathroom, Charlie's room, airing cupboard—a hot press, Mrs Burke had called it last night, whatever that meant—and Mrs Burke's room. There was no sign of a Mr Burke, and Kai wasn't going to ask. Everyone had secrets. He had enough of his own.

He took a towel from the airing cupboard and slipped into the bathroom with his toiletry bag. He locked the door and tried the handle to make sure no one could enter. Mrs Burke or Charlie didn't need to see him in the shower. He didn't even like seeing himself naked let alone having anyone else bear witness to his skinny ass.

He was quick to shower, and he put on fresh clothes before going downstairs.

The smell of fried meat greeted him, and Charlie was sitting at the kitchen table that had been set for four, while Mrs Burke hovered over the stove.

"*Salut*," Kai said, then corrected himself. "Good morning."

"Sit here," Charlie said, slapping the chair beside him.

"Did you sleep well?" Mrs Burke asked. "I know you're probably used to a continental breakfast, but I couldn't let your first morning in Ireland go by without offering you a full Irish breakfast." She sat a plate in front of him.

Kai's eyes widened. The plate had sausage, bacon, eggs, mushrooms, beans, half a grilled tomato, and a thick triangle of something that looked like it should have been bread but wasn't.

"Soda farl," Charlie explained.

There was a jug of orange juice on the table and a stack of toast, and Kai didn't know where to begin.

When the back door opened and Caleb came in, Kai lowered his gaze. "Good morning."

"Hey." Caleb grabbed a slice of toast and said, "I'm going to go shower." He was wearing a sweatshirt and jogging pants and there was a sheen of sweat glistening in the hollow of his neck.

"Sit down," Mrs Burke said. "We're having breakfast as a family."

Caleb sat and Charlie said, "He stinks."

"You stink." To Kai, Caleb said, "This doesn't happen every day. You're lucky to get cereal around here most days."

"Thank you," Kai said because he didn't know what else to say.

He noticed a distinct lack of coffee, but he didn't want to say anything. A teapot steamed in the centre of the table next to the orange juice.

He picked at his breakfast as best he could. Mrs Burke had been half right. The French ate a much lighter meal this time of day—continental, as she called it—but in his house, coffee was often enough to get you going for the day.

"You don't have to eat with us all the time," Mrs Burke said as she joined them at the table, "but I always cook too much, so you're welcome to join us any time. I've cleared out a cupboard for you over there and a shelf in the fridge in case you want to buy anything special. Dig in before it goes cold."

Kai ate the mushrooms first. And as he cut into the fried egg and it bled across his plate, Charlie said, "How do you say 'hello' in French?"

"*Bonjour.*"

"And how do you say, 'Shut up'?"

"*Tais-toi.*"

"Tay-twah," Charlie said, sounding it out.

Mrs Burke said, "How do you say, 'Eat your breakfast and stop harassing the guests,'?" She clicked her fingers at Charlie, and he shovelled a forkful of baked beans into his mouth.

Kai couldn't eat anymore. The grease lay heavy in his stomach and he knew he'd regret it in half an hour, but he cut a sausage into pieces and continued to eat for fear of being rude.

Caleb was quiet as he picked at some eggs and what they'd called soda farl, dipping it in the soft yolk. There was no meat on his plate, but he couldn't have been vegetarian because he'd had the chicken alfredo in the restaurant last night. Kai watched as Caleb chewed, his eyes on his phone, typing with one hand, and he couldn't help but wonder what kind of body was hidden under those sweat clothes. An athletic one, for sure. Skinny people don't go jogging at seven A.M. and the photos in his room proved his love of sports. Kai ate his sausage and had to look away when Caleb glanced up.

"What do you hope to get out of studying in Ireland?" Mrs Burke said.

Kai shrugged. "It's not France."

"That's a very good reason," Caleb said. The tone of his voice implied a joke, not an insult, and Kai smiled.

"In my family, I am expected to have good grades and do my homework and come home from school and help my father with work. Here, I can experience another culture while I study, and can benefit from not being seen by my parents all the time."

"He's nothing if not honest," Caleb said.

Mrs Burke poured some more tea. "I'm not the kind of person to look over your shoulder while you're here, but if you want me to make sure you've done your homework and tuck you in at night, that'll cost extra." She was smiling. Everyone in Ireland was smiling.

"Maybe you can take turns tucking me in," Kai said, glancing between her and Caleb and then staring at his plate. He couldn't look up or they'd see how enflamed his freckles were.

There was silence.

And then Mrs Burke laughed.

"He tells jokes," Caleb said. "He can stay."

Charlie punched Kai's shoulder. "Yay, we can keep him."

With the breakfast things cleared away and Caleb in the shower, Kai returned to the bedroom and called his mum. He missed her, even though it had been less than twenty-four hours since he'd left France.

"Is your host nice?"

"Yes, she's wonderful. She made breakfast for me this morning."

"And your room is lovely?"

He didn't mention Caleb or Charlie, and as he looked around Caleb's room, he didn't know what reaction she'd have to him sharing with another man. "It's big. And the bed is comfortable."

"That's good."

"Mrs Burke is going to take me shopping for school supplies soon. I should go."

"Promise to call me every day."

"Mum."

"Okay, every other day. And if you meet a nice girl, you must have a chaperone at all times. All right?"

"Yes, Mum."

"You should wait until you come home and meet a nice French girl, anyway. You are nineteen. Maybe I should ask your father to speak to your *pépé*."

"No," Kai said, and the word came out too sharply. Fatima had had an arranged marriage planned with Zameer and look how that ended.

"It was only a suggestion, Kaiser."

Caleb came into the room then, wearing a T-shirt and pair of boxers, his hair wet and mussed. He was about to say something when he spotted Kai on the phone.

"I should go," Kai said.

Mum said, "Be good. And don't give your host any trouble. Speak soon, my love."

When he hung up, Caleb said, "You sound really different speaking French than you do when you're talking English. I like it."

"Do you speak French?"

"I know a couple of swear words."

"I can teach you some more." He grabbed his jacket from the hook on the back of the door. "Mrs Burke is going to take me shopping. Do you wish to come?"

"I'm good, thanks."

This time, Kai kept his gaze on Caleb's face, because if he looked lower he'd want to count the pale brown hairs that crept up his exposed legs.

"I've got some things to do," Caleb added. "But, tonight, maybe we can go to the pub?"

"Shouldn't we work to tidy the spare room?"

Caleb shrugged. And Kai could have kicked himself. Caleb

was offering him an evening alone, just the two of them, and Kai shot him down.

Caleb sat on the edge of the bed and pulled on a pair of jeans, hiding those strong legs. Their conversation was over.

Mrs Burke drove him into the city. "That's your campus. And over there, they do really nice coffee." She turned the car around and drove to St. Stephen's Green Shopping Centre.

It was huge. Three storeys of white and green décor and a glass roof that made him feel as though they were in a greenhouse.

"If you get lost, just follow your nose and I'll be in the food court. Take your time. We can drive home whenever you're ready."

"Thank you, Mrs Burke."

"I told you. You can call me Charlotte."

He nodded. He didn't think he could ever call her by her first name. His father would slap the back of his head if he tried that back home.

He browsed the shops for a while, unsure what he needed to buy. Notepads and pens. Some new clothes. He hadn't received the reading list from university yet, but he expected the campus would have a shop where he could buy the required reading material. He walked into a bookshop in the mall and realised he could lose himself there and be content for the rest of his life. He bought a few books from the two-for-one table and then continued shopping.

By the time he got to the food court, he had six bags filled with books, clothes, and some writing supplies, as well as a moka pot and two bags of ground coffee. Mrs Burke was at a small round table for two, a pot of tea in front of her and a book in her hand. He bought a coffee and joined her.

"Find everything you need?"

"Yes, thanks."

She topped up her cup from the teapot and Kai savoured his first cup of coffee since before he left France.

"I think I got lost three times," he said, unsure how to hold a conversation with her. He wanted to ask her about Caleb, find out everything he could learn about him, but he didn't want to raise suspicions.

Mrs Burke had put her book aside. "You'll love it here. Ireland is beautiful. And I promise I won't try to be a parent to you. All I ask is that you don't bring anyone into my home."

"Who would I bring into your home?"

"You know," she said, winking. "I have a young son. Charlie doesn't need to see random girls or guys coming and going at all hours."

Kai swallowed, unable to look at her. He turned his coffee cup around just to have something to do with his hands. "Girls or guys," she had said. As if it made no difference to her. He didn't know if she could tell he wasn't interested in girls, or if she was just covering all bases in a very open way.

"I promise," Kai said. "I will not bring anyone into your house."

"I mean, friends are okay. If you need to study. But no overnight guests."

"I understand."

"Tell me, do you have any brothers or sisters?"

Kai's breath caught in his throat. He hadn't expected the

question, but he realised as she asked it that it was just an ordinary enquiry. He was surprised it hadn't been asked sooner.

"No," he said. And it sounded so final.

"I'm sorry, I don't mean to pry."

"No. It's just—I did have a sister. But she's," he tried to find a word that wasn't going to tear the bottom out of his day, "gone. She's gone now."

"Oh, dear, God. I'm so sorry."

"It was six years ago."

"Do you want to talk about it?"

He looked up at her. He didn't know what words she wanted to hear. "She drowned," he said. "It was an accident," he said.

And when she flattened her lips in sympathy and touched his arm, he wanted to add, "But that's not the truth. The truth is—my parents did it."

6.

CALEB

aleb took his pills just after breakfast. This was his life, his day divided in two. He would take his meds at eight A.M., usually when he came back from a short run, and then again at eight in the evening. He took anti-rejection medication, anti-infection pills, anti-hypertension, steroids, and vitamins. Some, he only needed in the mornings. Some, twice a day. It had felt like a lot, but as Dr Hughes said when he was fifteen and hooked up to a drip in anticipation of his surgery, "Better a cocktail of pills than a coffin full of dirt."

"I'm broken-hearted," Caleb had told him.

"Then you're in luck because I just so happen to be a specialist in mending broken hearts."

Caleb didn't remember the days leading up to his surgery. He was in and out of consciousness and pumped full of so many drugs that even if he wasn't unconscious, he was sleeping. The heart he was born with was giving out, and as he was taken down to surgery and his donor heart was being flown in by air ambulance, he wished he could remember that evening, with his parents standing at either side of his bed, and Charlie in Mum's arms. There'd have been tears. And prayers. And when the old heart was cut from his chest, he wanted to say there had been a bright light, a voice calling to him from above—but there was nothing.

"But you didn't have a near-death experience," Mum said later. "Your life was in the hands of Dr Hughes—literally. He kept you going, so you wouldn't have seen a light at the end of a tunnel. You were here the whole time."

The weeks that followed were tough on everyone. Caleb's medications were being adjusted and readjusted, nurses were at his side for continued surveillance, and Mum and Dad sat in constant vigil. They were waiting for the word from Dr Hughes. Until he said Caleb's body wasn't rejecting the heart, it seemed like everybody was expecting the new organ to explode at any minute.

And even when he was discharged, he was told to take it easy. To Caleb, that meant no fatty foods and not so much exercise. To Mum, it meant helping him out of bed in the mornings and walking him to the sofa where she would tuck a blanket around him. It meant asking him if he needed anything and then asking him again two minutes later. And it meant telling him off if he dared get off the couch to reach for the TV remote.

"I could have got it for you."

"You were in the kitchen."

"You could have called me."

"I literally moved two feet."

"Do you need anything else while I'm here?"

"No."

"Are you sure?"

She didn't stop. She fussed around him when he'd got his strength back, even when Dr Hughes reported the success of his dosages and agreed that more exercise was essential for the recovery of his mind as well as his body.

For the first six months, he'd had weekly visits with Dr Hughes' transplant team, as well as bi-monthly meetings with Dr Ange—"Ange for angina," Caleb called her. She refused to be known as a psychologist, but she was checking on his mental state.

"You're not suffering from any anxiety? Depression?"

"Why should I be? I've got my life back, pretty much."

And for the most part, Caleb wasn't suicidal. He was happy. He knew it was a long road to recovery, but he was finding it easier to climb the stairs at home without feeling out of breath and—not that he'd admit it to anyone—his teenage libido had returned with gusto. He'd been worrying about that since his surgery but didn't know how to ask anyone. Thankfully, he woke one morning about four months after the transplant, and everything was in miraculous working order.

His only concern was the sports he'd played. The track team won silver at the summer meet, but his Under 16s football team was suffering without him.

For weeks, that summer, he would sit in the garden under a blanket and stare at the basketball hoop his dad had installed back when he was eight. In those early days, he didn't have the energy to pick up a ball, let alone dunk one. But the further out from surgery he got—what he referred to as Day Zero—the stronger he became. He started walking on a treadmill and soon he was able to jog.

Now, at twenty, he was running eight kilometres a day and his heart—Alice's heart—was doing well. And he couldn't be certain, but he thought that Alice had improved his game. His baskets were more precise, and his dribbling was on fire.

Alice was his superpower. Some guys get invisibility; Caleb got Alice.

He got dressed when Kai left to go shopping with his mum, and Caleb looked around the room. He'd been there only one night and already the place was a mess. Caleb needed order. If something was out of place, it messed with his ch'i. It's why he swallowed his pills in the same order every day, took the same route on his run, and always put his clothes in the hamper instead of on the floor.

Three large suitcases were stacked in the corner of the room, and a fourth was open, its contents strewn across the bed— shirts, jeans, socks. He picked up one of the shirts and sniffed it, smelling the clean scent of fabric conditioner, before he stuffed it into the suitcase with everything else, zipped the case closed, and put it with the others.

He neatened up the bed, put Kai's T-shirt from yesterday in the hamper in the bathroom, and then he moved the furniture around so that there was a clear divide. Kai could have the bed and the chest of drawers, and Caleb would have the other half of the room. He wasn't given to being so petty, but he hated a mess, and if Kai was going to be one of those guests until they'd cleaned out the spare room, he had to lay down the ground rules immediately.

He'd offered to take him to the local pub that evening but Kai turned him down, saying they ought to work on the guest room. And as much as Caleb had been hoping for some time alone with him to get to know him better, when he looked around his room he knew that making space for their guest was a much better use of their time.

But moving his own bedroom furniture around had made him sweat, and he grabbed a bottle of water from the fridge and took it out to the yard. Charlie was playing on his console and Mum and Kai were still out, so he dropped a few shots in the hoop until his phone buzzed and broke his concentration.

"Pablo's Pizzas," he said, putting on an Italian accent, "where our puns are always cheesy."

He could almost hear the eye roll in Jayne's voice. "I'm bored," she coughed, "not suicidal."

"Hey. Stop telling me off. You don't pepper-own-me."

"Oh my God, stop already."

"Another one bites the crust," he said. When she didn't laugh, he said, "You all right?"

"They just took Mr Michaels down for surgery."

"They got him a transplant? That's awesome news."

"He's the first one since I got here," Jayne said. Although she'd been on the donor list for months, she'd only been in the unit for a few weeks. She'd taken a bad turn at home and was moved onto the super-urgent transplant list. It was part of the reason Caleb thought of Alice as his special power—you go from the waiting list to the urgent list to the super-urgent list. It's got "super" right there in the name.

"Are you nervous?" Caleb asked Jayne.

"I'm not nervous. It's just weird. Am I going to get like he was?"

Mr Michaels was one of the older patients. He'd been in the ward for three months and he'd already had surgery to prolong the life of his existing heart as he waited for a donor. Caleb had tried to talk to him a few times, but he was either sleeping or grumpy. And for the last few days, he'd been unconscious.

"I hate to tell you this, Jayne," Caleb said, "but you will never be a grumpy old man."

"But he got so grey."

Caleb sat on the picnic table in the corner of the garden and watched a plane leave a vapour trail overhead. He longed to be up there, touching the heavens. The plane was too high up to be coming in for a landing at Dublin. Given the direction it was going, he reckoned it was on its way to Shannon.

"Grey is our colour, Jayne. It should be our international flag. When you go that colour, it means you're ready."

"Ready for what?"

Death was what he meant. Instead, he said, "Ready for a donor."

He waited while she coughed and took a minute to catch her breath, and then she said, "What if he doesn't wake up?"

"I can't answer that, Jayne." The plane had disappeared, but the trail was there, marking its passing, two jet streams clouding into one thick scar across the sky. He wasn't going to lie to her. He told her parents that the first time he'd met them.

"She's only thirteen," Mr Goddard had said.

"But she's going through something that only she can understand," Caleb told him. "If you don't want me answering her questions, I won't visit her, but I've been where she is now. I know what's going through her head."

"What?" Mrs Goddard asked. "What's on her mind?"

"Honestly? The only thing she's thinking about is the end. It doesn't matter how hopeful she is or how positive she's trying to be around you. She knows, more than anyone, that if she doesn't get a heart in time, it's game over. You can't sugar-coat that."

"Do you know her prognosis?"

"I'm not a doctor. I'm just a volunteer. If she asks me any medical question, I will direct her to the transplant team."

"And if she asks you for an opinion, as someone who's been through it already?"

Caleb had shrugged. "I'll be honest with her. I owe her that much."

"Okay," Mr and Mrs Goddard told him.

And that was why he now said, "Mr Michaels is fighting his own battle. And I have first-hand experience that the DTC team is top-notch. But there are always factors we can't account for. Every case is different, Jayne. We've got to hope that he wakes up and everything's a success. But if he doesn't? It's nobody's fault. And what happens if they don't try? Maybe he wouldn't have woken up tomorrow anyway. At least with the surgery, he has a fighting chance. Without it, he's as good as gone."

"I liked it better when you were doing pizza puns," Jayne said.

"Then you know what Mr Michaels would tell you if he wasn't such a grumpy old git. He'd tell you to go out there and cheese the day."

"Praise cheeses," she said.

That evening, while Mum was working a shift in the ticket office of the local theatre, Caleb ordered pizza and he, Kai and Charlie tackled the spare room. It was a mess, and the more they shunted boxes from one side to the other, it only got worse. There was no end in sight.

Charlie said, "How can we have collected so much junk since Xui was here?"

"Who?" Kai asked.

"We hosted a girl last year. And we had to do the same thing then."

Caleb handed Charlie a stack of bank statements. "Put these on the pile for shredding. They're all online anyway, I don't know why Mum insists on keeping them."

Kai said, "What was she like?"

"Who?"

"The girl from last year."

"Boring," Charlie said. "She never wanted to play video games. Not even Fortnite."

"Shut up," Caleb said. "Nobody plays Fortnite anymore. Anyway, she was all right. I had to bunk in with this crazy critter so she could have my bed until we sorted out the spare room."

"Critter?"

"Critter. Like an animal."

"I'm not an animal," Charlie said. He took more than he could chew from a slice of pizza and the cheese dangled like floss from his lips.

"Only an animal puts pineapple on his half."

Kai lowered his eyes and handed Caleb a shoebox full of old birthday cards. "I like pineapple."

"On pizza?"

He nodded, and Caleb couldn't help trying to count the freckles on his face. He realised he was staring when Kai looked away and scratched the back of his head.

Charlie was on his knees with his head bowed, and his shoulders rocked as if he was laughing.

"That wasn't funny," Caleb said.

Charlie looked up.

His face was flushed, and his mouth was open.

He wasn't laughing. He was choking. A chunk of pineapple fell from his lips and as he looked at Caleb, he could see strings of melted cheese between his teeth.

Charlie's eyes were bulging.

And Caleb froze.

He had spent his life around death. And here he was, in the presence of it, and he didn't know what to do.

"Charlie?"

A strangled noise came from the back of his brother's throat.

And then he fell forward, his fingers curling into the carpet pile. Saliva spilled from his mouth and pooled into the open pizza box.

"Charlie?"

Caleb couldn't move. He couldn't tear his eyes away from Charlie's reddened face.

Somewhere outside of himself, in the furthest reaches of the universe, he heard Kai say, "Charlie, are you okay?"

And he watched as Kai got behind Charlie, wrapping his arms around his waist, his hands clasped together, and he squeezed.

Squeezed again.

And again.

Charlie's face was so red it was becoming purple. The gurgling in his throat was raw and wet. And his eyes were fixed on Caleb as if he was accusing him.

Kai heaved again.

And Charlie coughed.

A wet chunk of pizza hit the floor.

Charlie gasped. And cried. And curled up on the floor in a foetal ball.

And Caleb still didn't know what to do.

He stared at his little brother, a sobbing mess in front of a box of half-eaten pizza, and more than his own mortality, he realised how fragile the whole world was.

He got on the floor beside Charlie and pulled him into his arms. "You're okay. You're all right."

Kai stroked Charlie's hair. And Caleb wanted to hold him too.

"You saved his life."

"If I wasn't here, you would have done it."

"Thank you," Caleb said, and Charlie pulled away from him. "I'm okay."

"Are you sure?"

Charlie nodded, wiping the tears from his eyes.

And Caleb said, "Don't tell Mum, okay?"

7.
KAI

K ai was in bed by the time Caleb had brushed his teeth and settled down on the mattress on the floor. He was wearing a fitted T-shirt that had shown off his athletic body when he came into their room, and as he slipped out of his jogging pants under the dim glow of the lamp on the bedside table, Kai closed his eyes. He didn't want to stare.

He'd yet to see Caleb shirtless, but he knew that when he did he wouldn't be disappointed. Kai twisted on the bed, making sure he was under the duvet.

"Light off?" he asked.

"Sure."

In the darkness, Caleb's face was lit by his phone screen as he browsed Instagram or whatever app he was scrolling through. For a few minutes, they were silent, and Kai had opened his mouth to say something twice and thought better of it.

And then Caleb flicked his phone screen off and the memory of his face danced across Kai's vision before the room settled into darkness.

"You awake?" Caleb asked. His voice was muffled and sleepy.

He didn't know why, but Kai considered not responding. He buried his head deeper into the pillows. "Yes."

"Who taught you the Heimlich?"

"We learned it at school."

"I was taught it around Charlie's age," Caleb said. They were talking in whispers and Kai had to lift his head to hear him. "I just—froze."

"It's okay."

"No. He was choking, and I did nothing."

He heard movement from Caleb's mattress and Kai held his breath. But the sound of moving fabric stopped; he wasn't coming closer.

"If I wasn't there, you'd have helped him," Kai said.

"What if I couldn't?"

Kai sat up, staring at the place where he knew Caleb was but could barely make out the shape of him in the dark. "You would, Caleb."

That was the first time he'd said Caleb's name out loud. It felt silky on his lips.

"Kai?"

Maybe Caleb was testing out the sound of Kai's name, too. "Yes?"

"Thank you for saving my brother."

"You're welcome."

They said no more for a few minutes and Kai thought perhaps Caleb had turned away from him, eyes closed for sleep.

But when Caleb spoke again, his voice was stronger, louder. "I owe you."

Kai pushed his hands behind his head and stared at the dark ceiling. "Next time, I'll choke, and you can save me. Then we'll be even."

"Don't joke about it. I might let you die if you keep messing up my room."

"Sorry."

"I was joking."

"Banter," Kai said. He knew the word.

"Just craic," Caleb told him.

And soon Caleb's soft snores filled the room and Kai closed his eyes. When Mrs Burke had come home from her job, Charlie didn't tell her he choked. And neither Kai nor Caleb offered up the information. The spare room was forgotten about for the rest of the evening, and the four of them watched TV until Mrs Burke suggested it was Charlie's bedtime. Still tired from the nerves of travelling and from a day of shopping, it wasn't long before Kai had turned in for the night, too.

But once he was in Caleb's bed, he couldn't sleep. He kept thinking about how large the mattress was and how uncomfortable Caleb must be on the floor. But he didn't dare offer to share.

Although he'd come to terms with his sexuality a few years ago when Louis Chastain from gym class pinned him against the locker room wall and kissed him so hard that his lips hurt when they were done, Kai was not prepared to come out. His parents would never allow it. Not only was his mother Catholic, but they were also Algerian. There could be no worse combination in Kai's mind. And Dad, even though he had given up his religion for her when they got married, could not shake his ingrained Sunni Islam ways even as he shook off the yoke of its servitude.

Fatima knew it. It was why she'd kept it a secret that she was dating Avery Truffaut, and that time when she crawled in through his bedroom window and he demanded to know where she'd been, she was reluctant to tell him.

"She's my girlfriend," she'd said at last. And then, "You wouldn't understand."

In the weeks that followed, Kai covered for her. At twelve, he was not old enough to chaperone her dates with Zameer, the man their grandparents had arranged for her to marry. But when he came for dinner, Kai made a point of sitting between them like a cute contraceptive, always smiling, asking Zameer questions when it seemed he was getting too close to Fatima.

They had not set a date, and when pressed by their mother, Fatima would say, "I am too young. Maybe next year."

"You do not want your ovaries to dry up and wilt," Mum said.

"But I am sixteen. I have many years ahead."

Dad would take Zameer to the garage where he worked when he was not at the shop, and he showed him the different types of wood that he worked with, and what each one was best used for. All the things Kai had heard before and forgotten. He had no interest in carpentry, even if—as Mum put it—it was "the profession of St Joseph."

Kai loved books. Literature was his passion and he had chosen Trinity College Dublin for its magnificent library that contained over two hundred thousand old texts, encased in dark oak shelves. TCD housed the Book of Kells, a ninth-century illuminated manuscript famed for its majestic illustrations, and Kai had already purchased a ticket to view it during Freshers' Week.

Fatima often bribed him with battered copies of Guillaume Musso novels that she borrowed from Avery, and Kai would huddle under his blankets with a flashlight and devour every word. And it was Avery who had introduced him to the classics—Camus, Dumas, Hugo—when she met up with Fatima after school one day and she handed Kai a hardcover copy of *Madame Bovary*. Although some of the words were difficult to digest, Kai fell in love with Emma, the titular character, who, just like him, would lose herself in romance novels.

His dream was to fall for a book nerd and live happily ever after, reading side by side in front of an open fire. But here, lying in somebody else's bed in Ireland, far from home and the comforts that he'd come to think of as meaningful, he couldn't shake the thoughts of athletic Caleb, a man who had no books to speak of in his bedroom save for a copy of a light aircraft training manual.

If Kai had a type, Caleb wouldn't be it. He thought he wanted broody and well-read, but the truth was, Caleb's athletic body slithered inside his brain and wrapped its powerful arms around him. And even when he didn't want it, it wouldn't let go.

Caleb's soothing snores were like music as Kai lay awake in the dark, listening to his deep breathing. Eventually, he had to get up, pull the blanket from the bed, and spend the rest of the night on the couch. Not because Caleb's nasal breathing was annoying, but because if he lay there any longer, he might have slipped out of bed and onto the mattress beside him.

And that wasn't worth the two seconds of excitement it would create in his body.

In the morning, Mrs Burke woke him with a whisper. "We'll sort your room out today. I know he snores, but I didn't think it would be enough to disturb your sleep."

"It isn't that," Kai said, sitting up and covering his cold legs with the blanket that had slipped from him during the night.

"Oh?"

But he couldn't tell her anything else, so he made a snoring sound at the back of his throat, and she laughed.

"Say no more. I'm making breakfast. Do you want anything?"

"I'll just make some coffee, if that's okay."

He knew it should be weird, standing in the kitchen in a T-shirt and boxers, watching the moka pot on the stove as Mrs Burke chopped a banana into a bowl of bran flakes, but it felt natural, as though he'd been living there for years instead of two days.

When he poured the extra-strong coffee into a small cup and sat at the table opposite her, he savoured the smell of his drink and the early-morning birdsong outside. And he realised that, even last night, behind the pleasant sounds of Caleb's snoring, Ireland was not a quiet place. If it wasn't birds or traffic, it was distant sheep or cattle.

"Was it my snoring?" Caleb said from the doorway.

When Kai looked over his shoulder, he saw that he was

dressed in sweatpants and a hoodie. He didn't think it was possible to look sexier. "You were like a train," he smiled. "I'm just glad you don't smell like the Paris Metro."

Caleb raised an arm and sniffed his armpit. "I smell like roses."

Mrs Burke said, "You won't when you come back from your run. Don't forget your tablets."

"Stop treating me like a child."

"Stop smelling like a teenager."

"Love you," Caleb shouted as he left through the back door, and the words made Kai's neck itch with a wholesome fever.

Mrs Burke finished her breakfast, rinsed the bowl, and put it in the dishwasher.

"Tablets?" Kai asked. He knew he shouldn't, but the word came out of his mouth before he could stop himself.

She looked at him. "Vitamins. That's all. You should take some too. Especially Vitamin D as we go into winter." She busied herself at the sink. "I can pick some up for you later if you want. What are your plans for today?"

Kai topped up his cup and said, "I thought I would explore Dublin while I can."

"Put our address in your phone. And you should buy a Leap Card. Public transport is cheaper that way."

She left the kitchen and Kai could hear her upstairs, trying to wake Charlie.

By the time he'd reached the city centre on the Luas tram system, a light rain dampened the streets, but the buskers didn't care. One guy, with an umbrella wedged over his shoulder, played the guitar and sang Irish revolutionary songs to the people who passed by and ignored him. Kai dropped a two-Euro coin into the open guitar case in front of him and walked on.

Dublin city was a lot like Paris. The statues were made of bronze, greened by their age, whereas Parisian sculptures were stone, but the streets were bustling, and the hawkers were just as loud.

He stopped by the statue of James Joyce, just off O'Connell Street, and then made his way to Merrion Square Park where he took a selfie with Oscar Wilde.

And when he felt hungry, he found a small café on a narrow side street that had three tables outside and six on the inside. The rain had stopped, and the sky was clear, so he ordered a sandwich and a coffee and sat at one of the round tables on the open street. A woman in a head scarf asked him to buy a magazine from her, but the waitress came out with his sandwich and the woman hurried away.

When he'd eaten, he sat there to enjoy the rest of his coffee and he worried about his parents. He didn't know what kind of people they were before they had children, but with Fatima gone and him overseas, he feared the worst. They would either find their love again, falling into each other's arms in the dark of a lonely night, or they would fall apart. What happened to married couples when their children were all gone? He didn't know.

Without Kai to bridge the massive gulf between them, he thought Dad would dive deeper into work and Mum would spend more time at church. Perhaps him being in Ireland, away from them, would spell their end.

He hoped not.

As he looked across the street at the people who passed by,

he spotted two men walking towards him. They looked both ways and then crossed the road, and as they entered the café, he saw that they were holding hands.

Two men. Holding hands. In public.

The future was here.

But one of the men spotted him staring and before he went inside said, "Take a picture, it'll last longer."

And Kai blushed.

The future was tempered by a troubled past.

He wanted to say something, to tell them he wasn't staring in disgust but admiration, but the bell above the door tinkled as it closed, and he was alone.

He'd seen Fatima and Avery holding hands once. It wasn't long before she'd gone missing and Mum made Dad take the car out to look for her. Kai had been late home, working on a project that kept him at Sacré-Cœur later than he intended, and as he walked home through the dark October streets, kicking leaves out of the way, he came around the corner of Rue Saint-Rustique, and he stopped on the cobbles when he recognised Fatima at a table outside a café. Her arm was stretched across the tabletop, holding Avery's hand, and Kai was about to shout and wave at them when Avery leaned across and kissed Fatima.

Kai had taken a step back. He knew they were girlfriends. And he knew what that meant. But he hadn't expected to ever see his older sister kiss another woman.

It was weird. Even though he wanted to kiss boys, seeing her kiss Avery was the strangest thing he'd ever encountered in his thirteen years.

And the night she disappeared, Kai sat in the back of Dad's

car and watched the blue lights swirl across their street when they pulled into the drive. With no sign of Fatima across all of Paris, Kai wished he'd gone up to them at the café outside Saint-Rustique and hugged them both.

But he hadn't.

He got out of the back seat of Dad's car and Dad ran up the driveway, taking Kai's mother in his arms. And the policeman in his dark blue uniform was holding up a large plastic bag and was gesticulating east of them, across the Gobelins, and towards the Seine beyond it.

As Kai came to his parents, the zip toggle of his coat between his lips in anticipation, he saw Fatima's denim jacket in the bag. It was hers without question. He'd watched her sew the butterfly patch on the left shoulder six months earlier, and when he asked her about it, she'd looked around to make sure Mum and Dad weren't nearby, and said, "Avery turned me into a butterfly. I used to be an ugly caterpillar. But she set me free."

And as he stood on the driveway between his parents, staring at the wet jacket in the plastic bag, the policeman asked him, "Do you know what happened to your sister, son?"

And Kai looked at his dad. And then his mum.

And he said, "No, sir."

Mum cried. And even though he knew his text messages wouldn't reach her, when he'd crawled into bed that night, just before the sun came up, he typed on his phone and pressed send anyway.

And then he switched his phone off in case Mum would look at it while he slept.

His text message, unsent, said, *I can't lie anymore.*

8.

CALEB

The wet paving stones under Caleb's running shoes stretched out as he swallowed the road. He checked his smartwatch to make sure his heart rate was still under 130 and he tapped the screen to skip the current track that was playing in his earbuds. As he turned into the east side of Marlay Park behind the GAA club, the drizzling rain had stopped but it dripped under the park's trees and dampened his hoodie. He continued around the cricket grounds and passed the tennis courts before doubling back and stopping at a café for a bottle of water. Jogging on the spot as he drank, he had a lot to smile about. His first flying lesson was this afternoon, so long as the rain held off, and he was nervously excited.

He ran back the way he came and made it home in just over forty-five minutes, and when he came in through the kitchen,

Mum was sitting at the table, looking over a couple of bills.

"Has Kai gone out?" he asked. He tried to make it sound as though he was disinterested, but he was already disappointed to wake up to an empty room this morning, and when he'd come downstairs and saw the blanket rolled up on the couch, his heart sank lower. Kai needed his own room, and Caleb would have to deal with that.

It didn't matter that the French student had only been there for a couple of nights; Caleb's room would feel empty without him.

Mum looked up. "Sorry?"

"Is Kai out?"

"He's gone to town."

Caleb looked over her shoulder at the bills. "Do we have enough to cover them?"

"We're fine."

"Mum."

"We're fine. It's not your place to worry."

"I'm going to take a shower."

She got up and filled the kettle. "Wake your brother, will you? I need the three of us to tackle Kai's room before he gets home, please."

When he was showered and dressed, he joined Mum and Charlie in the spare room. They were knee-deep in boxes, and Caleb thought Charlie looked pale, as though they were both remembering his choking fit from the night before. Caleb mouthed, "You okay?"

And Charlie ignored him. "Where do you want these, Mum?"

Mum looked at the contents of the box and said, "Put it on the 'keep' pile."

When he'd left the room, Caleb picked up a box of books and followed his younger brother to the garage.

"What's going on?"

"Nothing."

"So, why won't you even look at me?"

Charlie put his heavy box on the largest stack and shrugged without turning to him.

"Are you angry about last night? You didn't choke, you were fine."

"Forget about it."

Little brothers have a knack for making you feel guilty. Caleb said, "You didn't tell Mum, did you? I can give you that twenty Euros back if you want."

Charlie glared at him. "It's not about that, dickhead."

"What, then?"

"Nothing."

As he walked out of the garage and back into the kitchen, Caleb grabbed his arm. "Charlie, come on. What the hell's wrong with you?"

"You are."

"What have I done?"

"Dad couldn't be bothered to make it to my birthday last month. And now he's going to show up for your first flying lesson."

"Is he?" Caleb hadn't spoken to his father in weeks. "I didn't ask him to."

"He called Mum while you were in the shower. He's

supposed to meet you there."

"I'll tell him not to come."

Charlie pulled out of his grip. "Don't bother. He loves you more than me."

"No, he doesn't."

"No. It's fucking Alice that he loves."

Caleb almost punched him, but he restrained himself. It wasn't Charlie's fault. It was Dad's. And his little brother was right—Dad paid more attention to Caleb since he had his transplant than he did to Mum or Charlie. Caleb watched him stomp back up the stairs and he waited for a few minutes before joining them. It was best to let Charlie cool down before speaking again.

When he got back to the spare room, Charlie and Mum were sitting on the floor, right where Charlie had almost choked to death, and Mum had her arm around him as they leafed through an old photo album of Mum when she was a kid.

Charlie looked up. "Didn't you say you found that twenty quid I dropped yesterday?" His smile said that he'd forgiven Caleb for having somebody else's heart—but only if Caleb was willing to pay for it.

He pulled the note from his pocket. "Yeah. You got to be more careful, buddy. Stop throwing money around."

They worked all morning and by the time they'd stopped for lunch, the room was cleared of boxes, and the boys carried the mattress back in to put on the bed. Mum added fresh linen and Caleb put his own room back in order. He wheeled Kai's suitcases in and stacked them in the corner.

"Is this room bigger than mine?" Charlie asked.

"You can fight Kai for it."

From downstairs, Mum said lunch was ready. She'd made omelettes and, when Charlie had finished and gone to play something on his console, she said to Caleb, "Are you excited to be up in the air?"

"You spoke to Dad?"

"Charlie told you? Your father wanted to surprise you at the airfield."

"Why? He couldn't even show up for Charlie on his birthday."

"He had to work that day. You know what it's like."

"Stop defending him. Charlie knows as well as you do—Dad's only sticking around because of me." Hypertrophic cardiomyopathy is hereditary and, although Dad had no symptoms of his own, it came from his side of the family.

"That's enough, Caleb. I won't have you bad-mouthing your father while he's not here to defend himself."

"It's the truth. I've said the same thing to his face. Anyway. I'm going to be late."

"Don't slam the—"

Caleb slammed the door. He grabbed his helmet, pushing the button for the garage door to tilt up and overhead, and he let the moped's engine hum underneath him for a minute before setting off. He, more than anyone, knew that driving angry would never end well. He'd almost killed himself last year when Gordy had dumped him. He'd pushed the moped too hard and the roads were wet. They'd only been dating for six months, but Caleb took the breakup badly. Later, he'd said that although he had somebody else's heart in his chest, Gordy had none.

At the airfield, Caleb signed in and was met by his instructor. Chief Pilot Colin Moore said, "You're the boy with the heart?"

Caleb tapped his chest. "I hope so."

"And you passed your Class Two medical?"

He handed over his medical certificate. Although Dr Hughes had signed him off for flight training, Caleb still had to attend a medical exam with the aviation authority. They gave him a clean bill of health, which he wasn't expecting. Having a heart transplant wasn't enough to ground you, it seemed.

Colin Moore glanced at it as he scratched his greying moustache, and then said, "You're not going to have a heart attack on me, are you?"

"I think the authorities would have a field day if I was *on* you while I had a heart attack."

"Your PPL application didn't say you were a funny man."

"Didn't it?"

Colin grinned. "This way, big man."

As Caleb followed him across the field, grateful that his dad hadn't turned up, his instructor explained the process. He'd have nine theory exams to pass before his practical flight exam as well as a minimum number of hours in the air. Today was just an introductory flight before Caleb decided if he wanted to commit to it or not. Colin would fly and Caleb was just along for the ride.

"Some people think they want to fly but as soon as they get up there, they realise all they wanted was to be in an aeroplane, heading off on holiday somewhere foreign, not manning the controls."

"I want this," Caleb said. "I need it."

As they entered the hangar, Caleb saw the magnificent flying machine that they'd be going up in.

"It's a Cessna 172 Skyhawk," Colin said. "I call her Maisie." He let Caleb in on the right side and Colin took his place in the pilot's seat. Caleb was stunned. He knew the instrument panel would be full of dials and gauges, but he wasn't expecting so many.

They sat for over twenty minutes as Colin explained important things about pre-flight checks and weather conditions and flight planning. "You'll learn all that in your theory tests. Did you join a ground school?"

"No," Caleb said, "I'm going to self-study. I can get everything I need online." He was confident he could study online and pass all nine exams within the eighteen-month period he was allowed and not need to spend extra on ground school, which wasn't a legal requirement anyway.

With their headsets on so they could communicate in the air, Colin performed his checks, radioed Ground Control, said, "Clear," and started the single engine. The twin-blade propeller gleamed to life as it spun and as the engine roared, so did Caleb.

Colin laughed. "Let's take her up, shall we?"

He talked him through the procedures as they taxied to the runway and waited for permission to take off. Colin talked the whole time, but Caleb found it difficult to concentrate as he felt the cabin vibrate around him and the excitement of take-off was too strong.

They got the word and Colin said, "Put your feet on the pedals and hold the wheel. They're connected to mine, so you'll be able to feel what I do as we fly."

They zipped down the runway and as Colin lifted the nose, Caleb felt the wheel pull back and Alice screeched with glee inside his chest.

They were up and, in just a few minutes, Dublin stretched out before them like a toy village.

"You always want to keep your nose on the horizon," Colin said. "That's your guide."

He took them across Dublin and did some sixty-degree turns over the Aviva stadium, and Caleb's stomach was tense with excitement.

As they drifted out over the coast, Colin said, "Having fun?"

"Fuck yes. I mean—yes. God yes."

"Swearing in the air is a ten-Euro fine."

"Really?"

"No." Colin's laugh was broken and nasally in Caleb's ear. He pointed. "See that mass on the coast over there? The inlet? That's where we're headed. Think you can handle it?"

"Me?"

"She's all yours. Keep her steady. You don't need to hold the wheel so tight. Relax."

They weren't as high as the clouds, but Caleb was already in heaven. When Colin had said most people think they want to learn to fly until they get up there, Caleb panicked that he'd feel the same. But sitting in the cramped cockpit, faced with a million dials and words that he'd never heard before, he knew this was what he wanted. He kept the wheel steady, watching the instrument panel—airspeed, altimeter, heading—and feeling the joy of flight. This was better than sex. Colin took his hands off the wheel to prove to Caleb that he was doing it on his own.

"Do you plan on going for your commercial license?" Colin asked as Caleb watched the plane's nose, making sure it was on the horizon. The noise of the engine became a permanence that underlined the bubbling excitement deep in Caleb's brain.

"I don't want to fly the big jumbos. Just something small and private. I'm not looking for a career, I just—I feel free up here. I don't know what I'm doing yet, but I know this is what I want."

He looked over Dublin as they approached along the coast. This high up, he could just about make out the traffic as it criss-crossed the streets, and here he was, the only plane for days, and his cheeks ached from smiling.

"You're a natural," Colin said.

He took them back to the airfield, and Caleb had never been so disappointed. He could have stayed up there forever.

On the ground, Caleb's legs were like jelly for a few minutes until he readjusted to the lack of vibration.

"You'll be coming back, then?"

"Every day if I could afford it."

"How about I get you in for your first actual lesson this time next week?"

"Deal." They shook hands and Caleb paid in advance for next week's lesson. As he left the office, his dad was waiting outside, leaning against the sports car he'd bought after the divorce, like a man in the middle of a life crisis.

"Dad."

"I saw you boys coming in for the landing. Was that you at the controls?"

"It was just an intro flight."

"She's a beauty."

"Why are you here?"

"I wanted to take you for coffee."

Caleb looked at the helmet in his hands. "I've got the bike."

"Leave it. I can bring you back for it when we're done."

Caleb sighed. Typical Dad, breezing in and out when he wanted to. He threw the helmet in the cramped back seat of the low-profile car and slid into the front. Fancy sports cars weren't his thing, and he wasn't impressed by how many horses his dad's car stabled. But Dad was covering half the cost of his private pilot's license and when he got the car two years ago, he let the boys sit in it and Caleb revved the engine. "Hear that? She's a beast, isn't she, boys?"

Charlie, nine at the time and still enamoured of his father, said, "I'm going to have one when I grow up," and Caleb smiled when he knew he needed to, for the sake of appearances.

Caleb wanted to tell him he was gay, right there in the front seat of his GT that day, thinking maybe it would spoil his dad's fun, but he knew he would be doing it out of spite, a month after his mum told him she already knew and, in truth, he didn't think Dad would care anyway.

When they pulled up at a coffee shop, his father let the engine settle before they went inside.

Caleb took a table while Dad ordered, and when he joined him a few minutes later, Dad said, "How're things? What's been going on?"

"You missed Charlie's birthday."

"I was overseas. Anyway, I spoke to him on the phone."

"Did you get him a present?"

"I put some money in his account."

"Yay," Caleb said, his voice as expressive as his flat white.

"Why are you being snarky?"

"I don't care if you let me down, but Charlie's eleven. He's just a kid."

"I'm going to take him camping next week."

"He starts school next week."

"The weekend, then."

Caleb shook his head. He stirred some sugar into his coffee and slapped the spoon down on the table. "Don't be one of those dads."

"And what kind of dad is that?"

"What am I even doing here, Dad? You missed Charlie's birthday, Mum's struggling to make ends meet, and here we are, playing happy families over coffee?"

"Why's she struggling?" Dad asked.

"That's not my point. Why are we here?"

Dad's arm twitched and Caleb realised he wanted to check his watch as though he had other things to do. He took a sip from his coffee and then scrunched a paper napkin in his fist. "I wanted to talk." Caleb rolled his hand, palm upturned, to indicate that he should continue. "I'm thinking of asking Joanne to move in with me."

Caleb's smile was tight-lipped. Joanne was thirty-one, sixteen years Darren Burke's junior. She'd be like a big sister to Caleb.

"I'm glad you felt the need to tell me that."

"I'm not telling you, Caleb, I'm asking you."

"Asking me? You're asking your son if you can move in with

your girlfriend?"

"I wanted to be courteous. When you boys come to visit, I don't want it to be awkward."

"How often do we come to visit you, Dad? By the time we do, you'll have moved on to somebody different, somebody younger."

"Not this time. Joanne's different."

"Different like Lucy? Or different like Maeve?"

"I didn't come here for your lip, Caleb."

"You can take me back to the airfield now."

They didn't speak on the way back. And as Caleb rode home, the visor of his helmet masking his face, he didn't want to go flying if it meant Dad would be involved.

Why do parents always get in the way?

9.
KAI

Kai shuffled under the blankets and looked around his new room. It was all his. A chest of drawers and a wardrobe for his clothes, a desk for studying, a wall-mounted TV that he could cast Netflix to if he felt like it, and a small bed just for him. He looked at the carpet where he'd knelt with Caleb and Charlie the evening before as they'd tried to clear some of the mess, and then he looked at the closed door that trapped him in, away from everyone else.

He was alone.

And for the first time, he hated it.

Since Fatima disappeared, and his parents closed themselves off, Kai had learned to be alone. He was better off in his own company, twisted around in the fancies of his own mind than trying to find the words that kept a conversation alive. Because inside, he was dying. His world had changed, and Mum spent those first months in frantic tears, and dad would go out and walk along the bank of the Seine and call Fatima's name as if she would reach out from the murky water and beg to be brought home. And Kai would sit at his bedroom window, watching the night, waiting for her to climb up to the garage roof and come in as if she'd just been gone a few hours and didn't want their parents to know she was out late.

His small group of friends grew smaller still as they fell away from him. He no longer wanted to play football or ride his bike with the others, and in time he was eating lunch alone, at a table on the edge of the school grounds that looked over the sports field. But he was okay with that. Because when he was alone, he didn't have to speak. And if he had to speak, he'd utter the truth.

And the truth was terrible.

He walked home alone, stopping at the library, and he'd curl up on a giant blue beanbag in the kids' corner, a thirteen-year-old among toddlers, and he'd read Éluard's *Capitale de la douleur*—Capital of Pain—and he would understand, intensely, every word of Éluard's poetry. Because he felt pain, too.

Silence became his voice. Words were to be derided, and in the first six months since Fatima's disappearance, he hadn't noticed that his voice was deepening in maturity. And when he did speak, answering a teacher's question or talking to the librarian about classical literature, his throat felt dusty and unused.

He was the silent black kid at the back of the class—because any degree darker than white was considered black to his class-mates—and, after a while, he became invisible. He jumped into the pages of a book, and he didn't want to come out.

And now he looked around his bedroom in Mrs Burke's house, and he felt utterly alone.

Caleb had come home from his flight lesson, full of laughter and boisterous energy. He poured prosecco into glasses for him, Kai and Mrs Burke, and they clinked a toast as Caleb told them about his exciting day. And no one had mentioned that Kai's life had been shuffled into another room until it was time for bed and Mrs Burke said, "We've got a surprise for you." She led him by the hand up to his new room, where his suitcases had been placed in a corner and the bed was made.

"Awesome," Kai said. "Thank you. You didn't have to do this."

He wished she hadn't. But he knew that he couldn't sleep in Caleb's bed forever. Caleb had been forced to sleep on a mattress on the floor and everyone was grateful that Kai now had a room of his own.

Everyone except Kai.

He turned and faced the wall, knowing Caleb was on the other side, and he buried himself in his pillows.

On Monday, he got the bus to campus even though Mrs Burke had offered to drive him there—he needed to do this for himself. When he moved into halls of residence next semester, he wouldn't have Mrs Burke to do everything for him.

The campus was huge and, even studying the map he'd been given, he still got lost on his first day. He sat in a large lecture hall later that week, listening to the professor talking about the underlying themes of Kafka's *The Trial*. His reading list was primarily made up of the Continental greats—Tolstoy, de Cervantes, Orczy; most of which he'd already read. He was pleased to see Austen on the list, having never read any of her works in English, but he wasn't looking forward to attempting James Joyce.

When he visited the Book of Kells, he was stunned by its beauty. The corners were age-worn but it had been so well pre-served that Kai couldn't believe the colourful depictions were still vibrant.

Later, he took a seat at a desk in the library, and he couldn't read. He sat in silence, like he'd done almost half of his life, and he listened to the soft noises that draped across the floor. Footsteps, whispers, the turning of pages, and the scratch of pens against paper.

Libraries were the best place to avoid conversations.

And they held more secrets than Kai did.

You don't know what you're going to get when you open the cover of a book, and that's what intrigued Kai. Each one was a promise. A gift.

And there was not enough time in his life to read every single one of them.

By the end of his third week at college, he hadn't made any friends, and as he sat in class, he blended into the masses. He participated in group discussions only as much as he needed to, and those people in his group would listen, but they didn't seem to be interested in his views of Tolstoy's work.

He rode the bus home every evening and he sat in the back garden at the picnic table, using his phone's torch to see by as the evening light faded, and he'd read a few chapters, taking notes in a spiral pad. He'd look through the kitchen window at

Mrs Burke as she stacked the dishwasher, and Charlie would come in and ask for something from the fridge, and Caleb would pace up and down as he talked on the phone to someone. And Mrs Burke would eat a biscuit from the cookie jar, holding one hand under her chin to catch the crumbs before she dusted her hands off and sat at the table with some papers. And when she wasn't looking, Charlie would sneak out and take the lid off the cookie jar before going upstairs, a biscuit in each hand. Upstairs, Caleb's shadow would pass across his window, and Kai would try not to stare.

This was family life. This was what his own family could no longer be. Not until the truth came out.

And maybe not even then.

Because when his parents found out, they would likely murder him for keeping this secret for six years. They wouldn't understand. Couldn't.

The only person who could was Fatima.

The night the policeman held up her soaked jacket in a plastic bag and told them that she'd fallen into the Seine, Kai shut his mouth and refused to open it. "He's in shock," Mum had said.

"He'll be all right," Dad said.

But he wanted them to ask. He needed them to say, "Do you know the truth? What happened to my daughter?" Because if they asked him—directly—he could not lie. That was his rule, his life.

That was his truth.

He marched his way into October, sitting through lectures and seminars and group workshops, and Kai kept to himself as much as he could. The days were getting shorter, and it wouldn't be long before his bus journey home would be dark and dreary.

"How's school?" Mum would ask him on the phone.

And Kai would say, "It's great. I'm learning so much."

"And what are your plans for Halloween?"

"There is a party on campus," he said, though he didn't point out that he wasn't going. "There will be lots of people there."

"And alcohol?"

"Yes, mother. We are grown-ups. We are allowed to drink."

"Do the Irish drink as much as they say?"

"I haven't noticed so much."

"And your host. Is she well?"

Kai answered her questions with as much feigned interest in his voice as he could muster. But, in truth, he missed her. "How is Dad?"

"Busy. Always busy. Work has picked up. There is a big job coming, he says."

"That's great, Mum."

"Are there any girls in your classes?"

"No, mother. Girls are not permitted to study here. It's so terribly backward."

"Don't joke, Kaiser. It is not long since women had any rights at all."

Every time, the same old questions. In the same order. How was school? How was Mrs Burke? Did you meet a girl?

He wanted to scream at her. "I'm gay. I don't want a girl. I like men." But he couldn't. For the same reason that Fatima couldn't tell them about Avery Truffaut. There would be no changing their minds. Kai had known this since he was thirteen.

When Fatima came to him that night, the night she disappeared, she'd been crying.

"What's wrong?" he asked. He thought maybe Avery had dumped her.

"Mum found out."

"Found out what?"

"About me. And Avery. And now I have to go."

"Go where?"

"Somewhere. Anywhere. I have to get away."

"What did Mum say? How did she find out?"

"Change the PIN on your phone, Kai. Don't let Mum into your life. She'll ruin it the way she's ruined mine."

"What are you talking about?" Kai asked. And when Fatima sat him down on the edge of his bed and told him what she was going to do, he said, "No. You can't. Dad will kill you."

"I'm dead either way," she said. "Dead to the family."

"Not to me."

"I know," she said, touching his warm cheek. And when he looked up at her, she said, "I'll miss you."

"Don't go."

"I have to."

"Can't you just pretend? Tell Mum she was wrong. Zameer is your fiancé. He's the one you'll be with forever. Just like Mum and Dad."

"I can't do that, Kai. If I can't be me, what's the point? If I can't tell the truth, I'm lying to myself."

"If you do this, I will have to lie. To everyone."

"You can do it. For me. Be strong."

"I'm not as strong as you, Tima. Just stay."

"I'm sorry," she said. She kissed his cheek and she winked. And she tied her wild hair back and that was the last time he saw her.

When her personal effects were released, Mum clung to her jacket for weeks, like a child with a blankie. They had a funeral for her, burying an empty casket, and the detective in charge of her case was there. He said, "I'm sorry for your loss," for the millionth time.

And Dad said, "I'm sorry you never drained the Seine to find her."

And Mum said, "Will you ever find her body?"

The detective said, "No. I'm sorry."

Caleb interrupted his thoughts. He came out of the back door as Kai sat at the picnic table, and he was dressed in his running gear. He jogged to the table and said, "What're you reading?"

"Nothing."

What he meant was that he hadn't been reading the book but was instead thinking about his life. But the word came out harder than he'd intended.

"Are you okay?"

Kai's phone vibrated and the screen lit up.

"I'm fine. I'm sorry." There was far too much sorrow in the world.

"For what?"

He said, "I," but he didn't know what words should follow it. He held up his book as his phone vibrated again. "*The Picture of Dorian Gray* by Oscar Wilde."

"For school?"

"No. Just for fun."

"Better you than me," Caleb said, and he turned away for his run. He would usually run in the morning, but he'd had an early flight lesson this morning and he'd told them all at dinner that he didn't have the time.

In the dark, Kai looked at his phone.

The smell of Caleb's deodorant lingered over the picnic table.

He unlocked the phone with his thumbprint and read the message. It was from a number whose contact name was simply *F*.

How are you, little bro?

10.

CALEB

Ater his fifth flying lesson, Caleb still had a long way to go. He needed at least another thirty-five hours in the air before he could obtain his license, but Colin Moore told him that almost nobody passed on the minimum requirements. He'd be more likely to need upwards of sixty hours just to feel competent enough to sit in the cockpit with an examiner.

Caleb didn't doubt it. He was struggling to keep the plane level, and every time he took his eye off the Cessna's nose, the attitude indicator—the instrument panel's artificial horizon—would bounce all over the place. But he was getting better at maintaining a cruise speed and, despite his struggles to keep the plane steady, he was in love with flying.

"There's no better feeling in the world," he told Kai one evening when he'd come downstairs and found the Frenchman eating ice cream straight from the container. "It's terrifying and exciting and my heart pounds when we come in for a landing. Like—what if I can't level out in time? What if I fly in too steep and the propeller churns into the tarmac and we explode?"

Kai's lips were glistening white from the ice cream. "How can you enjoy that feeling?"

"It's exhilarating."

"It's petrifying."

"Exactly." He took a spoon from the drawer and joined Kai at the table. "It's after twelve. Why are you sitting in the dark, eating ice cream like a loner?"

"Loner?"

"On your own."

Kai slid the tub towards Caleb. "No reason."

He sucked melting ice cream from the side of his thumb and Caleb had to look away. When he glanced up again, Kai's bright amber eyes were staring at him.

"What?"

"*Je ne sais pas quoi dire*," Kai said.

"I don't know what you said."

"It's okay. Never mind. I'm going to bed. Good night."

As Kai left the kitchen, Caleb called, "*Bonne nuit*." He hadn't learned much French over the years, but he remembered how to say good night.

The following evening, as he was piecing together a costume for the hospital's annual Halloween party that weekend, he looked out of his window and saw Kai sitting at the picnic table in the garden, a thick scarf pulled tight around his neck, and he was gesticulating with one hand while talking on the phone. Caleb couldn't hear him—not that he'd have understood him anyway if he was speaking French—but from his movements and the dark expression that knotted his eyebrows, he looked angry or scared.

Caleb closed his curtains, letting Kai have his privacy.

He'd struggled to come up with a suitable Halloween costume that didn't cost a fortune, but he'd asked Colin if he could take a few handfuls of straw from the bales that lined the sides of the airfield's runway, and he found a pair of oversized dungarees at a local charity shop. Together with a plaid shirt and one of Mum's old sunhats, he'd managed to turn himself into the scarecrow from *The Wizard of Oz*, with patches of straw stuffed into the neckline and cuffs of his shirt, and some more under the brim of the hat. He bought cheap Halloween makeup to add rouge to his nose and some freckles. It was far from perfect, and he looked nothing like the character from the old movie, but it would do.

As he came downstairs that evening, Mum was dressed as a witch, answering the door to trick-or-treaters, and Charlie was stretched out on the couch screaming into his headset as usual. Like most kids his age, he was too old for Halloween.

Fireworks exploded somewhere in the distance and the doorbell chimed again.

Mum said, "Get the door, will you? I need to straighten my makeup."

"Trick or treat," the kids yelled.

Caleb doled out miniature Snickers and tiny packets of Smarties, and when the kids walked across the lawn to the neighbour's house, Caleb closed the door and said, "Charlie, get the door if it goes again. Where's Kai?"

Charlie shrugged. "On your right, Danny. They're hiding behind the trees." He bashed the buttons of his controller.

Caleb called upstairs. "Mum. I'm going now."

On his way through the kitchen to the garage, he spotted Kai sitting at the picnic table outside again. He was a formless shape in the dark, huddled against the chill of late October, and Caleb wouldn't have seen him if it hadn't been for the glow of his phone.

Caleb watched him through the window for a minute, and when he stopped texting and his phone screen went dark, Caleb joined him, walking across the lawn like a brainless scarecrow.

Kai laughed, but there was no mirth in it.

"You okay?"

One of the neighbours set off a Catherine wheel and it hissed and sparked to the excited screeches of children.

Kai nodded. "What are you dressed as?"

"Isn't it obvious? I'm a friend of Dorothy's," Caleb said, hoping Kai would understand the double meaning. But Kai only narrowed his eyes in a question. "I'm the scarecrow from *The Wizard of Oz*."

"I see."

"Is it no good? I look stupid, don't I?"

"No. You look fine. It's good." The flat expression on his face had a sadness about it that Caleb couldn't ignore.

He checked the time on his phone screen, then sat at the table opposite him. "Are you all right? You seem to spend a lot of time out here on your own."

Kai looked at the house. "I had to take a call."

"Everything okay at home?"

"It's fine."

"Then why do you look so sad?"

"Do I?"

"I'm a good listener if you need to talk."

"It's just—*merde.* I have some things to deal with."

Caleb heard the darkness in Kai's voice, and he paused, waiting to see if he would elaborate. When he didn't, he said, "Are you homesick?"

"No."

"But you're not enjoying it here, are you?"

"I love it here. I'm just . . . lonely."

"All right, mister. You're coming with me." He stood up and reached out his hand. "I'm not taking no for an answer."

"Caleb."

"Come on." He took Kai's hand and dragged him off the bench, but the skin contact was electric, and he let go when Kai was standing. He led him upstairs and into his bedroom. "Stay here." Caleb went up to the attic and found a box of old Halloween costumes he'd worn in previous years. He never wanted to dress as the same thing twice, so the old costumes had been worn once, washed and put away in storage.

He took the box into his room and dumped it on the floor in front of Kai's feet. "Pick something."

Kai crouched and opened the box. "I don't understand."

"Don't ask me to say it in French because I can't. But you're coming with me to a Halloween party."

"I don't need your pity friendship."

"Suit yourself. But you're still coming."

Kai rummaged in the box and pulled out a hockey mask, followed by a purple Joker jacket. Beneath that was a clown mask and one shoulder guard from a stormtrooper costume.

"Are none of these outfits complete? Should I go as Jason the Stormtrooper-Joker-Clown?"

"You can go as a pantomime dame for all I care, just get undressed and pick something to wear." He folded his arms in mock impatience, and when Kai turned his back to get changed, Caleb didn't look.

He didn't see the smooth brown skin of his back.

Didn't see the white boxer briefs that framed his butt.

Or the fine hairs on his legs.

And when Kai turned, smiling through his costume, Caleb made a point of not looking even harder.

As they rode across town on Caleb's moped, a scarecrow at the front, with Jason Voorhees' arms wrapped around his waist, Caleb laughed.

He pulled up outside the hospital and when he cut the engine, Kai took his helmet off and slipped on his mask. "Why are we here?"

"For the party."

"At a hospital?"

They walked towards the entrance as an ambulance siren wailed across the night. He'd forgotten Kai didn't know about his transplant and he didn't feel like explaining it now. "I volunteer here. For the sick kids."

"It's a kids' party?"

"Sorry," Caleb said. "Were you expecting alcohol and beer pong? It's not all kids. Mostly teenagers and the staff. Is that okay?"

"I couldn't leave now if I wanted to," Kai winked.

"Party of the century," Caleb said as they went inside. He waved at the security officer and then they took the stairs to the third floor.

"I can't see in this mask."

Caleb appraised him. The navy boilersuit was far from flattering, but the soft French accent that was muffled by the hockey mask was still appealing. "You look good," he said. "Listen. Before we go in. You should know—this is a transplant unit. It's not just teens, there are some adults too. Some of them will be too sick to come out of their rooms. Some won't look very healthy. Just so you know."

Kai nodded. "How did you end up volunteering in a transplant unit?"

Caleb held the door open for him. "Just lucky, I guess. Come on."

The party was in full swing. In the open family area that was separated from the private rooms by the nurses' station, teenagers and adults who weren't at risk of infection were in various costumes, milling around, holding cups of juice and paper plates filled with cakes and sweets. Soft party music danced from hidden speakers overhead and the walls were decorated with skeletons, cobwebs and a few childish paintings of ghosts and vampires.

Caleb spotted Abigail, the ward manager, who was wearing a cloak and pointed hat and had a fake nose and green face paint. "Abi, this is Kai. He's been staying with us for a while."

Kai raised his mask and smiled. "*Bonjour*. Hello."

"*Bonjour* to you, too," she said, shaking his hand. "It's good of you guys to join us."

"You know I wouldn't miss it."

"Jayne's in her room. She's not doing so well."

"Should I go see her?" Caleb asked. To Kai, he said, "I won't be long."

Abigail said, "Take your friend. Maybe the company will help. Sanitise your hands, please. And don't forget your masks."

They went around the nurses' station and into Jayne's room where her parents were sitting at her bedside. He introduced them to Kai and then looked at Jayne. She was ashen-faced, and her eyes drooped with tiredness.

"Not too much stimulation, okay?" Mrs Goddard said, and she and her husband stepped out of the room.

Caleb touched the back of Jayne's warm hand, and she opened her eyes.

She tried to speak but choked on her words and Kai came to her side as if he could do something to help her. The fact that he didn't flee was enough of an indication to Caleb that he was one of the good guys.

Kai took his Halloween mask off.

When she could speak, Jayne said, "Put it back on. You're far scarier without it." Her breath was laboured but her smile was genuine.

Kai said, "Not as scary as Caleb without the makeup."

Jayne laughed.

"How are you?" Caleb asked. It was hard to believe she was only thirteen; her puffy skin made her appear haggard and ancient.

"Tired."

"Any news?"

"Nothing yet."

To Kai, Caleb said, "Jayne's on the heart transplant list. Super-urgent. I'm sure they'll find a match soon."

"Not soon enough," Jayne said.

"Ah. You're in one of those moods." He hopped up on the bed beside her, careful of her dripline, and he stretched out, making a point of getting cosy.

"Should you be doing that?" Kai asked.

"Jayne doesn't mind. Do you, Jayne?"

"It's not like it's turning either one of us on."

Caleb laughed. "You're too young to know about being turned on."

"You're not getting me hot under the collar, anyway."

"Good."

"Good."

"Good," Kai agreed. And they all laughed. Kai said, "It's nice to meet you, Jayne. I'm going to go and find some cake." He touched her arm, and then he smiled at Caleb and left.

"Is he your Prince Charming?" Jayne asked.

"If only. He's the one I told you about, the guy who's staying at ours for a semester while he goes to Trinity."

"He's cute."

"No, he's not. He's fit."

"Proper fit."

"Yeah." Caleb turned on the bed to face her. "How're you doing?"

"I'm okay."

"Jayne."

Her face crumpled and she broke into tears.

"Hey," he soothed, putting an arm over her shoulders.

She sobbed against him for a minute. "They pump me full of so much stuff to numb the pain, but it still hurts. Half the time I can't breathe, and I can feel my heartbeat stopping and starting. I'm swelling up like a balloon and my feet are as big as footballs. And now there's blood in my mucus."

He stroked her hair back out of her face. "It's always darkest—"

"Don't come at me with your kitschy sayings, Caleb. I don't need that right now."

"What do you need?"

"Use your brain."

Caleb tapped his straw hat. "I don't have a brain."

"You don't need a costume to prove that."

"Very funny."

Jayne wiped her eyes with the back of her hand. "Your straw tickles." He turned over and stared at the ceiling. They did this before. Abigail didn't approve of him being on the bed with Jayne, and her mother thought it might interfere with the sterility of her room, but Jayne liked him lying beside her, looking at a spot on the ceiling so that neither of them could see each other.

Only then would she ask the hardest questions. And their rule was that they couldn't lie. When they assumed the position, every word had to be the truth.

"How terrified were you of dying?" she asked him.

"On a scale of one to a hundred? About one hundred and

fifty. How scared are you?"

"One hundred and forty-nine."

"Truth," he said.

"I don't want to go to sleep in case I never wake up." He felt her fingers reach for his hand. "Am I going to die?"

He didn't pause. Pausing was the sign of a lie. "One day."

"Which day?"

"I don't know."

"Could it be tomorrow?"

"Pass."

"Could it be tomorrow?"

"It could be," he said. And he couldn't contradict himself. As much as he wanted to, he couldn't say, "But maybe it won't be." Her rules were strict. He'd been where she was. And as they lay beside each other and stared at the ceiling, he had to be honest. But so did she. "Do you think you will die tomorrow?"

"No," she said.

"If they find you a heart, do you think you'll survive the surgery?"

"Yes." Then she said, "Did your parents' constant tears make you angry?"

"Always."

She didn't ask another question and Caleb turned his head to look at her. She was crying again, silent tears this time, and they rolled over her cheekbones to her ears.

"I don't want to die," she whispered.

"I don't want you to die, either." He brushed a thumb over her cheek. "I have to take you to prom, remember? What did you ask me for? The waltz, wasn't it? I've been practising."

"No, you haven't."

"No. But I will. It's on my bucket list to take a girl to prom."

"Sure it is. What about that gorgeous Frenchman?"

"You can ask him for a dance when I'm done with him."

Jayne pretended to gag, but she choked instead, a thick, wet sound that rattled around the room. He rolled her onto her side and rubbed her back until she stopped coughing.

He got off the bed when Kai came back in with three cups of juice in his hands. "I wasn't sure what you were allowed to drink?"

Jayne nodded and took the cup, but she didn't drink from it.

"Everything is okay?" he asked, his mask pushed on top of his head and his accent strong.

"Say something in French," Jayne said.

Kai smiled. "*Quelque chose en français.*"

"What does that mean?"

"You asked me to say something in French. It means, 'something in French.'"

Jayne closed her eyes. "Everyone's a funny man."

They sat with her for a few more minutes, but when she looked exhausted, they said their goodbyes. Outside her room, when Caleb closed her door, he touched Kai's back to get his attention.

Kai turned.

"Thank you."

"What for?"

And Caleb pulled him into a hug. "For being here. And for treating her like a person."

11.
KAI

Kai felt a tingle of anticipation as Caleb's arms wrapped around his neck. But Caleb pulled away after a few seconds, and his smile was shy.

"Come on. Let's get back to the party."

He didn't know what to expect when they'd pulled up on Caleb's moped outside the hospital in their Halloween costumes, but he hadn't counted on being surrounded by so many sick teenagers. In the family area, one girl was dressed as a zombie with peeling skin and knotted hair, and Kai wasn't sure how much of her sickly pallor was makeup and how much was real. He kept his hockey mask on in the hopes that he wasn't breathing out any nasty spores that could harm the kids.

A young boy, eight or nine years old, came towards him in a wheelchair, and from the loose neck of his hospital gown, Kai saw an angry red scar on his chest that looked fresh, as though at any moment it could tear open and bleed.

"That's some amazing makeup," Caleb told him. "Tony hasn't had any surgery yet."

"It looks so real. Is it not in poor taste?"

"These kids have a sick sense of humour. They have to or they'd just curl up and wait for death."

Kai's phone vibrated in his pocket. "You know a lot about these children?"

"I've been volunteering here for years. Are you going to answer that?"

Kai pulled his phone out and slid the call option to Reject. "It's not important. What kind are these?" he asked, pointing at a plate of cakes. He knew what they were, but he was trying to change the subject. Fatima could wait.

But his phone rang again before he could put it away.

"Chocolate brownies. One of the parents must have made them. Whoever is calling you is pretty insistent."

Kai swiped the screen again.

Caleb said, "If you need to get that, I don't mind."

"We're at a party. It can wait."

Caleb nodded, though there was a flash of doubt across his face. "Wait here. I'm going to find Roger. He's one of the nurses. If I know him like I think I do, he'll have a little flask of something stronger than cherryade."

Alone, Kai looked at his phone. As well as two missed calls, there was a text message. *Call me. Urgent.*

She'd been gone for six years, and now she had something urgent to say?

When she first disappeared, it had taken her almost eight months to get in touch. A single text message from a number with the +371 country code that he didn't recognise pinged one night while he slept. He woke up as his phone danced on the bedside table.

I'm safe. Love you. Delete this.

He replied, *Where are you?* But Fatima didn't respond. He deleted the message and pushed the phone under his pillow. He couldn't sleep for the rest of the night, and every time he thought he heard his phone ping, he looked at the blank screen and then shoved it under the pillow again.

On his fourteenth birthday, he received another message, this time from a different country code. *Happy cake day.*

Her messages were in English, as though that would make them harder for Mum or Dad to interpret if they ever found Kai's phone, and he typed his replies in English, too. Not that she ever responded.

Not until he was fifteen. He'd gone on a week-long field trip to Montpellier with school when he got a text from Fatima that read, *Still travelling. Still miss you.*

He replied, *Can we talk?*

She didn't respond until he sent a follow-up message. *I'm in Montpellier with school. Mum and Dad aren't here.*

In two minutes, his phone rang, and he excused himself from the hotel lobby where he'd been sitting with some class-mates. Outside the hotel, staring down the wide road towards the Porte du Peyrou arch, he answered the phone, pressed it to his ear, and held his breath.

He didn't speak.

A muffled voice said, "Is that you?"

"Yes. Is it really you?"

"Yes," Fatima said, and he heard the tears in her voice.

They talked until his phone beeped. "My battery is going to die."

"Charge it."

"I'm outside."

"How long are you in Montpellier?"

"Until Saturday."

His phone died before she could respond.

She'd been halfway across the world and back since leaving her jacket and her shoes on the bank of the Seine. When Kai told her they'd only found one of those shoes, she laughed. "That makes it better," she'd said. "If they ever find the other shoe downriver, they'll know I was washed away."

"How could you do that?" Kai demanded. "Mum and Dad's world has been ruined. I didn't think Dad could cry until you went away. It's been two years and I still hear them sobbing at night."

"I didn't do this, Kaiser. They did."

"Where's Avery?"

"She's here."

Avery Truffaut didn't disappear on the same night. She held Kai's hand in the days that followed, and they joined the search party along the banks of the Seine, calling Fatima's name into the river as if they could entice her back. She squeezed Kai's fingers when he cried, and she kissed his cheek and whispered, "Tell no one. You made a promise."

"Why won't she come home?" he asked her.

"You know why."

She stayed with her parents until the end of the summer, and then she went to university—somewhere abroad, Kai heard—and she never returned.

Caleb nudged him with an elbow and handed him a plastic cup. When Kai looked up, he realised he'd been staring at his phone. He put it away.

"I know I've asked you before, but are you okay? Really? You look whiter than me."

"Sorry."

"What's going on?"

Kai shook his head. "I'm fine. This is a great party. I'm glad you invited me."

"You don't look it."

"How can you tell behind my mask?"

Caleb smiled. "I have a sixth sense."

And Kai's phone rang again.

"Seriously, man. Answer your phone, before I answer it for you."

He slipped his mask off, swallowed the contents of his cup, the unexpected warmth of alcohol burning in his chest, and he stepped out of the ward to answer the phone.

"Why didn't you pick up?" Fatima asked as he jogged down the stairs, across the lobby and into the cold night air.

"I was busy."

"Have you heard from Mum?"

"No. Why? Have you?"

"Avery heard from a friend of a friend," Fatima said. "They've started another petition to search the Seine."

"Again?"

"You have to stop them."

Kai didn't know what to say. Mum had petitioned the courts every six months since Fatima disappeared, but her request was never granted. As far as the courts were concerned, her daughter's body could be in the English Channel by now. Sonar, coupled with a team of divers, would never find a body and, even if they did spot something, identifying the remains would lead detectives to someone else entirely. But he realised that Fatima wasn't aware of this.

"She's asked before. They never say yes."

"What if they say yes this time?" Fatima asked.

"They won't. And if they do, so what? Just because they don't find a body doesn't mean there isn't one down there somewhere. Where are you now anyway?"

"Sweden."

Kai sat on a bench outside the hospital and looked up at the cloudy sky. Fireworks erupted somewhere in the north. "Why do you move around so often? It's not like Mum and Dad are chasing you."

"Nowhere feels like home."

"That's because you're not home."

"I can't go back, Kai."

"What about Provence or somewhere far away from Paris? Somewhere that's still France."

"I can't be myself in France. Not while Mum and Dad are there."

She had explained, while he was in Montpellier that year, that her reason for leaving was because Mum had found out about her relationship with a girl. "You will get married to Zameer at once and forget this nonsense," Mum had told her. "You will not tarnish your father's name. I will not allow it."

They'd argued, and Fatima told Mum she would never marry Zameer.

"But it is arranged. You will marry him and that's final."

"Then I'll run away."

"You will destroy this family if you do," Mum had said.

In the broken-hearted confusion that followed Fatima's disappearance, Mum had even embraced Avery when she came to pay her respects at the funeral. Kai could see that she was too distraught to recognise her daughter's girlfriend.

For years, Kai hated Avery. She was the one that broke his family in two. She was the one who made Fatima leave. But the older he got, and the more his Mum asked him about girls, the more he admired Fatima for getting out.

"I'm gay," he admitted to his sister a month before leaving for Ireland.

She was silent for a second, her breathing loud as he pressed the phone to his ear. He was leaning out of his bedroom window, hoping his parents wouldn't hear him.

Fatima said, "Welcome to Gay Club. The first rule of Gay Club is: don't tell Mum."

He never would.

Ever since Louis Chastain kissed him in the locker room at school, he knew he liked boys. Maybe even before then. But being gay was a sin in both of his parents' religions. In Algeria, he could be imprisoned for it, and his Muslim father would disown him—or worse. And Mum's Christian faith meant that no matter where he went he would always be an abomination to her.

To his dad, he would burn in Jahannam for all eternity.

To his mum, he'd never enter the kingdom of Heaven.

"I'm going to Ireland for university," he'd told Fatima that night as he leaned out of his window. "She'll never find out."

Fatima said, "Because you know if she does, you're dead, right?"

"I know."

"Do you have a boyfriend?"

"No." Louis Chastain kept coming back for more kisses in the weeks that followed, but they'd never taken it any further, and he hadn't been with anyone since.

Now, under the warm glow from the hospital windows, Kai said, "You should come to Ireland. You probably wouldn't even recognise me after all this time."

"Of course I'd recognise you, freckle-face."

"Piss off."

He heard Avery's soft voice in the background.

"I have to go."

Kai stood. "Yeah. Me too. I'm at a party."

"Happy Halloween."

He ended the call.

He was glad that she was happy, but he could never understand the need to fake her death. It was the kind of thing you'd see in the movies, and he remembered thinking, at thirteen, that she'd never get away with it. She'd get to the Spanish border, or Germany or Switzerland, and they'd stop her. He thought— had hoped—that a day or two after she disappeared, she'd be brought home in the back of a police car, her hair covering a sorrowful face, with a promise to marry Zameer and never see Avery again.

But that hadn't happened. And the longer it got, the smaller his hope became. And now, standing on the edge of a hospital carpark, dressed as Jason Vorhees, he almost wished she'd taken him with her. They could have gone on the run, just the two of them, and maybe fate would have brought them to Ireland anyway. Maybe Kai would have met Caleb regardless. And maybe, if he ever plucked up the courage, he'd ask the wannabe pilot for a kiss.

If only.

He went back upstairs.

Caleb was in conversation with the ward manager when Kai approached, and he put an arm around Kai's shoulders. "This guy," he said, "can speak perfect French. Go on, ask him to say something."

"No kidding," Abigail said. She winked at Kai, then said, "*Salut Kai. Moi c'est Abigail. Ça va? Il est très drôle.*" She rolled her eyes with exaggeration when she called Caleb really funny.

Kai laughed.

Caleb said, "What? What'd she say?"

"Nothing," he told him, and Abigail winked.

"I'm glad you're both here," she said. "Caleb, you were one of our Christmas elves last year. This year, I've had two cancellations. And you're both about the same size. What do you say?"

"Christmas elves?" Kai asked.

Caleb said, "Every year, Santa Claus visits the ward and

hands out gifts to the patients. It's actually really fun. Are you interested?"

"And we have to dress up?"

"You can't be an elf without some elf clothes," Abigail said.

To Kai, Caleb said, "You're going home for Christmas, though, right?"

"That was the plan. Sorry, Abigail. If I was staying, I'd definitely help out."

"It was worth a shot," Abigail said, and she fist bumped them before walking away.

Caleb said, "Was your call important?"

"No. But I'm glad I took it."

He picked at a plate of cocktail sausages and mini sausage rolls, and then held it out to share. "I'm sorry. When I invited you to a party, I should have told you it was a kids' thing."

"No, it's fine. The DJ is *très drôle*." Behind a makeshift DJ table with two laptops and a floor speaker, a brightly coloured clown was twisting a balloon into an animal.

"Shall we go home?" Caleb suggested.

"Don't you want to stay?"

"We can always go and eat whatever sweets are left at home."

"Your place or mine?" Kai asked, and he was grateful for the hockey mask that hid his blush.

On the back of Caleb's moped, Kai put his arms around his waist, linking his fingers together, and he felt the warmth of Caleb's body. He clung to him as they rode home and leaned with him as they rounded the corners.

And when they stopped at a set of traffic lights, Caleb flipped his visor up and turned his head. "You okay?"

"Perfect," Kai said.
And he meant it.

12.

CALEB

Caleb lay in bed, swallowed in his thick duvet, and listened to the sounds of Kai as he came out of his bedroom and went into the bathroom. He heard the door close, an electric toothbrush whir, and then the water was turned on and the shower door slid closed on its runner.

When they got back from the hospital party last night, Kai went upstairs, changed out of his Halloween costume, and came back down to the kitchen in a pair of loose-fitting, maroon pyjama bottoms and a plain white T-shirt. He'd folded the boiler suit and he sat it on the kitchen table, with the hockey mask on top. "I'll wash it in the morning."

"It's fine," Caleb had said. "Mum'll do it."

"I had a good night. Thank you."

"It doesn't have to be over."

Kai looked at him. He had a dimple on his left cheek when he smiled, as though someone had stolen the other one.

Caleb turned away from him, opening cupboard doors. "It's still early. And I'm almost certain we have a bottle of crème de menthe left over from Easter." He found the bottle and grabbed two shot glasses. "Sit," he said, pulling a chair out from the table.

Kai sat opposite him without a word, the Jason Vorhees costume between them like a memorial.

Caleb filled the glasses with the thick green liquid and slid one across the table. "*Sláinte*."

"Is that Irish?"

"Yes. It means 'cheers' or 'good health'."

Kai raised his glass. "In France we say *Santé*."

"*Santé*," Caleb repeated, sounding it out. The word wasn't too dissimilar from its Irish equivalent. They drank and he poured another round. "Do you miss home?"

"No." The word was quick on his lips. But he added, "I mean, I guess I miss my parents. But I don't miss Paris."

"Why not?"

Kai indicated that he wanted the bottle and when Caleb passed it to him, he poured two more shots. "Do you ever try to run away from your memories?"

"Every day."

"This is why I do not miss Paris."

"You must have some good memories."

"Yes. Some."

Instead of reaching across the table for the bottle, Caleb slid into a chair closer to Kai. "What is your worst memory?"

"What?"

"Your worst-ever memory. What is it?"

Kai took another shot before answering. "The day my sister's coat and shoe were found floating in the River Seine and we never saw her again."

"Shit. Fuck. Sorry."

Kai put his hand on Caleb's. "Don't. It's okay."

"No, I'm sorry. I shouldn't have asked that. I didn't even know you had a sister."

"I don't talk about it often."

"I'm so sorry."

Kai shook his head. "I can't tell you what happened. I want to, but—"

"I'm sorry."

"Stop apologising."

Kai's hand was still on top of his. He could feel the heat of his skin.

"What is *your* worst memory?" Kai asked.

"Why don't we do best memories instead?" When Kai pulled his hand away, Caleb felt as though his own fingers had a fever. He could have mentioned his heart—should have. But he changed the subject. He wasn't sure why.

"Okay. My favourite memory," Kai said, thinking about it as he poured more shots, "is Christmas when I was eight. My father—he's a carpenter. There was very little work that year. From September until the following February, Mum took an evening job as a cleaner at my school. Just so they could afford to buy food. Dad would come home from seeking work and Mum would kiss his cheek and tell Fatima and I—that's my sister— to do our homework. And she would go to work, cleaning the school, and I would be in bed by the time she returned. When I woke, Dad would have gone out looking for employment and Mum would be cleaning the house. For months, that was all she did. She cleaned the house and then she cleaned the school. She was tired; I could see it in her eyes. And Dad would look for work and come home in the evenings and say that there were still no jobs. And Mum would kiss his cheek and go to the school again."

Caleb poured more shots. "This doesn't sound like a good memory."

"Just wait. *Santé*. In November, our parents called a family meeting and they said, 'There is little money. Pick one thing that you would like from Père Noël.' That is the year that I knew Father Christmas was make-believe. I had been begging my dad for a bicycle since the summer. And when I knew that Père Noël couldn't afford it because he was just my father in a red coat, I said, 'I do not need a bicycle. I can walk to school. Therefore, I would like a dictionary. A big one.' You see, I already had a dictionary, from school, but it was a pocket one. I wanted one that would fill my desk like in the movies. Not a book but a tome."

When he smiled, Caleb saw the memory dance across his face.

Kai said, "After evening Mass on Christmas Eve, when Père Noël leaves his presents, there was one waiting for me. It was a dictionary—this big. Huge. And I was happy. The jacket was crumpled a little near the spine, and inside the front flap, my parents had tried to erase the pencil mark where it had been priced. I knew it was second-hand, but I didn't care. Is it starting to sound like a happy memory now?"

"A little," Caleb said.

"Inside the dictionary, there was a bookmark. One of those laminated bookmarks with a quote. It said, *Words are the most powerful drug used by mankind*. It is by Rudyard Kipling. And the bookmark was inserted in a page of words beginning with V. And halfway down the page, the word *vélo* was circled in pencil. And when I looked up at my parents, my father had left the room. And when he came back, he was pushing a bicycle. *Vélo* is the French word for bicycle. It was old. It was rusted under the seat, but it was mine. My father helped me restore it. And I never loved him more than I did that Christmas."

The silence that followed his words was thick with wonder. Caleb could imagine an eight-year-old Kai, riding a bike up and down the road outside his home with a giant smile splitting his freckled cheeks. And his dimple would be deep and hold all the promises that the world could throw at him.

And this morning, listening to the sounds of Kai in the bathroom, Caleb smiled. When Kai had asked him what his own favourite memory was, he couldn't think of any. There was the day he woke up with Alice's heart in his chest, but that would require too much explanation. There was the day he realised he wanted to kiss Johnny Appleby, but he wasn't sure if that was a favourite memory or just a preteen fantasy.

"I guess it could be the day Charlie was born," he'd said. "I was nine and I'd spent my whole life as an only child. And when Mum told me she was pregnant, I was so angry. I didn't want to share her love with anyone, especially not an ugly brother. I was her little boy. But the minute I saw Charlie, when Mum was still in the hospital, I fell in love with him. He was so small. So vulnerable. Don't tell him I said this, but when Mum put him into my arms for the first time, I kissed the top of his soft head and said, 'I'm your big brother. I'm your protector now.'"

"Amazing," Kai said.

And Caleb laughed. "These days, I'd rather have the dictionary and the bike."

"You don't mean that."

Caleb had poured the last of the bottle into their shot glasses. "When you've lived with him more than a couple of months, you'll feel the same."

He listened as Kai left the bathroom and returned to his room. And before anybody else could get up, Caleb took a shower. By the time he'd finished, Kai had already gone to college.

At the airfield that morning, Colin Moore tapped his headset and said, "Take a breath. Contact Ground Control. You remember what to say?"

They'd been practising standard radio dialogues. Caleb glanced at the corner of his folder where he'd written down the frequencies for Ground Control and Tower, and into his headset he said, "Dublin Ground, this is Cessna EL-YBY at Alpha, requesting taxi to active, with information Delta." He'd spelled out their tail number using the NATO phonetic alphabet, which he had to recite in his head a few times before speaking. Before his lesson, he'd written on the back of his hand: Echo, Lima, Yankee, Bravo, Yankee.

Ground Control was quick to respond. "Cessna EL-YBY, Dublin Ground. Taxi to Runway 2 Left via Alpha, Alpha 3."

"Taxiing to Runway 2 Left via Alpha to Alpha 3. YBY,"

Caleb confirmed. Then he added, "Thank you. Have a nice day."

"Never forget your manners," Colin had told him on day one.

When he'd taxied to the runway boundary, he switched frequency and requested permission for take-off from the Tower.

Tower said, "Cessna EL-YBY, Dublin Tower. Hold short on Runway 2." A minute later, they said, "Cleared for take-off. Fly runway heading; left turn approved."

Caleb confirmed the instruction and signed off. He loved this part. As he gained speed on the runway and pulled the wheel back, he felt the air take them, and as he levelled out at his assigned altitude, his stomach dropped the way it does on a rollercoaster.

Colin shook his head. "If that grin gets any bigger, you'll swallow yourself."

He maintained an altitude of 3,000 feet, dropping and rising at Colin's request, and the longer he flew, the better he was at keeping the plane's nose straight.

Below them, Dublin was a myriad of moving parts, a machine that survived only because each part knew what the other was doing.

Colin questioned him at every point of their lesson, and he was correcting him less than in previous flights.

"Good going," he said when they'd circled out over the coast three times. "Time to take her on home."

Six kilometres from the airfield, Caleb radioed Dublin Tower to request permission to land. He remembered his tail number without looking at his hand, and Tower told him which runway to come in on. But because he was still so far out, they said, "Report on approach."

He said to Colin, "I think it's time we start booking a few two-hour sessions."

"I know you're keen to pass, Caleb, but let's stick to what we're doing for now. Your patterns are still a bit sloppy."

"Then two-hour flights would help, right?"

"You'd be braindead halfway through the second hour."

He began his descent. "You're a spoilsport," he laughed, taking his eyes off the panel to glare at Colin.

And as soon as he did, Colin held up one hand and smacked the dash with the other. "Engine failure," he said.

For a second, Caleb took his hands off the wheel. He panicked. He knew the engine was fine and that Colin was testing him, but he couldn't remember the procedure for in-flight engine failure. He gripped the wheel again before it pulled and he said, "Trim to eighty. There's a field down there. Is it long enough? I think it's long enough. Attempt engine restart." He indicated but didn't touch the relevant switches as he said, "If no restart, squawk 7500. Check seat and seatbelt. Stow loose or sharp objects. Flip doors before touchdown. And land with all the grace of a baby dalmatian on ice."

Colin said, "And when you land, you'll have the international authorities gunning you down. What did you do wrong?"

Caleb didn't have a clue.

"What was your squawk code?"

"7500?" He'd been trying to memorise the codes that would be entered into the transponder depending on the situation.

"That's not the emergency code, is it?"

"Shit."

"What did you tell ATC?"

Caleb shook his head. He was annoyed with himself. Instead of telling Air Traffic Control that he was in engine distress, he'd announced that they were being hijacked. "Damn it."

"And this is why we don't let students squawk emergencies for real," Colin said. "What should your squawk code have been?"

"7700. I know it. I swear I do."

"Get your codes right," Colin said. "You're not going solo until you do." On the ground, he took control, leading them back to the hangar, and he laughed. "You were going to land with all the grace of a what?"

"Baby dalmatian on ice."

"Never mind your squawk codes, you need better analogies."

"My analogies are just fine," Caleb said, and then his shoulders slumped when he saw his dad's car in the parking lot.

"Yo, kiddo. Fancy lunch?"

"Does Mum push my iCal to your phone, or do you just follow me everywhere I go?"

"I'm paying for these suckers. Of course I'm going to know when you're flying."

Dad drove him to a pub for lunch and when they got there, Joanne waved. Dad's girlfriend managed to grab a small round table and she'd pushed a third chair toward it. The fact that Dad didn't tell him she'd be there made Caleb puff his cheeks up and sigh. When he saw Kai later, he'd have a new worst memory to share.

But Dad said, "We've got something to ask you."

And Caleb said, "I'm not giving you away."

Joanne laughed. "I'm not marrying the old geezer, I'm just in it for the sex."

"Jesus, Joanne. The kid doesn't need to hear that."

"Relax," she said. "He's not a kid. And he knows I'm only joking."

Dad scowled and went to the bar. When they were alone, Caleb said, "I'm glad you're joking because I'm not calling you Stepmum. What's going on?" She was only eleven years older than him and even thinking about her with his dad was weird.

"You know he loves you, right?"

"Sure."

"And you know we live ten kilometres closer to the airfield than your mum does, right?"

"What're you getting at?"

"You know what I'm getting at," she said. "Here he comes. Act surprised when he asks you."

Dad sat their drinks on the table and Caleb pulled his pint towards him. "It's not happening," he said.

"What isn't?" Dad asked.

"Whatever you're about to ask me."

To Joanne, Dad said, "You told him?"

"No, he just guessed."

Dad put his hand on Caleb's arm. "You know it makes sense. Your mum has Charlie and that new lodger. And we have a tonne of space. You can have your freedom. And I can drive you to the airfield every week. Joanne can have a room ready for you by the weekend. What do you say, kiddo?"

Caleb didn't want to consider the idea. Getting out from under Mum's thumb would be amazing. But living with Dad and Joanne would likely kill him.

And being away from Kai's wide smile and that single dimple would make him miserable.

"What do I say?" Caleb asked. "I say stop calling me kiddo."

And Joanne slapped the back of Darren Burke's head. "I told you not to call him that."

13.

KAI

When he got to the library just before nine, it was empty. Even the bus ride into town had been quiet, with only a few passengers and the driver who looked like he was still in last night's Halloween makeup.

Kai took a seat at one of the wide tables and checked the time on his phone. He was sure the sign-up sheet for his study group had said nine o'clock, although he imagined there'd be some hangovers this morning. Halloween seemed to be a huge deal in Ireland and the smell of spent fireworks hung on the air as he'd waited for the bus in the cold gloom of a November morning. It wasn't raining, but the sky was black and angry. And as he pulled a volume of works by Samuel Beckett from the shelves and returned to his table, he heard the sky crack as a flash of lightning illuminated the large windows and the rain drummed against the pane beside him.

It was like the morning that Fatima's empty casket was buried. Paris had been dulled by a grubby storm that dogged the city since the night before, as Kai sat on the edge of his bed, staring at the window, at the gullies of rain that washed it clean, and he begged God to make Fatima change her mind and come home. Before it was too late.

Mum had bought him a black suit and he'd tried it on that afternoon. The shirt was too big in the neck, and the jacket sleeves extended down to his knuckles, but when Mum asked him, "How does it feel?" he said, "Sad."

"I know," she said, and she didn't make any alterations. He didn't have the heart to ask her.

The suit hung on the back of his door, watching over him that night as he pretended to sleep. And in the morning, the rain hadn't let up and Fatima hadn't come home.

The church was packed. Fatima's classmates were there, many in tears as they hugged each other. "Such a horrible way to go," someone said.

The neck of Kai's shirt had bunched up at the sides where Dad had pulled the tie too tight. And Kai sat in the front row, unable to look up at the casket whose lid was closed and there was no body inside. But it wasn't empty.

The detective in charge of Fatima's case said they'd collected all the flowers and teddy bears that had been left on the banks of the Seine where her jacket had been found, and he asked Dad if the family would like to have them.

"It's gruesome," Dad had said.

But Mum said, "Let's put them in the casket. As a memorial."

Mum said Kai could add something too, something personal, and Kai stood in Fatima's bedroom that day, looking at all her belongings, crying because he knew the truth and couldn't say it. If he spoke up now, Dad would find Fatima and kill her. And then they'd really have a body to bury.

Kai chose Fatima's art brushes, and he tied them together with a ribbon and placed them in the casket alongside everything else. She had walked away from everything, every half-squeezed tube of paint, every unused canvas, and the brushes whose soft heads had hardened because they weren't cleaned right. She'd turned her back on them. And on Kai.

And in the church, he kept his eyes on the polished stone floor and he tugged at the neck of his shirt, and Mum put her hand on his leg. And the handkerchief that was scrunched between her fingers was one of Dad's, his initials curled up in the corner of it like the remnants of a happier life.

The priest said his prayers and the congregation responded through their tears. And Kai shook his head when the priest indicated that it was time to come up and recite the poem his Mum had chosen for him to read.

The old priest beckoned him with a crooked smile and a gentle nod. Dad put his hand on Kai's shoulder, and Mum kissed his cheek, right on the same spot that Fatima had kissed him the night she ran away.

Kai stood up but his legs wouldn't work. The priest came down from the altar and led him up to the lectern. And the words on the page in his hands bounced like the rain outside. And when he looked up at the congregation, he saw Avery Truffaut standing in the doorway, framed by the flash of light that shocked the clouds outside.

He sat the sheet of paper on the lectern to stop it from shaking, and he opened his mouth.

He didn't know what words came out.

He didn't know if he was reading the poem or speaking his truth. But when his voice cracked, he looked up at his parents, Mum's hands in Dad's, Dad's forehead pressed against her temple, and Kai said, "I can't."

Mum smiled through her tears. She nodded. Yes, you can, it said. Carry on.

But he didn't know how far down the page he'd read, and his eyes were so thick with tears that he couldn't see it anyway.

Mum came to him. And she rubbed his back and read the words that he could not. And as the pallbearers carried the casket out of the church, the congregation lay their hands on him as though they were prophets and he a sick thing to be healed.

"Sorry for your loss."

"You're so brave."

"She's in a better place."

"You look just like her."

And when they were standing in the cemetery, huddled under black umbrellas, Kai looked around. Avery was no longer there.

And Kai buried his truth inside an empty coffin. And he had to believe that Fatima was gone. She was never coming back. Because, for Mum and Dad, she was dead. To the world, she was gone. That was his new truth, a fake truth, one that had been willed into existence because the more people believed it to be so, the stronger its essence became.

In the library, Kai looked up when someone said, "Nothing to be done."

He studied her face. "Excuse me?"

"I'm beginning to come round to that opinion," she said, and he realised she was quoting the opening lines of dialogue from Beckett's *Waiting for Godot*, the book that was open in front of him but that he couldn't concentrate on.

She unwrapped her scarf from her neck and shook the rain off her coat. "Did you know Beckett originally wrote it in French?"

"No."

"He did."

"That explains the Eiffel Tower reference."

"I'm Emily," she said, taking a seat beside him and unzipping her backpack.

"I know." He'd seen her in class and maybe they'd said hello once or twice, but they'd never had a conversation. He hadn't really had a conversation with anyone since he got here. His classmates seemed to keep to themselves, as though none of them had a clue how to behave in a world of new people. Their professor asked questions at the head of the room, and no one answered him. "And what do we think is the symbolic significance of the meteor in *The Scarlet Letter*?" he asked, and everyone looked at their empty notepads as though the answer would appear there.

For weeks, Kai had taken as many notes as he could, switching out blue biro for red when he needed to write something with emphasis, underlining in green ink, and cramming additional notes in the margins. But he hated Hawthorne's *The*

Scarlet Letter, and Shakespeare in English was just as confusing as Shakespeare in French. Even *The Iliad*, that one classic that would consistently make him smile, left him feeling cold when he read from it.

He didn't know why. Reading used to be fun.

But as September gave way to October, his notetaking became less, and his multicoloured writing technique slipped into a wall of blue text, which became pencil. And by Halloween, not two months into his degree, there were times he didn't even open his notepad during class. And in the evenings, he struggled to read even a few pages.

Fatima was on his mind.

And Caleb was running laps in his head—Caleb with the cheeky smile and the bright eyes and the desire to help sick kids when he had no reason to even think about them. Caleb with a head for heights, who longed to throw himself into the sky and see how high he could get.

And Kai was feeling more isolated by the day.

"It's Kaiser, right?" Emily said. She'd taken her notepad out of her bag but hadn't opened it. There was a biro stuffed through the spiral spine.

"Kai."

She was pretty, in a frizzy-haired kind of way. She wore a sweater that swallowed her body so that he couldn't tell quite how large she was, and the deep red of her lipstick drew a stark contrast to her pale skin.

He smiled. Looked at the words of Samuel Beckett. Watched the rain gush down the large windowpane.

And then someone else arrived, bringing a draught of cold

air with him, and as he slumped into a chair opposite them, he said, "Man, I'm so hungover."

It was easier in a crowd. You could disappear. Kai had perfected the ability to fit in by wearing the right clothes—nothing too loud or too sombre—and speaking occasionally but saying very little. He could stand just close enough to the centre of attention to be part of the circle, but far enough away from the nucleus that his opinion wasn't called upon too often.

In the weeks that followed, he would spend most days in the library, skipping the occasional class, asking Emily if he'd missed anything important when they met for study group, and he'd have conversations by text message with Fatima. Now that he wasn't living at home, she was texting with more frequency. It was easier to talk when they both knew Mum wasn't going to find their exchange.

Kai would cut class and walk through campus in the rain, keeping his head down, hood up, and he'd kick the autumn leaves out of his way and wonder why the hell he was even here. He couldn't bring himself to open a book anymore.

The one thing that kept him in Ireland was Caleb. It was foolish, of course, but Caleb made him feel things he hadn't known were possible. They'd never talked about their feelings or their sexuality, and maybe Caleb was tactile with all of his friends. Once, as they passed on the stairs, Caleb put his hands on Kai's waist after they'd done the side-stepping dance for too long, and he moved him aside with a gentle touch.

"Pleasure doing business with you," he'd said as he continued up the stairs.

And Kai wanted to say, "You smell good," but instead he

said, "Thanks."

And he heard Caleb's laughter as he turned around the corner on the landing.

But when he wasn't in Caleb's presence, he knew that he was lonely. "Depression," Mum had called it when, after Fatima's funeral, Kai refused to speak. "He's suffering from depression," he'd heard her tell Dad.

He understood now that depression came in many forms. When Fatima ran away from home, he was depressed. And when *he* ran away from home, fleeing the country to read books in Ireland, he'd felt worse.

And he still didn't have a job, so flying home for Christmas was looking less likely. Not that he'd be any happier in Paris. He'd fled from his parents for a reason, in almost the same way that Fatima had. What were the odds that they were both gay? It seemed remarkable. But he knew that if he left home the same way she did, their parents would die. And as much as he hated their close-minded views, he didn't want to hurt them. They were still *Maman* and *Papa* regardless of their homophobia. They might not want him to live if they knew the truth, but it's all he wanted for them.

By the first week of December, standing outside the library, he called Mum and said that he couldn't afford to fly home. "But flights in January will be much cheaper," he said.

"You know your father and I would love to help you pay for your flights, don't you?"

"I know."

"But we do not have the spare cash. I'm sorry."

"I understand." His dad was finding it difficult to get work and it made Kai glad that he wasn't there, eating their food and wasting their electricity. "Is the house at risk?" he asked.

"No," she said. "You have no need to worry."

When he hung up the phone, Emily was walking across campus towards him. Every week, she took the chair beside him and tried to involve him in conversation. He smiled when he needed to, and answered her questions, and he hoped that next week she'd sit somewhere else. She was friendly, but he wasn't looking for friends.

"Howerya?" she said as if the greeting was just one word. "Aren't you in the group chat? We're not meeting today. Tommy's got a cold and Sarah had to go to the STI clinic." She held up her hands. "Don't ask."

"Shit," Kai said, and he liked how the English word was harsher than the French.

"Fancy a pint?"

Kai checked his phone.

"I don't bite."

He shrugged. "Okay."

She led him through campus and across the road to O'Neills. She ordered a couple of drinks and paid for them both, and Kai sat at the small round table opposite her as she dipped her finger in her glass to swirl the ice.

"You don't say much, do you?"

"I say enough."

"That's the thing," Emily said. "You say just enough to fly under the radar. It's cute."

She asked him about his life in France, about his family, and he told her very little. And even though he didn't ask, she said, "My dad's on his third marriage, and Mum's popping more wingers than a hedonistic headbanger. And my little sister is up the duff at fifteen, if you can believe it."

"I don't understand half of those words," he admitted.

"All I'm saying is you might have a fucked-up life that you don't want to talk about, but some of us have it worse. Are you Muslim?" she asked.

He was taken aback by her forthright question, but when he had the time to think about it later, he admired her for asking it so bluntly. "Christian."

"Practicing?"

"I go when my mum forces me to. She's quite strict about going to church."

Emily nodded as though she'd just cracked a code. "So, she doesn't know you're gay?"

Kai choked on his beer, and he mopped his chin with the back of his hand.

"It's okay if you are. In Ireland, we don't give a shit."

He held onto his glass so that he had something to do with his hands. And he couldn't meet her eyes. "Is it obvious?"

"Probably not to anyone else. But my ex-boyfriend turned out to be gay. So I kind of have an inside track. You're not out to many people, are you?"

"Just my—just a girl from Paris."

"Well," Emily said. "Now you've doubled your inner circle. One hundred percent increase in confidantes. Not bad for a day's work, eh?"

Kai smiled. He couldn't help it. She had this infectious way about her that drew him in. He hadn't been looking for a friend, but he'd found one anyway.

"Can I say it out loud?" he asked.

Emily grinned. She stuck out her hand. "Hi. I'm Emily and I'm straight."

"Hi, Emily. I'm Kai," he said. "And I'm gay."

And it felt good, saying it openly, without fear of rejection.

14.
CALEB

Mum and Charlie were putting up the Christmas decorations when Caleb said it was time for his appointment.

"Crap," Mum said. "Is it two o'clock already?"

"If you're too busy, you don't have to come. I can go on my own. I'm a big kid now."

She draped a strand of tinsel around his neck and patted his cheek. "You will never be a big kid to me."

"Don't I know it."

"Be thankful you have a mother who cares."

"Can't she care a little less?"

"Never."

Charlie stepped over the box of baubles and grabbed his PlayStation controller, but Mum took it from him and put it in her handbag.

"Your job's not done. I want that tree to look immaculate by the time we're home. But leave the angel until I get back. I need a photo of you putting it on like we always do."

When she stepped out of the room, Charlie said, "She knows I've got another controller, right?"

"Mum," Caleb called with a grin, and Charlie punched his arm. Caleb pulled him into a headlock and gave him a noogie. When he squirmed away, Caleb said, "I want that tree looking immaculate. Like the Conception."

He didn't know Mum had come back into the room until she smacked the back of his head with a suppressed laugh. "Come on, you don't want to be late."

In the car, Caleb said, "Did Kai tell you when he's going home for Christmas?"

"I was going to talk to the pair of you about that."

"Oh?"

"He doesn't get his next Student Support grant until the middle of January, and I think his parents are struggling a bit, financially. He's going to be staying with us over the holiday."

"Okay. Cool."

"'Okay, cool?'" Mum asked. "You're all right with him staying over Christmas?"

"Why wouldn't I be?"

"I'd hoped you'd be fine with it, but I expected a little bit more drama than, 'Okay, cool.' You'd say, 'Jeez, does he have to stay?' and I'd say, 'Yes, I'm putting my foot down,' and then maybe there'd be some slamming of doors and stomping of feet. And eventually, you'd see that letting him stay with us for Christmas is the right thing to do."

Caleb punched the dashboard. "Jeez, does he have to stay?"

"Yes," Mum said, laughing.

"But he's so French."

"What do you have against the French?"

He wanted his body against the French, but he didn't say that. "Charlie will be cool with it, too."

"You think?"

"If anyone will wilfully go up against him on the PlayStation and lose consistently, Charlie wouldn't care if you invited Robespierre."

"Look at you being geographically topical." She pulled into the hospital carpark, found a parking spot, and cut the engine. "Do you really think he'll be okay with it? I've been putting off telling you guys all week."

"Mum, we're three weeks out from Christmas. If he doesn't go home soon, we'd have figured it out anyway. Charlie will be fine. He's a good kid."

"You're both good kids."

"I'm not a kid."

"Santa isn't real," she said.

Caleb clutched his heart. "You're killing me."

She pulled him into a hug and brushed his hair back from his face. "Sometimes I think about killing you just so I can keep you young and innocent."

"You're scaring me now. Besides. I haven't been young or innocent for many years."

"You think I'm kidding? I don't want you to grow up."

"Growing up is just something that happens, Mum. We can't avoid it."

She cupped his face and kissed his forehead. "Four and a half years ago, I didn't think you'd be around to grow up."

"And twenty years from now, when I'm picking out your nursing home, you'll wish I wasn't here."

"Twenty years from now, I'll be moving in with you and your husband so you can look after me."

"What—there was no room in Charlie's bachelor pad?"

"Charlie doesn't need me the way you do."

"You're kidding, right?"

He got out of the car. Dr Hughes' office was on the ground floor, but he looked up at the third-floor windows where the transplant unit was. He could see Jayne's room from the car-park, even if he couldn't see inside. His time in hospital, before and after his surgery, had been a welcome break from Mum's incessant care. She wasn't joking. If she could live with him forever, she would. She needed to be a part of his recovery, even though the work was already done.

That was why she confined him to the couch when he came out of the hospital, and why she insisted on coming to each of his check-ups. She wasn't controlling in terms of dictating what he did all day, but she demanded to know his every move. He wouldn't be surprised if she'd installed a tracking app on his phone, or if she had half of Dublin reporting back to her when he was out of the house.

She meant well. He knew that. She was worried about his health, about the possibility of his heart being spontaneously rejected. "If you collapse somewhere away from home and I don't know it, how can I help you?" she'd said on many occasions.

It didn't matter that he had her marked as his *In Case of*

Emergency contact on his phone and that his smartwatch had a heart rate monitor that sounded a notification when it went above or below a certain rate. "I need to be there for you, even if that means getting on your nerves," she'd told him.

Ordinarily, he could deal with it. But, sometimes, it was too much.

In the waiting room outside Dr Hughes' office, Mum sat in a seat and leafed through a magazine while Caleb paced the room. Sitting still wasn't something he could maintain for long. He had two more flying lessons before Christmas, and he was gearing up for his first solo flight. Only in the air, when he was three thousand feet off the ground, did his brain stop shouting at him. That, and when he was near Kai.

Colin Moore's Cessna and Kai had the same effect on him. They focused his mind. In the cockpit, he had learned what each dial and switch on the instrument panel did and he could recite them in his sleep. And he was learning to concentrate on the skyline without always having to keep his eye on the plane's nose. And when he was in conversation with Kai, sitting at the kitchen table or out at the picnic bench in the yard, Caleb could look at him and hear his words. And there was nothing else in the world to get in his way.

But, right now, he didn't have Kai or Colin Moore's Cessna. And he circled the waiting room, flexing his fingers into fists and thumping the air like a boxer. And his thoughts were all over the place. Kai was staying for Christmas. And that meant Christmas was going to be different. But weird. But nice.

And a nurse said, "Caleb Burke?"

Mum stood up like she always did. And Caleb said, "Sit

down," like he always did. Today was one of those days that her constant watch on him was infuriating.

He went into Dr Hughes' office and closed the door.

"Charlotte isn't with you today?" Dr Hughes asked.

"She's in the waiting room. She has a Christmas present for you."

"She didn't have to."

"She knows that." He stripped his shirt off. There was a thin scratch of downy hair on the left of his chest but, otherwise, it was still smooth. Back when he'd just had his stitches removed and his scar was dark and raised and red, Dr Hughes had given him a cream to rub on it twice a day. Now, the scar was still visible—always would be—but it was white, and its terrain wasn't raised as much as it had been.

Hughes pointed at the treadmill, hooked his electrodes up to the monitor, and they went through the standard battery of tests. "A little faster," he said at intervals. "How are the flying lessons?"

"Man, you have no idea. I love it up there. It's just me against the sky. Nothing else matters. When I strap into that aircraft, I become something I've never been before."

"And what's that?"

"Alive."

"Caleb. You've been alive your whole life."

"Not like this."

"You're hurting my feelings."

"Sorry, Doc. You gave me Alice. You gave me life. But you didn't give me an altimeter."

"I can order you a set of aircraft wings, if that helps?"

Dr Hughes took some notes on his computer and told Caleb to sit down. He wrapped a blood-pressure cuff to his arm and pushed a button to auto-inflate the band. And he pressed his stethoscope to Caleb's back and listened to his lungs.

And when he was done, he said, "I'm concerned about your blood pressure. It's a little elevated."

"A little?"

"Enough that I'm concerned."

"So, not a little, then."

"It's manageable. I'm going to prescribe you something to help bring it down again."

"Is it my HCM?" It had been so long since he'd said hyper-trophic cardiomyopathy out loud that he'd almost convinced himself it wasn't a real thing.

"No," Dr Hughes said. "It's a common side effect of your immunosuppressants. But like I said, it's manageable. It means adding an extra pill to your daily cocktail. Do you think you can manage that?"

"I don't know, Doc. I'm already taking a million pills. I'm not sure my stomach has the room for another one."

"If you want to live, you'll make the room."

"You're a cruel man, Dr Hughes."

"You don't get anywhere in life by being nice. Remember that."

"Don't tell my mum about the new prescription, okay?" He sat there, shirtless in the cold room, playing with the hole in the knee of his jeans.

"What's on your mind, Caleb? I've known you long enough to know when you have questions."

"How much longer do you think this heart has, Doc?"

"It's impossible to say. Ten years? Twenty? All we can do is keep an eye on it."

They'd had this discussion before. When a heart transplant is performed on someone so young, the chances of them needing repeat surgery in the future are moderately high. The slightest factor can affect a donated organ. Before he passed away last year, Caleb knew one of the DTC patients who'd been waiting on his third transplant. The longest surviving heart transplant on record was less than thirty years and Caleb knew Alice wasn't going to beat that. But Dr Hughes said they'd monitor it, looking for signs of rejection or disease, and one day he would say, "It's time."

Which meant he was out of time.

"And when that day comes," Caleb said, "we'll be right back where we started, looking for a donor. I was lucky the first time, Doc. What if we don't get a donor heart so fast the next time?"

"More people join the donor register every day. What has gotten into you, Caleb? You're normally so upbeat."

Caleb shrugged. It was hard to put his thoughts into words. "I feel like I finally have something to live for."

"And that's making you worry about the future?"

He nodded.

Dr Hughes said, "I can't guarantee how long you have left with Alice. But what I can say is that when that day comes, you and I are going to do our best to beat it again. All right?"

When he'd put his shirt back on and Dr Hughes walked with him out to the waiting room, his Mum was still flicking through the same magazine. But the edge of her thumb was in her mouth and Caleb heard the crack of her nail as she chewed it.

"Merry Christmas, Jerry," she said, and Dr Hughes embraced her. "This is for you."

"You shouldn't have."

"I needed to."

"But I didn't get you anything."

"Yes, you did," Mum said. And Caleb rolled his eyes.

Dr Hughes held the wrapped gift and said, "If this box has a heart in it, I'm going to be a little freaked out."

Caleb mimicked Brad Pitt from that old movie when he mimed, "What's in the box? What's in the box?"

When Mum and Dr Hughes had done their pleasantries, Caleb told her to meet him at the car. He went upstairs.

Abigail looked exhausted, like she'd been on shift for five days straight, and Caleb said, "I came to see Jayne, but how the hell are you doing?"

"I'll be happy when I retire. Put a mask on. She's not doing so well."

Caleb wrapped the strings of his surgical mask over his ears and put on a disposable apron before he went into Jayne's room. She looked asleep.

Or dead.

But when he cleared his throat, she opened her eyes. "Hey."

"Hi."

She didn't have the energy to sit up. She said, "Where's the cutie?"

"He's at college. And you weren't supposed to remember how cute he was. How're you doing?"

"I'm dying."

"That's a terrible reason to be lying in bed."

"You're right. Let's go dress shopping."

Her cheeks were flushed and sweaty, but when he touched her hand it was cold. "Not this again."

"Got to look pretty for prom."

"You don't need a dress to look pretty."

"Piss off," she said, and she choked on her own words. He helped her roll onto her side, and he rubbed her back until she'd hacked up all of her pain.

She held his hand, and he told her about his flying lessons, and about Kai, who was staying with them for Christmas, which was going to be utterly weird.

"Does he know you like him?"

"No."

"You should tell him."

"Why?"

"Why not?"

"Because that would change everything."

Jayne coughed and cupped her mouth with her hands. Her shoulders bunched against her ears and when her energy was spent, she rolled onto her side to face the wall.

"Things change every day," she said. "Mostly, you don't get a say in the matter. But this time, if you tell him, you will make things change, one way or the other."

Caleb said, "What if it changes the other way? Not the way I want it to change."

"At least you'll know. At least the mystery will be over."

"I like the mystery."

"That's your problem."

He offered to get on the bed beside her, to stare at the ceiling and speak the truth, but she was too tired, too sick. He took his mask and apron off in the corridor and dropped them into a clinical-waste bin. And Abigail said she'd text him if there was any change in her condition.

"Merry Christmas," he said. He went downstairs with a cloying sadness in his chest. He wasn't convinced Jayne would live long enough to get a new heart.

In the car park, Mum turned the radio off when he got in the car. "Ice cream?" she asked.

"Not today," Caleb said.

"It's tradition."

"Mum. Can we not?"

"Are you okay?"

"I'm fine. Let's go home."

"But we go for ice cream after every check-up."

He didn't mean to snap. He knew she was right. "Jesus Christ. Can you just take me home, okay? I'm tired."

"What the hell, Caleb? I thought we were having a good day."

He looked up at Jayne's window. She may never know what a good day was.

And on the ride home, Caleb tried to focus his mind. He thought about his next flight lesson, about the wheel and the pedals and the switches. He thought about the open sky, the fresh air that was his and his alone, and he knew that there was nothing on the ground that could take his focus away.

Nothing except Kai.

Kai, who looked perpetually sad. Who closed his mouth when people were around, as though he was about to say something he didn't want to utter. As though he would spill a secret so dark that when he did say the words his tongue would turn to ash and float away on the wind.

Caleb closed his eyes.

If there was a way through Christmas, to understand the cruelties of the world and the light of life, it was with Kai at his side.

He looked at his mum as she turned into the end of their street. "Sorry, Mum."

"Want to talk about it?"

"Not today."

And when they got home, while Kai was still at university, Charlie had strung the ornaments on the tree, and the angel was still in her box. He paused his game on the TV and Mum readied her phone to take a picture.

Caleb lifted Charlie by the waist, even though he was tall enough to reach.

And Charlie put the angel on the treetop.

When she snapped her photo, Mum said, "You're both growing up too fast. That's my wish for Santa this year. To slow you down."

Caleb put his arm around Charlie's neck, and he said, "Run, kid. It's too late for me. Get out while you still can."

And Charlie said, "What the fudge are you talking about?"

"Don't swear," Mum said.

"I didn't swear."

Caleb looked towards the window. It was too cold to snow;

that's what they said. It didn't make sense—it would snow if it needed to; there was no such thing as too cold. But the sky was blue and clear.

"Kai's staying for Christmas," he told his little brother.

"I know. He told me, like, a week ago."

And Caleb was annoyed that Kai could talk to Charlie and not him. Didn't he matter as much?

15.

KAI

When he got off the bus, Emily waved. Christmas Eve shopping was not something Kai had expected to be doing with his new college friend, but she had talked him into it while they were sitting on the brown leather couch at the back of the campus library on the last day of school. The leather was worn and cracked and reminded him of the picture of his grandfather. Before Fatima's disappearance, they would gather around the kitchen table once a month and pass the phone among them as they told their grandparents about their lives. Kai's Kabyle language skills were non-existent, but Dad had taught him a few phrases to greet his grandparents with.

After Fatima's funeral, the family phone calls became less frequent, and eventually Mum would have to remind Dad to call home. And Dad would say, "I'll do it later."

"You always say later but you never do."

"Later," Dad reiterated.

But he never did.

Emily pulled him into her arms as he approached. Ever since they started chatting in the library, she'd been the most tactile person he knew. More than Caleb.

She linked her arm through his. "Let's do the toy stores first. I need to buy something for my little brother. Do you need to buy anything?"

He shook his head. He hadn't mentioned Caleb to her yet because there wasn't anything to tell. But he wanted to get him something special. He'd already found a gift for Charlie and Mrs Burke, but he was struggling to think of something worthwhile for Caleb.

Mrs Burke had told him not to, but he insisted. He was disturbing their usual Christmas plans by being there, and it was the least he could do. But she made him promise not to spend too much money on them. Which was good because he didn't have much anyway.

He'd already sent a small package home with a gift for his parents, and the box they'd mailed to him was tucked into the corner of his room between the chest of drawers and the wardrobe. They told him not to open it until Christmas.

As they walked towards the shopping mall, under the bright white lights that formed a ceiling between the buildings, Kai adjusted his scarf. His breath smouldered into fog in front of his face and the rain was so fine that you couldn't see it but it still got you wet. Christmas music spilled out of the shopfronts, and the lit-up *Nollaig Shona* signs—"It means Merry

Christmas in Irish," Emily explained—were accompanied by charity Santas and a great deal of festive cheer. If he hadn't felt so miserable, it would have been beautiful.

But there was an ache in Kai's chest that he couldn't smother. He had woken with it that morning and carried it around with him since breakfast. He was away from home at Christmas for the first time in his life, and although the season was a depressing one for his parents, they tried to make it special for him. But Fatima's disappearance and the secret that he bore at the back of his throat would dampen the mood of Christmas and, when they came home from evening Mass on Christmas Eve, their gift-giving ceremony was one of little cheer. The laughter was forced and, in bed on Christmas night, Kai would listen to the cries of his mother and the soothing tones of his father, and he would clench his fists to his ears to drown out the agony that his secret had caused.

But it's not my secret, he'd tell himself. It's Fatima's. Not that that made it any easier to bear.

Emily dragged him through the toy stores, acting like a kid, pushing the "Try Me" buttons on plastic ambulances and police cars, pulling the string on the backs of dolls to make them talk. She threw a basketball over the shelves into the next aisle before casually walking away. To one of the elderly shoppers, she said, "Kids, eh?"

Her joy should have been infectious. He should have been in his element, joining in with her fun. But he couldn't.

Inside the foyer of the mall, a collection of carollers sang *God Rest Ye Merry Gentlemen* and, further down, a line of toddlers and their parents queued to see Father Christmas one last time before the big day. Animatronic polar bears waved at the shoppers and a bearded man dressed as a fairy godmother was handing out leaflets that heralded the early arrival of the January Sales on December twenty-sixth.

Each shop seemed to have its own playlist of festive tunes, and by the time they'd made it to the food court with his stomach in turmoil for no reason, Kai had heard *Silent Night* half a dozen times.

Emily grabbed a table while Kai stood in line at Starbucks, and he stuffed his hands in his coat pockets. The knot in his chest was tighter than his fists. He could make out two distinct Christmas songs competing with each other, and the echo of the carollers downstairs was floating up the escalators. Children were laughing. Parents were telling them off, and the man in the queue behind him bumped against him as he reached for a serviette from the counter. He didn't apologise.

And there was a burning at the corners of his eyes. But he knew that if he brushed his knuckle against them, the tears would spill. Christmas was dark. Darker than it should have been. There was a weight on his shoulders that wasn't his to carry. And no one to help ease the pain.

His breath caught in his chest when the girl behind the counter said, "Next, please," and he had to swallow twice before he could get his words out.

He took their coffees to the table and when he sat opposite her, Emily's smile turned from one of delight into a downturned question. "What's wrong?"

"Nothing," he said. But as soon as he said it he felt his lower lip tremble like a pathetic little child that was scared of the dark. He blinked to fight back the tears, but a sob ripped from his throat, and he covered his mouth to hide it.

But it was too late. It was out. And so were the tears.

"Oh, babe," Emily said, her voice low, her hand stretching across the table to comfort him. "What's happened?"

He couldn't speak. Emily dragged her chair around the table and pulled him into her arms, and he sobbed quietly against her sweater as she rubbed his back in a coffee shop full of witnesses. His natural reaction would be to push her away and hide his embarrassment, but there was no shame. He'd gone beyond that.

When his tears had stopped and his cheeks tingled, he slipped out of her arms and offered her a sheepish laugh as he blew his nose.

Emily sipped her coffee. "Do you want to tell me what the heck that was all about?"

"I don't know."

"Are you homesick?"

He shook his head, then nodded. "I guess. I miss my parents. I've never been away from home at Christmas before. But it's not just that."

"What, then?"

"It's everything." He puffed up his cheeks and exhaled before saying, "I don't know what I'm doing here."

"Shopping."

"No, I mean here in Ireland."

"Do you really hate class so much?"

"It's just not what I thought it would be. I used to love reading. I love the classics. But now? Now I can't stand them.

Analysing them like this; it's destroying my love of books. Where's the magic when you dissect every sentence like a frog in a biology exam?"

"If you hate it so much, why don't you quit and go home? No one would think any less of you."

"I would. My parents would. Besides, I can't go home."

"Why not?"

Kai spooned some of the froth from his coffee cup into his mouth. "If I go back to France I'd have to be straight."

"You're not exactly being very gay over here—do you even have a boyfriend?"

"No."

"See? Look. I know you said your Mum's a strict Christian, but do you honestly think they'd disown you for being gay?"

"Yes."

"What about unconditional love?"

"It goes hand in hand with unconditional homophobia."

"I can't believe that."

"You don't know my parents."

"No." She pinched his cheeks together, making his lips pucker. "But look at this face. How could anybody hate it?"

"This face hides a lot of secrets."

"Smile more. People will never know it."

He forced a smile.

They sat among the bustle of Christmas Eve shoppers, and he told her things he had never spoken aloud before. Not about Fatima or his interest in Caleb, but about his Mum, his Dad, his one and only trip to Algeria that he had no recollection of, about his fear of hating the one thing that had brought him comfort his entire life—books.

"You need to drop out, Kai. Before it's too late. Or at least switch your major."

"To what?"

"The History of Being a Repressed Queer in Twenty-First Century Europe."

"That's not very funny."

She shrugged. "It's winter break. You have some time to figure it out. But if you don't want to go back to France, you either need to swap your degree for something else or find a job."

"Easier said than done. You try being a person of colour in Dublin at Christmas."

"Anyway," she said. "What are your plans for tomorrow?"

"I was supposed to be in France, but now that I'm staying here, I promised to be a Christmas elf at the hospital."

"You did what?"

"I know, right? It was a spur-of-the-moment thing."

"Sounds more like a momentary madness."

"You have no idea."

By the time he got home, he'd found a suitable gift for Caleb, and he had Emily's words hovering over his head. In a couple of weeks, he'd be back in class.

Or he wouldn't.

That was his choice.

He locked himself in his room and wrapped his gifts for the family that, since September, had felt like his own. They'd welcomed him into their home, and they were the nicest people he could think to share a house with. Even Charlie who, at eleven, was far too boisterous for Kai's liking, had settled into a comfortable routine of offering to play computer games with him and then asking him about his day when Kai said he'd love to play but had other things to do.

Mrs Burke knocked on his door that evening and when he opened it, with Sellotape stuck to the back of his hand and glitter from a Christmas card embedded under his fingernails, she handed him a box and said, "We have a tradition in this house. We wear matching pyjamas and have Christmas Eve dinner together. Last year, my ex-husband joined us, which wasn't awkward in the slightest, but I think he and Caleb have had a bit of a falling out recently, so it's just us."

He took the box from her when she pushed it into his arms. "Mrs Burke, I'm not even part of your family."

"You're never going to call me Charlotte, are you?"

"Sorry."

"And besides. You live here, so you're part of this household, which makes you part of the family. And I won't have you all alone at Christmas. You have twenty minutes." She tapped the box. "Put these on, and I'll see you at the table."

When he went downstairs later, in a pair of red tartan button-down pyjamas that fit him so perfectly it was as though they were made to measure, Mrs Burke, Caleb and Charlie were sitting at the table. They were all dressed in the same red tartan. And Charlie blew a party horn that unfurled in front of his face with a screech that made Mrs Burke laugh.

Caleb pulled out the chair beside him. "You can sit here, closer to the wine. We're going to need it when Mr and Mrs Pavarotti here start singing Christmas carols. Nice pyjamas," he added as Kai sat down.

"You, too. Are we still doing the elf thing tomorrow?"

"I wouldn't miss it."

Caleb held out a cracker for him to pull. The little plastic toy skittered across the table and Kai unrolled the joke card.

"What do you get if you cross Father Christmas with a duck?"

"I don't know," Charlie said. "What *do* you get if you cross Father Christmas with a duck?"

"A Christmas quacker."

Charlie cracked up. And Kai grinned.

Mrs Burke handed him the bowl of creamed potatoes and said, "Dig in."

It reminded him of his first morning in Ireland, sitting at this very table, eating more food for breakfast that day than he had in the entire year before, and the comfortable feeling that had settled on him then was stronger now.

When dessert plates were empty and Charlie was licking cream from his fingers, Kai stood and raised his wine glass. "Can I make a toast?"

"Speech, speech, speech," Charlie said, slapping the table.

"I don't have the words in English to express my gratitude to you all."

"Say it in French," Caleb said.

Kai smiled. "I don't even have the words in French. You have all accepted me into your home and made me feel welcome. And now I am going to be here during your Christmas, and I don't want to get in the way."

"You're not in the way," Mrs Burke said.

"I know. And this is my toast: to Christmas with strangers

who feel like family."

"To family," Caleb said.

And Mrs Burke cried and hugged them all.

On the way up to his room later, when Charlie had been ordered to bed and Mrs Burke was bringing presents in from the garage, Caleb came out of the bathroom as Kai reached the landing. The top two buttons of his pyjama shirt were undone. The overhead light was dimmed, and the glow was soft, but Kai could have sworn he'd seen a mark on Caleb's chest.

But Caleb buttoned up before Kai could stare. "Happy Christmas, Kai." He extended his arms for a hug.

Kai stared at the ground. "Merry Christmas." And when Caleb slipped his arms around his shoulders and pulled him in, Kai held his breath. He wondered if Caleb could feel the rapid-fire rifle shots of his heart.

Caleb's hands lingered on his back for a second before he pulled away.

"Good night."

And he disappeared into his room.

Kai's chest ached again, but it was different from the heavy feeling he'd had this morning.

He climbed into bed and checked the time. It was eleven P.M., midnight in France, and he called home.

"*Joyeux Noël, mon fils*," Mum said. She sounded formal, her voice clipped, and he could tell she'd been crying. "Do you miss me?"

"Of course."

"I wish you were here."

"Me, too," he said. But he didn't mean it.

16.
CALEB

Caleb pretended to be asleep when he heard his bedroom door opening and the sound of Charlie trying his hardest not to make a noise.

Christmas morning was packed with traditions, and this was the first of many. Charlie tiptoed across Caleb's room and Caleb buried his face under the covers to aid the illusion that he was asleep. When Charlie was close enough and his quiet breath turned into a stifled chuckle, Caleb reached up from the covers with a roar and enveloped his little brother in the duvet, pulling him down onto the bed.

Charlie screamed. "Let me go."

"Krampus always gets the naughty kids," Caleb said, and he tickled him.

Charlie cried out for his mum.

Caleb pulled him into a tight hug. "Merry Christmas, Squirt."

"Happy Christmas."

Mum appeared in the open doorway, tying the belt of her dressing gown. "You boys cannot be awake already. It's not even six A.M." When Charlie made an exaggerated snoring noise, flopping down beside Caleb in mock sleep, Mum said, "Keep it down. Try not to wake Kai so early."

But Kai's door opened, and he stood behind her. "Too late." He was smiling and his hair was mussed up at the back. He'd slept in the red tartan pyjama bottoms that she'd given him yesterday and the cuff of one leg was ruffled up around his calf.

"Merry Christmas," Caleb said, rolling Charlie off him and sitting up.

Kai tried to flatten his hair. "*Joyeux Noël*."

Mum kissed both his cheeks and Charlie said, "Can we go downstairs now?"

This was another of their traditions. Nobody could go downstairs on Christmas morning until everyone was awake. In previous years, before Dad moved out, Charlie would be pacing the landing from five in the morning and Dad would refuse to budge before seven.

"Go back to bed," he'd say. "Santa hasn't come yet."

"He came at two A.M. I heard him."

Two years ago, when Dad moved out, Charlie—nine years old and slipping out of innocence—came to Caleb and said, "Who's going to be Santa now that Dad's gone?"

"What do you mean, buddy? Dad isn't Santa."

"I'm not stupid. I've known Santa isn't real since last year."

"Don't tell Mum."

"But who's going to be Santa now that he's gone?"

"Mum will buy the presents. But now that Dad's moved out, don't be expecting anything big this year. Dad will still get us something when we go and visit him."

And even though the illusion of Father Christmas had been broken for years, last night, Charlie still put out milk and cookies, and a carrot for Rudolph.

Before he went to bed, Caleb whispered, "Why do you still do that even though you know the truth?"

And Charlie, with a weary smile, said, "I'm giving Mum one more year of joy."

This morning, with Mum and Kai standing in his doorway and Charlie wrapped in the duvet beside him, Caleb knew this Christmas was going to be different.

"So? Can we go downstairs yet?"

Kai said, "Can I use the bathroom first?"

"Good idea," Mum told them. "Everyone should brush their teeth before we go down."

"Me first," Charlie shouted. He rolled off the bed and dashed into the bathroom, and Mum went back into her room.

Kai scratched the back of his head, and Caleb pulled the duvet around himself as though he was embarrassed to be lying in bed when everyone else was up.

"Merry Christmas," he said, realising as he did that he'd already said it a moment ago.

Kai smiled and his cheeks were flushed.

And Caleb reached under his bed, pulling out a present. "Here. This is for you."

Kai came into the room and accepted the gift. "What is it?"

"Open it." Caleb patted the edge of the bed and Kai sat.

When he'd unwrapped the gift, he smiled. It was a dictionary, just like the one he'd told Caleb about before.

"I haven't got you a bike, don't worry."

Caleb felt the weight of him on the bed and they stared at each other.

"This is where you say, 'Thank you.'"

Kai blushed. "Thank you."

"Don't you like it?"

"I love it. I really do. I've got something for you, too, but I put it under the tree last night. So you'll have to wait."

Caleb got out of bed. He'd taken the pyjamas off last night and slept in his boxers and a T-shirt, and he turned his back on Kai to avoid any embarrassment as he pulled on a pair of sweatpants. When he turned around again, Kai was leafing through the dictionary as though it contained a world of secrets.

When Charlie came out of the bathroom with toothpaste foam on his chin, and he stood at the top of the stairs, he called to them with impatience as they took turns in the loo. Mum was last and Charlie was already three stairs down when she opened the bathroom door.

"Now?" he asked.

"Now," she said.

And Charlie was gone.

By the time they'd joined him in the living room, he'd already opened two of his gifts and was sorting through the rest of the presents under the tree. "Mine, Caleb's, Caleb's, mine. Here's one for you, Kai."

Caleb saw Kai glance at Mum as Charlie held the gift out to him.

Mum shrugged. "Santa must know where everyone lives at Christmas, I guess."

Thank you, Kai mouthed. "Santa is very clever." And only Caleb saw Charlie roll his eyes at the Santa references.

Kai put the present aside and reached under the tree. The gifts he handed to them were wrapped so neatly that Caleb almost didn't want to open his. The box had been covered with gold paper and a red bow was tied around it. His handwriting was as neat as the packaging. *To Caleb. Merry Christmas. Kai.*

His gift to Mum was a thick scarf that she draped around her neck and stroked the soft material as she stared in the mirror over the fireplace. "I adore it. Thank you."

To Charlie, he'd given a game for his console. Caleb knew his brother had already played it, but Charlie said, "Wow, thank you. It looks awesome. We can play teams later."

And then Kai turned to Caleb with anticipation lighting up his eyes.

Caleb looked at the present. "It's too pretty to open."

"I'll open it," Charlie said.

Caleb pulled the bow. When he unwrapped it, he grinned. It was an Airfix model aeroplane, the de Havilland Tiger Moth.

Kai said, "I couldn't find one exactly like the plane you fly. This is as close as I could get."

"It's amazing," Caleb said. He stood up and pulled Kai into a hug. "Thank you. Now the dictionary seems ridiculous."

"No, it's perfect."

They faced each other.

And Charlie said, "Get a room."

Kai blushed and Caleb coughed. And Mum pretended not to notice.

By the time Caleb had gone for a run, showered, and dressed in a Darth Maul Christmas sweater, he couldn't get the image of Kai's crimson face out of his head.

He joined the others at the table for Christmas lunch, and Mum sat the turkey in front of him, handing him the carving knife and fork. Last year, she'd carved it herself.

"Are you sure?"

"Don't cut yourself," she said.

"Would you rather I used those plastic scissors you get at Playschool?" Caleb stood and grated the blade against the side of the fork as if he was sharpening it. "Kai, as the guest, you get first choice. Leg, breast, or butt?"

Kai's knitted sweater was mustard with white trim, and he looked as tasty as a Christmas pudding.

Charlie said, "I want the butt," and he laughed.

Christmas carols were playing on the digital speaker and the lights around the tops of the cabinets twinkled in a brightly coloured orgy.

Kai said, "If Charlie wants the butt, I guess I'll have to have the breast."

"Wise choice," Caleb said, and he carved the meat.

As they ate, Mum said, "Kai, what are some Christmas traditions in France?"

"It isn't very different than what I've seen here. Except Father Christmas gives presents to good children, and *Le Père Fouettard* would smack you if you were naughty that year."

"Like a tag team," Caleb said.

"But mostly, we have *Le Réveillon*. I'm not sure what the English word is, but *Le Réveillon* is the Christmas meal. And it takes forever to eat. Sometimes we could be eating for six hours or more. There is foie gras and smoked salmon. Goose and turkey. Green beans cooked in garlic butter."

"Six hours?" Charlie said. "Then why are you so skinny?"

"Charlie," Mum snapped.

But Kai laughed. "Because my mother's cooking is—" He put his fingers in his mouth and pretended to gag.

"Same here," Charlie said, stuffing a whole roast potato into his grinning mouth, and Mum clipped the back of his head with her open hand and a laugh.

Kai said, "It's the nicest Christmas meal I've ever had."

Caleb had noticed Kai's English language skills were improving over the last few months. He no longer sounded so stilted. It wouldn't be long before he was drinking Guinness and swearing like a trooper.

Caleb had a glass of non-alcoholic Shloer with dinner, and when Mum suggested they should wait and let their food settle before attempting dessert, he said, "Actually, Kai and I need to get going. Save us some trifle. We'll be back in a couple of hours. Kai, are you ready?"

Kai joined him in the garage, wearing a heavy parka and a thick scarf, and as Caleb started his Vespa, Kai said, "How did you talk me into this?"

"Because you're a good person and I'm super charming."

"Agreed."

They rode across town to the hospital, with Caleb intimately aware of Kai's hands on his waist, and when they arrived, they dashed across the carpark. The pregnant clouds had exploded when they were still five minutes away, and as they stood in the hospital lobby, dripping on the polished floor, Kai smiled at him.

"Your rain is colder here than in France."

"I can only apologise on behalf of every Irishman who ever existed."

Abigail met them on the ground floor and handed them each a garment bag. "Let me get you a couple of towels. And you can get changed in Steve's office."

"Let the fun begin," Caleb said.

She left them alone in the psychologist's office which had no desk in it. There were three armchairs around a low coffee table and a couch along the far wall with a selection of toys and dolls in some storage boxes. Kai looked around and picked up one of the soft cloth dolls.

He held it out and said, "Show me on the doll where the bad man touched you."

"I thought you were the good guy."

He shrugged. "I have my wicked side. Don't you?"

Caleb unzipped the garment bag and held the sides wide. "I forgot how ugly these elf costumes were."

Kai rummaged in one of the toy boxes and then threw a stress ball towards him. "Will this help?"

Caleb gave it a squeeze. "Much better." He took the elf outfit from the hanger and said, "Time to get into character."

He turned his back and unsnapped his belt. He had stripped down to his boxers and socks when Kai said, "Caleb?"

"Yes?" He turned.

Kai was sitting on the edge of the couch, pulling on a pair of green elf leggings, and when he looked up, with his mouth open to speak, he stopped.

"God."

Caleb knew why he hesitated. He realised it even as he turned to face him. He was shirtless. And his scar was on display, that white jagged line that ran from just below his Adam's apple to the top of his stomach. He'd been hiding it from him for so long—why? Why was he doing that?—that when he faced him now, in his white boxer briefs and black socks, open and exposed like a weak sapling in a storm, he knew it was too late to cover it.

"I'm not God," he said, masking the uncomfortable feeling in the pit of his stomach, "but thanks for the vote of confidence."

Kai stood up, one leg in the elf costume, his jumper and T-shirt on the couch beside him. He couldn't take his eyes off Caleb's chest.

"I—"

"Yeah."

"Sorry." Kai met his eyes. "I didn't know."

"I didn't tell you."

Instinctively, Kai raised his hand to reach out, but he lowered it just as quickly.

Caleb said, "You can touch it."

"No, I'm sorry."

"It's okay. I don't mind."

Kai stepped closer. He raised his hand and let his cold fingertips brush over the white scar tissue. He pressed his palm against Caleb's chest. "I can feel it beating."

"That's a good sign."

"It's fast."

"I know."

"I'm sorry."

"Don't be."

Caleb flexed his fingers before pressing his own hand to Kai's naked chest. His nipples were dark and raised in the chill of revelation. He could feel Kai's heart racing, and he looked up at his face, at those shadowed eyes, the reddened cheeks that were splashed with dark freckles, and the thin lips that glistened under the overhead lights.

"Do you have any scars?"

"Only on the inside."

"Did your heart just skip?"

"I think so."

"Is that my fault?" Caleb asked.

"Yes."

"I'm sorry."

"Don't be."

And Abigail knocked on the office door. "Are you boys decent?"

They pulled apart. Kai slipped the other leg of his elf costume on, and Caleb held the garment bag in front of himself as she entered.

"What's taking so long?"

"We were comparing scars."

"Well, when the pair of you are finished flirting, can you get a wriggle on? Steve's waiting upstairs and he says his Santa beard is itching the heck out of him.'"

"I bet he didn't say 'heck', did he?"

"You know him too well." She closed the door.

Kai wouldn't look at him. Caleb turned his back again and got dressed in the red and green suit. Before they left the office, he pulled the pointed hat over his head, and said, "Are we okay?"

Kai kept his eyes low. "I hope so."

"Hey." Kai looked at him. "Smile. I don't like it when you frown."

And Kai smiled.

They exploded onto the ward ahead of Father Christmas, and those kids who were out of bed and waiting in the family room cheered.

Steve, with his best Santa laugh and fake beard hanging loose around his chin, handed out wrapped gifts to the boys and girls.

And when the patients had a chance to tell Santa their wishes—new organs all around—Caleb sought out Abigail.

"Where's Jayne?"

"She's confined to her room. No one gets in except medical professionals."

"Is she all right?"

"She's immunocompromised, Caleb. What do you think?"

Caleb hadn't suffered the same prolonged waiting period when he'd been hospitalised. He'd collapsed on the football pitch, spent a month slipping in and out of consciousness, and he'd had Alice's heart before he knew it.

"Can't I just nip back and see her? I'll scrub up and wear a mask and gloves."

"I'm sorry. I can't break the rules, even for a Christmas elf. You can stand at her door and wave through the glass if you want."

It would have to do. Kai went with him, and they stood at Jayne's closed door, shoulder to shoulder, staring through the glass window.

Caleb rapped on the pane and Jayne looked up. Her skin was splotched and inflamed.

She raised a weak hand and waved. Her eyes could hardly open.

A drip bag was her lifeline now.

"Is she okay?" Kai asked. He'd formed his mouth into a smile and his lips didn't move as he asked the question. Caleb figured he did it so that Jayne couldn't read his lips.

"She'll be doped up on tramadol. 200mg unless they've upped her dosage. I wouldn't be surprised if they have."

"But she'll be okay?"

Jayne lowered her waving hand, and she turned on the bed to face the wall.

"I hope so," Caleb said.

Kai faced him. "Will you tell me about your scar?"

"Not here. I can't tell that story in this ward. It's too hard."

"Then where?"

Caleb looked at Jayne again, and then he pressed his hand against the glass. The heat of his handprint left a mark on the window, and it faded as he walked away.

"Follow me."

17.
KAI

It made sense now, Caleb's need to volunteer at the transplant centre. Kai should have made the connection before, but as he followed Caleb down the corridor and they waited by the bank of elevators, he didn't know how to find the words he needed.

Caleb pushed the call button, and they stood in silence. The lift arrived and a young woman got out carrying a bouquet of flowers, and when they stepped in, Caleb pressed the top floor button, and the only sound was the whir of the motor.

Crossing the narrow corridor between closed ward rooms, Kai said, "Where are we going?"

Caleb didn't answer him.

They looked ridiculous in their elf costumes and pointed hats, but Kai trusted him as he followed behind.

Caleb led him to a stairwell at the far end of the ward and before opening the door to go up, he looked around to make sure no one was watching. They took the six steps to a metal fire door, and Caleb opened it without fear of any alarms going off.

They stepped outside.

The sun was setting and the sky was dark, but the rooftop was sheltered from the Christmas winds by a generator block at their backs.

Kai stood at the wall and looked across the Dublin skyline. He could see the Monument of Light in the distance, the tall spire that rose almost four hundred feet into the night and, beyond that, the purple sky was turning black.

"Wow."

Caleb stood beside him, closer than he needed to, and said, "Who knew Dublin could be so pretty, right?"

"It's beautiful."

"The first time I came up here was a week after my transplant. One of the volunteers brought me up when I was feeling sorry for myself. And I looked at the city below and realised I was such a small cog in a very big machine."

"What happened?" Kai asked.

"Not here. Come."

He followed Caleb around the rooftop. Across from them, the small lights that circled the helipad blinked in a relentless pulse. Behind the brick generator building, Kai watched as Caleb opened a service door. He pulled out a blanket and spread it on the rooftop between the wall of the generator and a huge fibreglass water tank. The rain had passed.

Caleb said, "There are enough provisions up here to stave

off the apocalypse. We've got blankets, bottles of water, ancient paperback novels, Playboy magazines from the early 2000s, and even an old kettle. Not that there's anywhere to plug it in. Either the nurses don't have a clue, or they know about this place and don't stop it, but kids have been coming up here since forever."

A brisk wind tore over the rooftop and toyed with the blanket until Caleb knelt on it to hold it down.

He lay on his back. "Here. Come down beside me. Jayne and I have this thing we do."

Kai shivered. The elf costume was a thin material and he wished he'd brought his coat. "What are we doing up here?"

"You wanted the truth."

"Yes."

"So, lie down beside me."

"Do I have to?"

"Yes."

He turned back to the service door and got another blanket, and then settled down beside Caleb, flipping the blanket over the top of them.

They lay on their backs and stared at the darkening sky.

"Take my hand," Caleb said, and Kai felt him reach across beneath the blanket. "Here's the deal. We don't look at each other. We hold hands, and whatever we say has to be the truth. Only the truth. And if you lie, I'll feel it in your hand. Okay?"

"Okay."

Caleb's fingers found his, and they linked together. "Ask me."

Kai didn't want to speak. He watched the dark clouds and felt the wind tousle his hair. Then he said, "What happened?"

Caleb's hand was warm, and their shoulders were touching. Kai glanced at him.

"Don't look at me." When Kai turned his head and closed his eyes, Caleb said, "I had hypertrophic cardiomyopathy. It's not contagious but it is hereditary. From my dad's side of the family. It means the walls of my heart were getting thicker and it couldn't pump the blood around my body the way it should. It had been getting worse for years and I didn't even know it. Not until I was about to kick a football and I collapsed on the pitch."

"How old were you?"

"Fifteen."

"Did it hurt?"

"I'd been tired and out of breath for a while but, no, I wasn't in any pain. Not really."

"Whose heart is it?" Kai asked.

"They never told me. But I call her Alice."

They were silent for a while, each in his own thoughts. Kai felt Caleb's fingers readjust around his hand, and the wind stirred the edges of the blanket.

He almost couldn't get the words out when he said, "Is Jayne going to die?"

"If she doesn't get a donor heart soon? Yes."

"And if she does get one?"

"There's still a chance. Transplant surgery can be risky. But she'll be fine." Caleb's fingers tightened.

"Is that a lie?"

"Yes," Caleb said. "I'm sorry. She won't be fine. Even if she got a new heart today, she'll be taking a fistful of pills twice a day for the rest of her life. And she's young; younger than I was.

If she survives, her body will outlive the donor heart and she'll need another one."

"Do you need another one?"

"Not yet."

Kai said, "Are you scared?"

Caleb didn't respond at first and Kai stole a glance at him. His eyes were shut and his lashes were wet. "Yes," he said. "Every day."

"This is why you fly aeroplanes and do crazy things."

"They're not crazy things. They're just things that make me feel alive."

"And Charlie? Does he have it too?"

"They test him twice a year, but so far he's okay. Chances are he'll be all right."

Kai let go of his hand. There was nothing more to be said. But Caleb reached out and gripped his fingers again.

"Your turn. Let me ask you something."

Kai stiffened. "What?" he whispered. He wasn't ready for his own truths.

Caleb took a breath. "Why are you always so sad?"

"Honestly?"

"The truth or I'll know it."

"I don't have a clue."

"Can I help you find out?"

"I'd like that."

Earlier in the week, as the madness of Christmas was fast approaching, Fatima had called him. She was cheerful and filled with laughter. She and Avery were heading to a forest cabin to spend Christmas alone and off the grid.

"But you haven't been on the grid for six years," Kai said. He'd gone outside to sit at the picnic table in the yard under a dark sky that harboured threatening rainclouds and, if they ruptured above him, he wouldn't mind getting soaked. Wet was just another feeling on top of all the other feelings.

"Stop it," Fatima giggled, and he knew she wasn't talking to him.

Classes had finished for the year, and the nights were long and lonely, and there was a lump in his throat that had been there for weeks. Mrs Burke had been busy preparing for Christmas, and Charlie was wrapped up in his games, shouting at his friends through a headset. And Caleb was out running every morning and flying as often as he could, and Kai had almost decided to leave. He was going to quit school and run away from Ireland. But he couldn't go home, and he didn't have the money to go to Sweden and stay with Fatima.

And seeing her after all this time, being in her company as she cuddled into Avery, would not be the reunion he needed.

"Why didn't you ever go back?" he asked her when her giggling had gone on long enough.

"Kai, that isn't fair. You know why."

"Do I?"

"Because of Mum."

"You could have talked to her." He looked up at Caleb's window and saw the flickering lights of his TV and he wondered if Caleb had any secrets. Before now, before the hospital rooftop, he thought Caleb's life was perfect. But as he sat on the bench in the yard that night, he heard the silence at the end of the line, and he hoped that nobody else would be forced to live with the lies he had to bear. "You should have said something," he told Fatima.

"And have her endless tears and dragging me to church by the hair to watch me burn? And what about Dad? You know he'd never understand. Even if I could have convinced Mum that my love for Avery was pure and good, like a gift from God or whatever, Dad would never come around. He'd hate me forever."

"He hates you for dying."

"Kai."

"And Mum hates you for falling into the river and not being strong enough to make it out."

"That's not fair."

"But you know what's worse?" Kai said. "I hated you for so long, too. I hated that you forced me to lie for you. If you were going to fake your death and run away, you should never have told me. You should have left me in the dark with Mum and Dad. I spent those first few months wishing you *were* dead, because then at least I wouldn't have to lie."

"Kai," she said. Her voice was soft, the laughter gone.

"You abandoned me, Fatima."

"I never meant to."

"No. Because you were only thinking about yourself."

"If I stayed, I'd have died."

"But you did die. Don't you see? To everyone back home, you were dead. And you left me. You left me there, Tima. On my own. I had to watch as Mum and Dad died too. You broke the family into pieces, and I can still hear Dad's sobs. We buried a coffin full of stuffed toys. And Dad bawled his eyes out that night. He was broken. And I'm broken," he said. He caught his breath and turned his back to the house that looked warm and inviting. "I'm broken."

"I'm sorry."

"What good is 'sorry' after all this time? Sorry doesn't make up for all the lies I had to tell. When the police asked me if I knew who you were with that night, or where you were going. When Mum took me by the shoulders and stared into my eyes the way she does when she's searching for the truth. When Dad took me out in the car that night to look for you. Where was 'sorry' then?"

Fatima said, "I know sorry isn't enough. I do. But you will never understand."

"I'm gay, too," he reminded her.

"But you're a man. You have no arranged marriage. They weren't forcing you into something you didn't want. I was lost, Kai. I was so confused. I had my family, and I had my secret life. You haven't felt the way I do about someone like this. I knew Avery was my life. When she wraps her arms around me, it's like a shield. She's the one who makes me feel whole. I couldn't live without her. And if I'd stayed, I'd be forced to marry Zameer and I'd have to get into bed with him and let him touch me. I'd have to bear his children and my skin would crawl when he looked at me or when he came home from work and expected me to have dinner prepared for him. That wouldn't be a life. It would be a prison sentence."

Kai was crying. And so was Fatima.

She said, "I know I left you behind and I'm sorry. I wanted to take you with me. But I didn't know that you were gay too.

You were thirteen, Kai. I thought your life would be normal and, if I wasn't there, there'd be no shame on the family name. You could get married one day and give Mum the grandchildren she so desperately wants. How was I to know that my actions were going to ruin your life? I never wanted that."

"What about Mum and Dad's lives? Don't they matter? You ruined them, too."

"I know. And it haunts me to this day. I was naïve. But I did what I did, and I have to live with that. I hope that one day you'll understand. I didn't leave because I wanted to hurt you or Mum and Dad. I did it because I couldn't hurt myself."

"I do understand," Kai said. "I hate that you had to do it, but I understand why. I knew you were supposed to get married to Zameer, but I didn't know what that meant. Not really."

"But now you see?"

"I get it. And you're right. I don't have someone like Avery. But I want that. I want what you have."

"You'll get it. One day."

"There is a boy," he said. "Here in Ireland. He's just a friend, but—I don't know."

"Is he nice?"

"Yes."

Fatima said, "Isn't that all we want? Someone who's nice?"

And on the hospital rooftop, lying under the blanket and holding that boy's hand, Caleb squeezed his fingers and said, "What are you thinking about?"

His answer was quick. "My sister."

"I have one more question for you. Is that okay?"

"Was that your question?"

185

"No."

"Then ask it. Ask me anything." He was ready now. If Caleb asked him, he would tell him all of his truths.

Caleb sniffed and Kai couldn't tell if it was from tears or from the cold. "In Steve's office, when you touched my scar and I felt your heart beating. Did you want to kiss me?"

Kai swallowed. That was not the truth he'd been contemplating. He nodded.

Looking at the black sky, Caleb said, "I can't tell if that was a nod or a headshake, so you'd better say it out loud."

"Yes," Kai said, and his voice cracked so he had to say it again.

"You can look at me now."

Kai turned his head and Caleb was staring at him. His eyes were flecked with light and even though most of his face was shadowed, Kai could tell he was smiling.

"And do you still want to kiss me now?"

He didn't trust his voice. He nodded again.

And Caleb leaned in.

When their lips touched, soft and warm, Kai knew that his heart was running fast, like the ticking of a clock on overdrive. And he let go of Caleb's hand, moving his fingers up to press them against Caleb's chest. And there, behind the scar, he felt his heart beating just as fast.

When they parted, Caleb raised his arm and looked at his watch.

"Do you have somewhere to go?"

"No," he said. "Just checking my heart rate. It's 112. Eighteen beats away from my alarm going off."

"What happens if it gets too high?"

Caleb smiled. "Kiss me again and let's find out."

Kai pressed his hand against Caleb's chest. "I don't want to hurt you."

"We're on a hospital roof. You can call for help."

"Caleb."

"I'm joking. My heart isn't going to explode. I'm always hitting 130 beats per minute during my run. The alarm is only a reminder. Alice isn't going to give out on me just because a cute boy is kissing me. Although she might get jealous."

"You're a terrible person," Kai smiled.

"And yet you still want to kiss me."

"I do."

And they kissed again.

18.

CALEB

He knew his heart was beating hard and he didn't care. Lying on the rooftop with Kai at his side, their bodies close, he could burn through seven hearts and still not want to stop kissing him.

When it started to rain, Kai pulled the blanket over their heads, but it wasn't enough.

"We should go."

"Do we have to?"

"No, but we already got soaked once today."

"Fine," Caleb said. "Way to ruin the mood."

"Blame your Irish weather, not me."

They stood and Caleb rolled the blankets into a ball and stuffed them behind the service door. Kai turned to make a dash for the entrance.

"Wait," Caleb said. "You forgot something."

Kai turned, standing in his thin elf costume, shivering under the rain. "What?"

"This." And Caleb pulled him into his arms to kiss him again.

But the rain was getting heavier, and Kai took him by the hand. "You're a walking cliché, you know that, right?"

They got back to Steve's office where their clothes were drying on the backs of the armchairs, and they got out of the wet outfits. Before he put his shirt back on, Caleb faced Kai one more time, exposing the past to his present. Kai touched the scar with reverence, and then he leaned down and kissed it, just below the collarbone.

"Merry Christmas," Kai said. And before they left the hospital, he took Caleb's hand. "I didn't think you liked me—that way."

"Are you kidding?" He cupped Kai's warm face. "I've been trying to tell you since the day you arrived."

When Kai smiled, his face glowed. And they stood in the lobby waiting for the rain to pass and listening to the soft sounds of Christmas carols from the wall speakers. Kai stood under the hot jet of air from the overhead heater in front of the automatic doors, and Caleb stood beside him, unspeaking, warmed by Kai's presence more than the heater, until Kai said, "The rain has stopped."

As they rode home, Caleb was certain Kai's arms were tighter around his waist, and when he pulled the scooter into the garage, they faced each other over the chassis and Caleb pulled his helmet off. He reached out and unclasped Kai's helmet, and when he lifted it from his head, he went in for another kiss.

"What if Charlie comes out?" Kai asked, though he didn't pull away.

"He won't."

"Or your Mum."

"So?"

"Won't they mind?"

"Are you scared?"

"Yes."

Caleb smiled. He put the helmets aside and came around the Vespa, putting his hands on Kai's shoulders. "When we walk through that door, we'll have no more privacy. Mum's far too clingy, especially this time of year, and Charlie pops up at the most inopportune times. So if you want to kiss me one more time tonight, this is your only chance."

"Will I never get to kiss you again?"

"You will. If you want to. We'll find a way. But we don't have to tell anyone. Not yet, if that's what you want. But I promise you, they won't have an issue."

Kai kissed him, his tongue parting soft lips and then they held each other, savouring the quiet of solitude before going inside.

And they spent the evening sitting beside each other on the couch as Charlie played a game on his console and Mum poured everyone a glass of prosecco.

"Me too?" Charlie asked.

"Half a glass," Mum said. "And don't tell your father."

"Not that he'd care."

Caleb said, "Didn't he come round while I was out?" It had

been two years. You'd think his parents would have figured out how to handle Christmas by now.

Upset with the world, Charlie said, "He called. He said to say happy Christmas to you. He's got presents for us, but we won't get them until we go and see him."

"Father of the year."

"Don't be so rude, boys," Mum said. "He's a busy man."

"Not too busy for Joanne," Charlie said, and Caleb kicked his thigh where he sat on the floor in front of him. He wasn't sure if Mum knew about Joanne moving in with their dad and this wasn't the time to mention it.

But Mum said, "What your dad does in his own home is nothing to do with us. Just be thankful he still cares about you. Most absent fathers never want to see their children."

"I don't think that's statistically accurate," Caleb said.

Charlie said, "You know he wants Caleb to move in with him."

"What?"

"I said no."

"When did he ask?"

Caleb glared at Charlie's back. Just because he was upset with Dad for not bringing gifts on Christmas Day, didn't mean he had to kick everyone else while they were down.

"A few weeks ago. But I said no."

Mum stood up.

Kai tried to look busy on his phone.

"Where does he get off?" Mum spat. "He knows you live here. He doesn't need to go offering you a place with him and that—child."

"Mum. Kai doesn't need to hear this. And she's not a child."

"She's half his age."

"Mum."

"Sorry. I'm sorry, Kai. Forgive me." She left the room and Caleb countered Kai's pained look with an apologetic face.

When Charlie had his back turned to them, Caleb slipped his hand down beside his leg, his pinkie finger stretching out to brush against the fabric of Kai's trousers. Kai pushed his leg closer.

When Mum came back, she brought the prosecco bottle.

And Charlie said, "Top me up."

Mum ignored him. "How was the hospital?" she asked.

"Wet," Caleb said, moving his hand away. Kai blushed.

They didn't get another minute alone that night as Mum fawned over him in a transparent bid to prove that living with her was better than moving into his dad's oversized house. And when he went to bed, Caleb lay on his side, staring at the wall that separated him from Kai, and he fell asleep with a smile on his face.

For the next three days, Mum and Charlie were forever in their way. One morning, Caleb went into the kitchen and saw Kai at the stove, making coffee. He crept up, touched Kai's back, and whispered, "Morning." But when Kai turned with a grin on his face, Charlie came in and Caleb pulled away.

"Are there any Sugar Puffs, sugar-puff?"

Caleb clipped the back of his head. "There's only Fruit Loops, fruit-loop."

And later, when Kai was sitting at the picnic table in the yard, Caleb spotted him from his bedroom window and went downstairs, but Mum was putting the bins out and by the time Caleb came out, she was standing by the bench, talking to their houseguest.

So, by the end of the week, when he was getting ready for his final flight lesson of the year, he jumped at the chance to offer Kai a ride when Kai said he was heading into town to meet a friend.

"Should I be jealous?" he asked as he handed Kai a helmet.

"Of Emily? I don't swing over there."

"Do you mean 'swing that way'?"

"Possibly."

Caleb knuckled his shoulder. "Good. Me neither. Now get on the bike before I change my mind."

The ride into town was slow as post-Christmas sales brought everyone out of their houses. He could feel Kai leaning into him, his arms tight around his waist and his chest against his back. And when he pulled up near campus and Kai got off, Caleb flipped up his visor. Their kiss was quick and awkward, both from Kai's shy embarrassment as well as the helmet getting in the way.

Caleb said, "I can pick you up again later if you want. Just text me."

"Have a good flight."

He rode to the airfield, feeling Kai's absence at his back. This would be his life now, snatched kisses when no one was around, and secret under-table knee-bumps on the few occasions that Kai joined them for dinner.

Kai seemed a little happier than before, but only when he was enveloped in Caleb's embrace, which was seldom. Never mind Dad's offer and Mum's desire to wrap him in cotton wool for the rest of his life; what Caleb needed was a place of his own. And Kai could stay with him, and they could kiss whenever they wanted.

Or more.

More would be better.

In the hangar, Colin said, "Happy New Year," even though it was still two days away. "I've got a late Christmas present for you."

"If it's one of those airfield baseball caps, I already stole one a few months ago."

"It isn't. And you'll owe me twenty Euros for that."

"In that case, how much are the pens, too? Because I must have about six of them."

Colin looked at his clipboard with the flight plan on it and a pen jammed under the spring. "So that's where all my pens have gone. Maybe I shouldn't give you this present after all."

"I have all the gifts I need," Caleb said.

"Who put the spring in your step?"

"Wouldn't you like to know?"

"My wife went through The Change eight years ago. You bet I want to know the details."

"Don't be a pervert, Colin."

"Fine." They got in the plane. "So do you want this gift or not?"

"Of course I do."

Colin handed him the flight plan. "I'll be checking on that pen when you're back."

"When I'm back? Wait. Are you saying what I think you're

saying?"

"Your first solo. Are you ready?"

"No," Caleb said, and his palms were already sweating.

Colin laughed as he opened his door. "You'll be fine. I have faith in you. Check your plan, you're just circling around the pattern today. Circle and down again, got it? Get the ATIS report before you taxi out, and most of all—don't crash. Let's see if we can manage three independent landings today."

"Are you for real?"

"I'll be on the radio if you need anything, but just listen to the traffic. You'll be fine. Now, remember. What's your priority?"

"Don't crash?"

"No, Caleb. Have fun. And fly." He held out his fist for Caleb to bump it.

When he was in the aircraft on his own, he closed his eyes and took a breath. He switched to the local ATIS frequency for the weather and terminal report, and then he made a note on the clipboard.

"Radio check," Colin said through the headset. "You good?"

"Call me Captain Caleb," he said. This is what he'd been waiting for. This was the beginning of his future. He'd remember his first solo flight for the rest of his life. The sky had that cold blue colour that was only found in late December, and the winds, remarkably, were light. He knew the Cessna would rise quicker without Colin in the co-pilot seat, and he'd been told how to compensate for that. It occurred to him that Colin was prepping him for this moment during their last lesson when he was hands-off for the entire flight.

He texted Kai before powering up the plane. *Oh my God. My*

first solo. Wish me luck.

Kai's reply was instant. *You got this, King of the Skies. Good luck.*

On the radio, Colin said, "In your own time. There's no pressure. I don't want you setting off until you're absolutely sure you're ready."

"I'm ready." He switched to Ground Control's frequency and requested permission to taxi. "Parking brake released." And on the dividing line before the runway, he contacted Air Traffic Control and asked for the green light.

"EL-YBY, this is Dublin Tower. Fly straight out; runway two. Cleared for take-off. And good luck up there."

Colin will have told Ground Control that this was Caleb's first solo flight, and it was obvious that they'd passed the information on to Tower.

Caleb manoeuvred onto the runway and, as he picked up speed, he said, "Gauge is in the green. Airspeed is alive." And then, on the open comms to Colin, he said, "Oh God, oh God, oh God."

"Keep her straight," Colin said. "You can do this."

The light aircraft left the tarmac, and Caleb was in the air. He held his breath until the top of the climb and when he exhaled, his stomach on the floor of the cockpit, he laughed. He was doing it. He was flying on his own.

He wished Kai was up there with him.

He looked across Dublin Bay beneath him and as he circled back towards the airfield, he knew that the world was his. It didn't matter what his father wanted for him, or why his mother was so protective. Up here, he felt alive, he was his own man.

And there was nothing on this earth that could hold him down.

From the sky, his problems seemed petty and trivial. He touched his chest. "This is for you, Alice. You got me here. No one else. Just you." He was never more aware of his good fortune than he was in the air.

He came back around. With Colin on the ground, Caleb had to concentrate on everything, but he realised as he requested permission to land that most of it was second nature and muscle memory. Colin was right. He was ready for this even if he hadn't known it himself.

As he began his descent, he said, "Final approach is clear."

And when the wheels touched the tarmac, he punched the air and laughed. Colin had him go again, and when he came back down for the third time, he taxied back to the hangar and Colin met him there.

"Well?" Colin asked. "How was that?"

Caleb hugged him. "The second-best thing to ever happen in my life."

"Only the second?"

"If you knew what the first was, you'd understand." And he let Colin think it was his heart transplant which, honestly, was up there on the list of most fabulous things in his life. But kissing Kai had pinched the number one spot.

Colin pulled a large pair of scissors from his back pocket. "You know what happens now, right?"

Caleb smiled and turned his back to him. "Don't cut too much, I love this shirt."

It was an aviation tradition Colin had told him. When a student pilot takes his first solo, he has his shirttail cut off. It was symbolic. Colin's office wall was lined with the shirttails of his previous students. Colin made him sign it.

As he walked back to his scooter with the back half of his shirt missing under his jacket, he checked his phone. He had a text from Kai. *Did you boss it?*

And there was a missed call from the hospital. He checked his voicemail. "Give me a call when you can, will you?" Abigail said. She sounded harried, but then, she always did. It had to be about Jayne. There was no other reason she'd call him.

He sat on his Vespa and dialled the hospital, then the Dedicated Transplant Centre's extension.

The nurse who answered put him on hold as they paged Abigail, and while he listened to the warbling music on the other end of the line, he ran through the likely scenarios. Her condition was deteriorating. She'd been moved down to ICU. Or she was dead.

One was likely. The others were probable.

The music cut short. Abigail said, "Caleb? Are you ready for this?"

"Just tell me."

"She's getting a heart."

"What?"

"There was an RTA two hours ago. It's viable. They're prepping her now."

"For real?"

"No, this is a prank call. What do you think? Of course it's for real."

"Can I come down?"

"No. She's scheduled for surgery as soon as the organ carrier gets here."

"Jesus. Are her parents there?"

"They're in with her now. They told me to call you. I've got to go. I just wanted to let you know."

"Thank you. Will you call me when she's out?"

"You'll be the first to know, Caleb. I don't know if you're the praying kind, but if you are, now's the time to get on your knees."

He knew the dangers. Heart transplant surgery, despite medical advancements, was still a risk. But she'd been on the waiting list for so long and he knew the outcome would be one of two things. She'd be alive.

Or she wouldn't.

I need a hug, he texted Kai.

And he watched as Kai typed a reply. Then the indicator disappeared, started again, and disappeared.

Finally, Kai said, *You and me both*.

19.
KAI

Kai's finger hovered over the trackpad on the laptop and Emily said, "What are you waiting for?"

He didn't want to press the button. On the screen in front of him was the Aer Lingus website and he was about to complete the booking for his flight home. But flying terrified him. And going home scared him even more.

He woke up this morning with a notification from his banking app that he'd received the second instalment of his grant payment. He wasn't expecting it until late January, so it was a welcome surprise. And when he joined Emily for coffee, he'd told her that he had promised to go home once he had the money to do so.

"You're coming back, though, right?"

"I don't even want to go."

"But it'll be nice to see your parents."

"I know." Part of him knew that going home was the best thing to do right now, to clear his head, away from college. But two weeks without Caleb's beautiful smile would be torture.

"There's a boy, isn't there?" Emily said the other day. "I can tell."

"What? No. Why would you say that?"

"Because you're denying it with the dirtiest grin on your face. Who is he? Is it someone from class?"

"No."

"Then who?"

"I don't want to say. It's too new."

"Oh my God, is it Professor Smythe?"

Kai retched against his fist. "Not even. What did you call him? Hella skank?"

"I literally never said those words in my life. But you're killing me. Who is it?"

"Please, Em. I don't even know if we're dating. We just kissed."

"Did you do the tango?"

"The what?" Emily winked and he said, "You have a filthy mind."

She continued to tease him in good spirits, but Kai blocked her words out. Were they dating? They didn't have that discussion yet or any real chance to talk much since Christmas Day because Mrs Burke always seemed to be in the way.

And now, he sat in a coffee shop with Emily's laptop in front of him and his bank card in his hand, and he was leaving for two weeks. "The cheapest flight is on the third of January. If

I go for ten days it means I'll miss a few days of school."

"You were skipping class before the break, anyway. A few more days won't matter. At least you'll have a break from it all and be able to decide what you want to do."

"It's going to be a week and a half of my mum asking me about girls."

"Tell her you met a gorgeous Irish girl called Emily. It's not a lie. You don't have to tell her that my touch would revile you. That the very thought of my naked flesh pressed against yours would bring you out in gay hives."

"Gay hives?" he laughed. He looked at the laptop screen. Ten days in Paris felt like an endless nightmare. But if he didn't go home, they would never forgive him. He did miss his parents—of course he did—but he could do without their lectures and their misery.

The reservation timer had been counting down while they spoke, and the time was running out before the system would release his reserved seat back into the pool. He held his finger over the button, and his phone lit up.

Caleb said, *I need a hug*.

And Kai typed a reply, distracted by the countdown timer. He mistyped twice before sending his response. *You and me both*.

"Is that him?" Emily asked. "Is that the boy?"

"No. Yeah." He sat his phone face down on the table. And he clicked the Confirm Booking button on the laptop screen. When the webpage offered him the option to print his boarding pass in advance, he sighed. He'd done it. And now he really could do with a hug from Caleb.

"Are you going to bring him to the party at Danny's

tomorrow night?"

"I'm not great at parties."

"How can you not be good at parties? You show up, you get so drunk you flash your boobs at strangers, you maybe dance on a coffee table and break a vase, and then you run when a neighbour calls the police."

"None of that sounds appealing," Kai said.

"Are you mad? It's brilliant fun. But fine, I'll do all that, and you can be boring and make out with your mystery man in the bathroom. You've got to come. Especially if you're jetting off to Paris for forever. It won't be the same without you."

"It's only for ten days."

"Forever."

He closed the laptop lid and pushed it across the table to her. "I don't even know if he has plans for New Year's Eve."

"You've got his number. Ask him. And for God's sake, make it official before you disappear for nearly two weeks and he moves on to somebody new."

That evening, while Mrs Burke was lecturing Caleb about the burdens of motherhood, Kai sat on the edge of his bed and called home. It rang once before Mum answered, as though she had the phone in her hand in expectation of his call.

"I was about to call you," she said. "We got word today that they've rejected our petition to search the riverbed again."

"I'm sorry," he said, and he meant it. He knew they would never find Fatima's body down there, but an active search would at least give his mother something to focus on six years after her disappearance. Every time the courts refused her requests, a little part of her hope faded. And he didn't know what would happen when she had none left.

He heard her breath bubbling with tears and he let her sob into the phone as though she was beside him, crying against his shoulder. When she sniffled and cleared her throat, he said, "The truth will come out eventually," and he didn't know why he chose those words. The truth.

"Not until we find her body, Kaiser."

He shrugged even though she couldn't see him. "But there's always hope."

Once, a few years ago, he'd asked his mother what she'd do if Fatima hadn't died in the Seine. "What if she walked through that door tomorrow, after all this time? With, like, amnesia. What if she hit her head and didn't know who she was for ages? Until she got another bump on the head and remembered everything and she walked five thousand kilometres just to get home."

Mum had studied his face. And then she said, "I'd hug her."

Dad said, "And I'd give her another bump on the head for being so foolish."

"We just want answers," Mum had said. But Fatima was right; it wasn't the truth they sought. They wanted a perfect lie. A happy family. And there was no room in that happy little saga for a gay child.

Never mind two of them.

He forced a smile onto his face before he spoke again, pressing the phone to his ear now that Mum's sobbing had ceased. "I'm coming home on the third of January. For ten days."

"That's wonderful news, Kaiser. Did you hear that, Ibrahim? Our son is coming home."

Kai couldn't hear Dad's muffled reply, but he imagined him sitting at the table, scowling at a piece of wood that wasn't taking the shape he wanted it to.

"Your father is excited."

"Can somebody pick me up from the airport? I'll email you my flight details, but I should get in around seven P.M."

He hung up when they'd confirmed the arrangements, and when he heard Caleb moving around in the room next to his, he knocked on his open doorway.

"Hey," Caleb said and when he smiled, Kai smiled. He couldn't help it.

Kai didn't enter the room. If he did, he knew they'd kiss and, as much as he needed that, he couldn't risk Charlie or Mrs Burke seeing. Maybe Caleb was right and she wouldn't mind, but he didn't want to jeopardise his place in her home.

"I've booked my flights for Paris and do you want to go to a party tomorrow night?"

"What? When are you leaving?"

"On the third. I'll be back in less than two weeks."

"Your parents must be pleased."

"Mum's ecstatic."

"I bet. Whose party is it?"

"Some guy from school. Emily has invited me and—well, I'd feel better if you were there, too. But if you have plans, I'll understand."

"Let me see," Caleb said, using his hands like weighing scales. "Spend the evening with Mum, who's only going to go on about Dad the whole time, or kiss you at midnight. Hm. It's a tough one."

The following evening, Kai put on a dress shirt and a smile to mask his misery, and he sat beside Caleb in the back of a taxi on their way to a stranger's house. Caleb brought a couple of bottles of vodka in a blue plastic carrier bag when he explained that you never turn up to a party empty-handed. And Kai said, "The French invented alcohol. I know the rules."

"No, you didn't. It was the Chinese."

"Okay, but the French perfected it."

"You have some decent wine. I'll give you that." In the back of the cab, he said, "Why do you look so nervous?"

Kai said, "We're going to be surrounded by strangers at a party in somebody's home in a city I don't really know yet."

"But I'm with you. What could go wrong?"

They pulled up at the house and Caleb paid the driver. It was three stories of swelling music and flickering lights, and when they stood at the garden gate, Kai said, "We can turn around and go home."

Caleb took his hand. "The taxi's already gone. And we're here now. If you get overwhelmed by the crowd, just tell me, okay? I won't let anything bad happen."

Kai steadied his breathing. It had been so long since he was invited to a party that he forgot how noisy they could be. Since Fatima's disappearance and he shut himself off from his friends with his inability to speak, a crowd of people was the last thing he wanted to be a part of.

"Shall we do this?"

He nodded and they pushed through the open door.

They'd been there more than ten minutes before Kai spotted Emily and she screamed as she came to him. She threw her arms around his neck. "Happy New Year, babe."

"Are you drunk?" he laughed.

"And then some." She turned to Caleb. "You must be the mystery man. I'm Emily." She pulled him into a tight hug and, over his shoulder, she made an approving sign to Kai with her hand. "Come and meet the guys."

She shouted names at them as they walked along the hallway and into the kitchen, and Kai was already overwhelmed. Emily had taken his arm and dragged him behind her, and Caleb was lost in the swell of bodies.

"Caleb?"

"I'm here," his voice said, but Kai couldn't see him.

"And this is Jamie and Graham. And that's Peadar but you can call him Paddy because he hates it." She pulled him deeper into the crowd. He could feel his lifeline slipping away.

"I've lost Caleb."

"Who?"

"Caleb. The guy I came with."

"He'll be around. And God is he fit. You didn't tell me he was fit. Stacy. Over here. Come and meet Kai."

Kai shouted hello over the noise of the music and Stacy called him Kay and said she was wasted.

Everyone was wasted.

Somebody bumped into him, and their drunken laughter circled around him. He saw Caleb through the people, six deep across the kitchen, and Caleb mouthed, *You okay?*

Kai nodded even though he wasn't.

He hadn't even poured a drink yet.

In the far corner of the kitchen, someone was guzzling a

bottle of whiskey as the people around him were chanting, "Chug, chug, chug." The guy emptied the bottle and then roared. A second later, he was running from the room in a white-faced panic.

Kai was jostled and bumped and pulled. And Caleb's calming influence was gone. He couldn't see him anywhere.

Emily stood on his foot and almost lost her balance. She gripped his sleeve. "I want to dance. Let's dance."

"It's too hot in here. Where's Caleb? I can't see him."

Emily's face was flushed and glistening with sweat. "Oh my God, I love this tune."

He looked around.

"Dance with me, Kai."

He couldn't find Caleb.

The music drummed in his head.

He heard something shatter in the next room.

Somebody elbowed him out of the way as they went to the fridge, and when Kai turned back, Emily was gone, too.

He was alone in a storm of revellers with nothing to anchor him down. He turned. "Caleb?" Turned again. "Caleb?"

He pushed through the crowd. Called Caleb's name again, turning in circles. But he was gone.

Kai slid the back door open and stepped into the night, trying to catch his breath. He hadn't had a panic attack since his flight to Ireland, and he didn't want one now. He should never have agreed to come.

He crouched with his elbows on his thighs and tried to slow his breathing, to focus his mind. But his thoughts were a jumble. France. Fatima. Caleb. Mum and Dad. Mrs Burke. Being gay. Having to hide it.

He clenched his jaw and inhaled in short, sharp breaths. It helped keep the tears back.

Emily had comforted him in the coffee shop when he'd started crying, and the woman on the plane helped to keep him calm during the turbulence. But he had no one here. Emily and Caleb had disappeared, and there was no kind stranger offering words of wisdom.

He stood up, feeling faint. And he wanted to scream.

And then there was a hand on his back.

"Kai?"

He turned into Caleb's arms.

And he let the tears out.

20.
CALEB

aleb held him. "What happened? I'm here. It's all right."

He'd only lost sight of Kai for a few minutes, and when he found him in the garden, a solitary figure in the darkness, he pulled him into his arms and held him tight. Kai sobbed against his neck and Caleb inched him across the yard, away from the house. They stood in the bleakness of New Year's Eve, the thumping house music spilling out from the open windows above them, the grass dewy and long at their ankles, and Caleb didn't let go until Kai's tears had stopped.

Someone approached them, clicking a cigarette lighter that wouldn't work, and Caleb pulled Kai into a firmer hug. He shook his head at the stranger, begging him to go away. The guy backed up with his palms raised in apology.

When Kai's breathing eventually levelled out, he said, "Shit."

"What?"

"I'm not a crier. I swear I'm not."

"I know. Want to talk about it?"

"Do you hate me?"

"Why would I hate you?"

"For ruining the party."

Caleb rubbed Kai's arm and then pointed at the patio furniture. As they sat, he said, "You didn't ruin it. Everyone's still having fun in there. And besides. Parties aren't really my thing."

"Then why did you come?"

"Because you asked me to."

"That's not a good enough reason."

"Sure it is."

"If I asked you to put your hand in a fire, would you?" Kai said. Caleb knew he was trying to be funny, but his voice was still full of baggage.

"I've walked on hot coals for charity. Me and fire have history." He took Kai's hand and folded the cold fingers into his own. "What happened in there?"

"Can we get out of here?"

"I can call an Uber."

"No, let's walk," Kai said.

Caleb stood up and held his hand out, but Kai stuffed his fists into his coat pockets.

As they walked away from the house, he said, "I panicked. I've been doing that a lot lately."

"Why?"

Kai shrugged.

"Don't do that. Don't shrug like it's nothing."

"I hate my life."

"Hey."

"No, I don't mean you. You're the only thing that's keeping me sane."

Caleb knew the feeling. With Dad on his back about moving in with him and Mum doing her best to protect him from the world, and Jayne's recovery from surgery hanging over his head, Caleb could only silence the mess in his mind when he was in Kai's presence. He didn't realise Kai had been going through something similar.

Abigail had called him that morning to say that Jayne's surgery was a success and she was in recovery. It would be a day or two before they could say she was not in any immediate danger as they waited for the anaesthesia to wear off and for Jayne to wake up. If transplant surgery was a risk, the first twenty-four hours was when Death could cash in on his returns policy. They'd be monitoring her in a constant vigil.

He wasn't a praying man, but when Abigail told him about the surgery, he said, "Keep her alive," to any god that would listen.

"I'm glad I keep you sane," he said to Kai, "but I need more than that if I'm going to help. Why do you hate your life?"

Kai couldn't look at him. "No reason . . . All the reasons."

"Which is it? None of them or all of them?"

Kai kicked a stone out of the way and ran the back of his hand over his nose. They were crossing the River Liffey on a narrow bridge and Kai had been dragging his fingers against the railings like a kid with a stick. He blinked a fresh wave of tears back before saying, "Can we lie down?"

"Here?"

"I want to do that thing. The truth game."

"There's an old carpark up ahead. Come on."

Caleb took Kai's hand and they ran along the dark street and scaled the low wall that bordered a small, seedy car park. There was space for about twenty cars, but only two of the bays were occupied, and a large, red industrial waste bin squatted in the far corner, its contents overflowing. They were on the outskirts of a shopping district and, at this time of night, there were very few people around to notice them.

The ground was cold but dry.

"I feel foolish," Kai said.

"Do you want to go home first? We can lie in the comfort of a warm room instead."

Kai shook his head. When they lay on the tarmac, away from the bin, and looked up at the black night, he said, "Do you remember the rules?"

"Of course I remember the rules. It's my game."

"Just checking."

They held hands. "No lies," Caleb said. "Do you want to start?"

"How's Jayne?"

"She's not out of the woods, exactly, but the surgery was a success."

"Has she woken up yet?"

"No."

"Okay. And how are the flying lessons?"

"You're stalling."

He heard Kai let out a long breath. Whatever brought on

his panic attack, he didn't want to face it. But that was the benefit of this game of truth. Lying on your back, staring at nothing, nobody can see the pain on your face as you speak. The words you say can float away. "I actually feel lighter now," Jayne had said the first time they did it. She flexed her neck and rotated her shoulders, and then she laughed, and even the sound of it was lighter. "Why is that?"

As he sat up, facing her across her hospital bed, he'd said, "Because the truth is unbearable."

Jayne frowned. "If the truth is unbearable, why do we keep it?"

"Because a lie is worse."

He felt Kai squeeze his hand. "Ask me what you want to know."

Caleb cleared his throat. He wasn't sure where to start. With Jayne, it had been obvious. She was dying; the truths she needed to speak had been his truths a few years ago. But Kai was a dark, empty chasm.

"I want to know everything," Caleb said. "But let's start with why you think you hate your life."

"I can't bear my degree. I used to love books, but now I don't want to open one. I'm a thousand kilometres from a home I don't want to go back to, although I do miss my parents. And Ireland is cold—it's always so cold here. My professors don't seem to care about their struggling students. They have less interest in being there than I do. And I haven't found a job yet. And then I look at you with your flying lessons and your amazing family, and you seem to have it all figured out. You know what you want from life and you take it."

As much as Caleb wanted to, he didn't interrupt.

"And then there's my sister."

He was silent. At length, when the silence became a knot between them, Caleb said, "What about her?"

"Fatima—the one I told you had drowned in the Seine? She didn't. She's still alive." He paused. Caleb wasn't sure if he was forming new words or reshaping old ones. "Nobody knows the truth. Not even my parents. You have no idea how hard it is to keep that secret. Is that terrible? Am I a horrible person? I have to face my mum and dad and lie to them every day." His breath caught in his throat and Caleb heard the rattle of it before he said, "Fatima had an arranged marriage. It wasn't by force, but once she had agreed to marry Zameer, there was no backing out of it. It was a binding contract. Mum and Dad—they were so happy. Fatima would give them grandchildren, and everything would be perfect for her. Except that's not what Fatima wanted. She wanted Avery, a girl from her class. Because Fatima is gay, too. She and Avery—they love each other."

Kai's fingers had curled tight in Caleb's hand, and Caleb watched a lonely blackbird flit across the sky above them.

"But that would kill my parents. They needed her to marry Zameer, but she wanted to be with Avery. And when Mum found out about her relationship with a girl, she was outraged. They threatened to lock her up until she begged God for forgiveness of her evil deeds. So Fatima did the only thing she could think of. She left. But running away wasn't enough. You don't know what my father is like. He's a quiet man. In all my years, I think I've only had a handful of conversations with him. He never says much. But when he does speak, everybody listens.

There are three gods in my house: the Christian one, Allah, and my father. And in his view, being a homosexual is worse than being a murderer. So if Fatima just ran away, my father would hunt her down. He would find her and drag her back to Paris and force her to marry Zameer against her will."

Caleb heard the crack in Kai's voice, the tears that he'd been holding in for the last six years.

"So instead of running away, she faked her death. She planted her jacket and shoes in the river and then she got on a bus out of town. I think she threw her phone in there, too, and it's probably still lying there, at the bottom of the Seine. They never found it.

"I texted her. Every day for months. But she didn't reply. Until one day she sent me a message from an unrecognised number. And now I'm the only one who knows that she's still alive. I'm the only person in the world, apart from Avery, that isn't looking for her at the bottom of the Seine." His voice lowered to a whisper and Caleb shuffled closer against his side. Kai's words came slow and were torn into ragged shreds. "I have kept her secret for years. And it has been eating my soul all that time. She's alive, and I'm grateful that she is. But because she is alive, I am dead. My spirit died when she gave me her lie and I made it my own. And now, in three days, I must stand before my parents and lie to them again.

"People say that lies of omission aren't so bad. But they are. When people lie openly, they say the words and put them out into the world. But when you omit the truth you keep those words inside, and they weigh you down. They live in you, feeding off you until there is nothing left to devour.

"Fatima knows it. That is why, instead of lying, she chose to leave. And that is why her lie has become my lie. And I hate my lie. I hate my life."

When he stopped talking, Caleb couldn't breathe. There was a weight on his chest that pinned him to the dull ground beneath him. He had no idea how somebody could keep a lie for so long. And it wasn't a little one, not like stealing a cookie before dinner. His poor parents, despite their appalling views on morality, must have been going out of their minds for the last six years since their daughter disappeared. And Kai, burdened by the truth but unable to say it aloud—what life must he have led?

Caleb turned to face him, and a car alarm blared in the distance. He stared at his flushed cheeks and the glassy eyes that looked to the heavens.

"The lie isn't yours now," he said. "It's ours. I will protect you from it."

"Thank you." Kai turned his head. "You don't hate me?"

"Never."

"I feel so weak."

"You are the strongest person I know."

"You give me strength."

"You give me kisses, so we're even."

Kai sighed, and Caleb felt the weight of his truth drifting away from them. Kai had been right; when you keep a lie in, it crushes you, compressing your soul like a spring. And when springs are wound too tight, one day they snap.

"What now?" Kai asked.

"Now I'd like to get up. I've been lying on a stone or

something. Right between my shoulder blades."

"This whole time? Why didn't you say something?"

"I didn't want to interrupt you."

"You're a fool, Caleb Burke."

"I know."

They kissed. And the car alarm stopped.

Caleb got to his feet and hauled Kai up. "I don't even know where we are anymore."

Kai took his hands and faced him. "You're beautiful."

"Shut up."

"It's true."

Caleb lowered his eyes. "I'm not as beautiful as you." He put his hand on Kai's chest. "You've held a dark secret for so long, I'm surprised you haven't gone insane."

"'*Take your beak from out my heart*,'" Kai recited.

"That sounds like a very bookish thing to say. I thought you hated books now."

"Some books are beyond hate."

They waited outside the carpark when Caleb ordered an Uber, and in the back seat, he pressed his shoulder against Kai's and leaned into him as they rode across Dublin. Standing in the driveway, watching the house, the living room lights were still on. It hadn't struck midnight yet, and Mum and Charlie would be watching the New Year's Eve festivities on TV, waiting for the countdown.

"Let's not go in there," he said.

"Why not?"

"Because they're having fun, and we're supposed to be at a party. It's the perfect chance to be alone. Come on, I have an idea." He grabbed Kai's hand and pulled him around the side of the garage. At the back, he used his keys to open the outer door and they slipped inside without a sound. The garage was cold but warmer than outside, and Kai straddled Caleb's Vespa, holding the handles and making a motorbike noise with his lips.

"Shush," Caleb said. "You don't want them to hear us."

"You should teach me to ride."

"Sure."

"Now?"

"No way."

"Why not?"

"Because—wouldn't you rather make out?"

"I didn't know that was an option."

Caleb stood with the front wheel of the scooter between his legs and he put his hands on top of Kai's, over the handles. "Making out is always an option."

Kai put his thumb and forefinger to his chin as though he was thinking about it before he said, "Okay, then."

They almost knocked the scooter over as they kissed.

The garage door rattled in the wind, and a hiss of cold air snaked in from the side window. Caleb grabbed an old duvet from one of the boxes and spread it on the dusty floor. And they lay there, folded into each other's arms, a chimera of limbs, as Caleb felt Kai's breath on his neck, his lips on his earlobe, and Kai's fingers found the nape of his neck, pulling him closer, tighter. And his back arched as Caleb slid a hand beneath him, gliding his fingers under the shirt and pushing up his back for better purchase.

He felt the slick dampness of sweat in the hollow of his spine.

And his phone chimed.

In the house, they heard Mum and Charlie cheering, ringing in the new year with a rendition of *Auld Lang Syne*.

The neighbours would be at their front doors in a second, and Mum and Charlie would join them in the street as they wished everyone a happy new year. It was a tradition that Caleb no longer saw the need to be a part of. He had new traditions to make.

Kai whispered, "*Bonne année.*"

"Happy new year." Caleb leaned back in for a kiss.

"Aren't you going to answer that text message?"

"It was probably just my mum."

"Then you should reply and stop being so rude."

Caleb groaned as he reached for his phone.

But it wasn't Mum.

It was Abigail at the hospital.

Happy New Heart. She's awake.

21.

KAI

The wheels screeched on the tarmac and Kai shuddered. He'd been holding his breath for the longest time and as they bounced and rattled to a halt, he let the air out of his lungs and tried to breathe normally. "*Bienvenue à Paris,*" the stewardess said.

Home. Not that it felt like home anymore. He'd been away for four months and already Paris seemed like a stranger. Outside the plane's windows, the sky was blue, and the buildings were chalky-white. It was eight degrees Celsius, the stewardess told them over the speakers, and she wished them a pleasant onward journey. "Please remain seated until the seatbelt signs have been turned off."

Kai switched his phone out of airplane mode and, as the passengers jostled in the aisle, he received a text from Caleb.

Facetime me whenever you need to. Good luck with your parents. It can't be worse than a freezing ocean, can it?

Kai smiled. On New Year's morning, Caleb had woken him before anyone else was up. He'd knocked on his door with a gentle rapping until Kai had rolled out of sleep and said, "Come in."

Caleb threw a towel at him. "Wear a pair of shorts under your clothes. We're going swimming."

"Swimming? But it's New Year's Day. There'll be nowhere open."

Caleb didn't wait around, and Kai had to lie in bed for a few more minutes until the strength of his dreams evaporated beneath the blankets. He clung to Caleb's waist on the back of his Vespa and, when he asked where they were going so early in the morning, he felt Caleb shrug and ramp up the little engine to its maximum power.

The sun was low and sparkling across Dublin Bay as they headed south along the coast road. They passed signs for Dún Laoghaire and the People's Park, and they turned off at Sandycove Castle. They continued along the road, past a small beach, and Caleb pulled into a busy parking lot under a banner that read, *Forty Foot New Year's Day Charity Swim.*

It was freezing, but Caleb wrapped his arms around him and said, "Are you ready to make memories?"

There were a few people in wetsuits, but for the most part, the adults and some children were walking around in shorts and T-shirts as though this was the height of summer.

The rocky outcrop gave way onto the Irish Sea, with a few steps down off the promontory, and the swimmers were spread out across the rocks.

"When you said we were going swimming, I thought you meant in a heated pool somewhere with a spa and a seaweed wrap."

"This is better. It'll wake you up."

"Why do we only have to swim forty feet?"

Caleb laughed. "The place is called Forty Foot. You can swim as much as you want."

"Why didn't you tell me?"

"You wouldn't have come if I did."

"Sure I would."

"Really?"

Kai grinned. He would never consider swimming in an icy ocean unless it was at Caleb's side. "Absolutely. Let's do this."

They paid their fee for charity, signed the waiver, and joined the others. Paper cups of tea and coffee were handed out and, as he slipped out of his jeans and the warmth of his coat, Kai was amazed at how many people were willing to brave the freezing plunge.

Caleb said, "It's tradition. Christmas Day and New Year's Day. Up and down the coast people join in for the big dip."

"Am I going to regret this?"

"Never."

When the time came, they lined up on the edge of the promontory, feet already like ice as they stood on the cold, wet stone, and when the organisers blasted their whistles, Caleb reached out and took Kai's hand.

They jumped.

For a moment, Kai wasn't sure they'd hit the water. The stun against his skinny body felt like he'd slammed into a wall. And then his head was submerged.

In the murky splash, he felt Caleb's hand slip out of his, and he struggled, kicking his legs and pulling with his arms at the darkness to reach the surface. He came up and groped for air, conscious of what the shock of cold water must have done to Caleb's heart, but when Caleb paddled over to him, he was laughing and coughing on a mouthful of water.

Kai had never been colder.

And never been happier.

Caleb pressed his body against him under the water, their loose T-shirts pooling up around their armpits, and he cupped Kai's lower back.

"Oh my God, it's freezing."

Kai laughed. "Do you want to get out?"

"No. Yes. Probably."

They weren't allowed to stay in the water for long. The organisers sounded their whistle after only a few minutes, and as Kai and Caleb climbed back up the side of the outcropping, they saw that most of the participants had already come in.

They made a dash to the Vespa and Caleb pulled two enormous towels from his backpack. Kai huddled under his towel and looked around. It should have been torture, plunging into the freezing ocean on the first day of the year, but everyone was in high spirits and the paramedics that strolled through the crowd needn't have been there.

"How was that?" Caleb asked him.

"Amazing."

They pulled off their wet shorts under the wrap of a towel

for privacy, and when they were dried and dressed, they bought some chicken soup that tasted as though it had been made from a powdered mix, but the warmth of it was welcome.

And as Kai stepped off the plane and headed towards Baggage Reclaim, he could still remember Caleb's soup-scented breath when he leaned in to kiss him, right there among the revellers of a New Year's Day swim.

"Making memories," Caleb had called it. New ones to replace a lifetime of misery. And it had worked. At least until Kai got in a taxi this morning and waved goodbye to Caleb at the front door of his house. Caleb had offered to take him to the airport and wait with him as long as he could before he had to go to the gate, but there was no room on the moped for his suitcase, even if it was a small one. Instead, Caleb waited until he was ten minutes away in the taxi, and he called him. He stayed on the phone until Kai had to board the plane, and he talked him through his initial panic at having to fly again.

Caleb said, "Once I have my license, I will fly you back to France myself so I can be with you the whole way."

"Can one of those little planes fly that far?" Kai asked, jostling forward in the queue, keeping the call active until the last possible second.

"On a full tank, we'd make it. But it'd be a damn expensive trip with the price of fuel."

He kept his earbuds in even as he found his seat and buckled his belt.

"You okay now?" Caleb asked.

"No."

"I wish I could have come with you."

225

"Me, too."

But that was never going to be possible. He couldn't introduce Caleb to his parents. He couldn't even say Caleb's name without his mum arriving at the truth.

He picked his bag off the luggage belt and walked out of the reclaim area into Arrivals.

His dad was there to greet him. He smiled, patting his hand on Kai's shoulder, and taking the suitcase from him.

"Your mother will be pleased."

Since Fatima's disappearance, Dad was devoid of emotion. Or perhaps he'd never had any feelings.

"How was Ireland?"

"Good."

"And your studies?"

"Good."

The car ride home was quiet, and the further they got from the airport, the lower Kai's spirits fell.

Mum welcomed him with tears and open arms. The house was awash with the smells of her cooking, and for an hour she didn't leave his side. "My baby is home."

She spoke to him mostly in French, with the occasional Kabyle word thrown in, as though without him there, his parents talked in their native tongue and now her words were jumbled.

Dad had taken up his customary spot at the kitchen table, sanding down a block of wood until Mum told him to clear his things away for dinner.

"Tomorrow," Mum said, "we will celebrate a second Christmas. It was not the same without you. Father Pierre is expecting us at Mass in the evening, and I have invited some neighbours to welcome you home."

He'd missed her cooking. Although Mrs Burke was a great cook, Kai didn't eat with the family often. He preferred to have his meals alone so that he didn't get in anyone's way. But the taste of Mum's Dolma, with just the right amount of cinnamon, was enough to warm even the coldest heart.

That night, sitting on the edge of his bed in his cold and sterile bedroom, he realised just how small his life had been. He didn't bother unpacking his suitcase. He would live out of it for the next ten days, and he couldn't wait to go back to Ireland. France wasn't home anymore. The warmth of Paris was an illusion.

And yet, even in Dublin, he didn't fit in. Despite having a bedroom in Paris and another in Caleb's house, he was homeless. Like an unpotted plant, he had nowhere to ground his roots.

He crawled into bed and sent a text to Caleb. *Rescue me.*

Caleb's reply was instant. *In a heartbeat.*

The next day, Mum fussed around him as though he'd been gone for years, and Dad, in a moment of unusual expression, called him the Prodigal Son. Kai walked through the motions. He had a two-minute call from Emily who said college was going to be boring without him, and Fatima sent him a coded text message that asked how their parents were. He'd changed her name in his phone in case Mum would spot it, and his reply—also coded—explained that they were the same as ever. Only worse.

In the evening, Mum forced him into a shirt and tie and

Dad grunted when they left to go to church. He might have given up his religion for her, but he wasn't prepared to pray to her God.

They sat in her customary pew and, listening to the priest reciting his words, Kai looked around. There were seven people in the congregation. Father Pierre didn't even need his microphone.

After the service, the priest greeted his parishioners by the main exit, and he took Kai's hands in his and held them as he spoke.

"It is good to see you, young man. I understand I should wish you a merry Christmas."

"Thank you, Father."

"How are your studies in Ireland?"

Mum touched his arm. "He is doing very well, Father. Just as I knew he would."

"That is good to hear. And do you attend Mass in Ireland, young man?"

"Yes, Father," he said, and he wondered if lying to a priest was worse than lying to your parents. But he was already up to his eyes in secrets and half-truths. One more wouldn't mar his soul.

"God bless you. Enjoy *Le Réveillon*."

"Thank you, Father," Mum said. She'd been cooking all day and, although it was the last thing Kai wanted, he told her he was looking forward to their pretend Christmas. He wanted to lock himself away in his room and call Caleb, not mingle with the neighbours and whatever young women Mum had lined up for him to meet.

They were home no more than twenty minutes when the neighbours arrived, and by nine o'clock the party was building momentum. Kai had already been introduced to two girls who blushed when he shook their hands, and he lost count of the number of times he'd said how great his degree was going. Every time somebody spoke to him, he smiled, nodded and thought of Caleb.

Dad took his elbow. "Come, son. Come and meet Mr Jabir. He has moved into town a few months ago."

Kai steeled himself. Being introduced to a man with such an Arabic name meant only one thing. Dad had picked a bride for him.

Dad kept a grip on his arm as he led him through the gathered crowd in the living room, and when they stood in front of a tall man with dark skin and a clipped beard, Dad said, "Here he is. Here is my wonderful son."

"*As-salamu 'alaikum*," Mr Jabir said, extending his hand.

Kai lowered his eyes and shook the man's hand. "*Wa 'alaikum as-salam.*"

"He is skinny," Mr Jabir said in French.

Dad said, "He gets this from his mother. But he is at his height now and soon he will fill out."

"He is nineteen?"

"He is nearing twenty, Mr Jabir. A very good age."

"But he does not have a profession."

"He studies. A man with a degree can receive a very good job, am I right?"

Mr Jabir did not look impressed. Behind him, his wife clung to the side of a girl who couldn't have been any older than fourteen or fifteen. They would not be married right away—not until she was of age—but both parties were allowed a say in the matter and either one could reject the proposal, if it ever got passed their fathers' discussions first.

The girl was almost boyish in appearance, Kai noted. Her features were flat, and her face was round. But he did not seek to marry a Muslim girl.

Or any girl.

He would wait until the party was over and he would refuse. It is not something to be said in front of the girl or her father.

But Mr Jabir shook his head. "Perhaps in a year or so when he fills out in the chest. You have my number."

Dad bowed as though it had been good news. "Thank you, Mr Jabir. I will feed him until he is broad and worthy." Mr Jabir swept out of the house with his family, and Dad said, "Go and eat some more of your mother's food. Eat plenty."

Kai retreated to the kitchen.

He checked his phone. He hadn't heard from Caleb for over an hour. Maybe he'd lost interest. Maybe he'd found a wife of his own.

He didn't think Mum would have approved of Dad setting him up with a prospective wife, but then Mum had been behind Fatima's engagement to Zameer. Her Christian ideals didn't extend as far as she'd like once Dad put his foot down.

At midnight, when the guests were gone, Mum led Kai to the kitchen table and the three of them sat under the photo of him and his grandfather. "Merry pretend Christmas," she said, sliding a box across the table to him.

"Mum. You didn't say we were doing presents. I haven't got

you anything."

"It's only a scarf," she said. And then she put her fingers to her lips. "I shouldn't have told you what it is until you opened it. Go on, open it."

Dad was sanding that infernal block of wood again.

"It's from both of us," Mum said.

He pulled it from the box and wrapped it around his neck. It was home-knitted in thick sky-blue wool.

Dad said, "You should give him meat to eat, not something to warm his skinny neck."

"Do not sulk," Mum told him. "Kaiser will find a lovely girl to marry when he is ready."

Kai cleared his throat. He didn't know he was going to say it until the words came out. "I met a girl. In Ireland. She is very nice."

Mum clapped her hands together.

"Is she Christian?"

"I think so."

"You should have asked. What is her name?"

Dad said, "There is no point in marrying a wild Irish girl if you are moving home when your degree is over."

Kai ignored him. "She's called Emily."

"A beautiful name," Mum said. "Is she as beautiful as her name? She must be to have caught your eye."

Kai smiled. He supposed she was beautiful, for a girl, but he didn't feel the need to say so.

"Tell me all about her," Mum said, and Kai added one more lie to his quiver. He told her how many dates they had been on and that no, they hadn't kissed yet, but it was only a matter of time. He'd be sure to peck her on the cheek when he got back to Ireland so that it wasn't entirely untrue.

By twelve-thirty, he was exhausted from trying to keep track of the lies he spoke, and when Mum said, "I wish Fatima was here to see what a wonderful young man you have become," Dad got up from the table and put away his block of wood.

"Good night," he said.

Mum put her hand on Kai's. "Are you happy to be home?"

Kai smiled. "I should go to bed."

"You didn't answer me."

"Yes, Mum. I am glad to be here."

He got into bed and faced the wall. He couldn't look at the window where Fatima used to climb in. And he couldn't look at the Crucifix on the wall beside the door or the Quran on his bookcase that stood out among the smaller paperback novels.

He told himself he wasn't going to cry.

But he did anyway.

22.
CALEB

he hospital was quiet. When Caleb pulled up in the carpark, the sun had barely risen, and many of the austere building's windows were still dark inside. He sat on his moped as the morning mist cleared, and he waited until he saw some activity from the third-floor windows as the nurses began their morning rounds.

Abigail had called him the night before to remind him of his promise to Jayne, not that he needed reminding. He said he'd be there when she was going to take her immunosuppressants for the first time. Her medication had been given intravenously for the first few days until she was strong enough to come off her IV and this morning was her chance to start a new tradition that would last for the rest of her life.

As he locked the chain around the front wheel of his Vespa,

Caleb remembered the first time he'd been presented with his cocktail of pills.

Dr Hughes had taken time out of his morning to stop by, and each capsule and tablet was laid out on the bed table in an arc in front of him. "Do you remember that rainbow song from kindergarten?" Dr Hughes asked. He sang, "*Red and yellow and . . .*"

Caleb frowned and refused to play along. "What age do you think I am, Doc?"

"Humour me. What comes after red and yellow?"

"I don't know. Pink and blue?"

Dr Hughes pointed. "Do you see any blue pills?"

"No."

"So try again."

"Pink and green?" The two-tone pill was laid out second in the order on the table and Caleb realised what Dr Hughes was driving at. "That's more magenta than pink, Doc."

"It's close enough. But you understand now, don't you? Take the pills in the same order as the song."

"I'm pretty sure there's no reference to grey in the song," Caleb said. There were three grey capsules on the table that looked the least appetising of all.

Dr Hughes grinned. "You can't have a rainbow without a little dull grey rain first, am I right?"

The song was helpful, despite making him feel like a child. As Dr Hughes had later explained, he didn't need to take the pills in that specific order, but the contents of one enhanced the compound of another, so getting them right was a sure-fire way of improving his chances against rejection.

The colourful printout that Dr Hughes gave him that morning explained his medication in more detail—Azathioprine, Bactrim, Cyclosporine, he had his own ABCs—but Mum found the lyrics to *I Can Sing a Rainbow* online and she printed them out for him and taped it above the bathroom mirror. And even though the page was long gone and he didn't need its mnemonic reminder, Caleb could still see the grease stains of the Blu Tack on the wall like ghosts of his fallen comrades.

He took the lift to the third floor, making sure his pill box was secure in his inside coat pocket. It was an oversized dosette box with fourteen compartments, an A.M. and P.M. section for each day of the week. It was bigger than the type of box you'd find on an old man's nightstand because it had to hold so many pills.

He walked down to the ward and realised the last time he was there was with Kai, dressed as Christmas elves and trying to hide the longing they felt for each other. He wanted to be on the roof, huddled under a blanket with Kai in his arms, sharing their first kiss again.

Caleb loved air travel, but since Kai got on a plane to go home, tearing him away from Caleb's side, a part of him wanted to hate flying as much as Kai did.

He filled his days with the mundanity of living, going for a run every morning, taking a ride on his moped in the afternoons, and swinging by the airfield even though Colin Moore was spending the first week of the year in Cumbria with his daughter. But his evenings were dull and quiet. He would lie on his bed with his hands behind his head, and he'd stare at the ceiling until sleep took him, wondering if Kai was lying on his own bed, thinking the same thought.

And the one thing that made his nights worse, that woke him in the sticky heat of fervour, was that Kai invaded his dreams. He was there, under the blankets, naked skin damp against him, his soft mouth pressed against the flesh of Caleb's breastbone. Or he'd step into the shower as Caleb scrubbed himself and wrap his arms around his waist as the hot water rained upon them like lava. Or Caleb would come up for air in the freezing Irish Sea and Kai would be there, taking off his towel to offer to him.

It made the mornings unbearable to know that Kai wasn't there to share those moments with. But today was five days into their forced separation. They were halfway there.

He'd sent him a text this morning, but he knew not to expect an instant reply. Kai was being cautious in case his parents were staring over his shoulder, and Caleb didn't understand the logic. His mum would never dream of invading his privacy in that way.

In the ward, Abigail nodded at him, and she paged Dr Hughes.

"Is she ready?" Caleb asked.

"Are you kidding? She's been pushing her call button since five-thirty. Why don't you go in? Dr Hughes will be up as soon as he can."

He stopped at the cleanroom and scrubbed up, putting on a pair of plastic shoe coverings, gloves, an apron and a haircap. Abigail tied a mask over his face. Jayne was no longer just immunocompromised; she was in a fight for her life, and any infection now could mean her death.

She opened Jayne's door and let him in. Her parents were there, wrapped up in their protective gear just as he was, and Jayne was propped up in bed. Her smile was weak but wide. Mr and Mrs Goddard hugged him, and Mrs Goddard was already crying. "It's a miracle," she said.

Jayne's face was pinker than the last time he saw her, but she was still weak and in pain. Her chest would ache when her medication wore off like she'd taken the full force of a blast from a torpedo but, for now, her smile swam in the post-glow of her epidural analgesia.

"How's the patient?" Caleb asked.

"Did you bring them?"

"Of course," he told her, patting his pocket. "I'm not a flake."

"And your dancing shoes?"

"Shoot. I left them at home."

"Next time," Jayne said.

Mrs Goddard tried to laugh. "It'll be a long time before you can dance, sweetheart."

He'd been an active athlete at the time, and Caleb knew how lethargic he felt after his surgery. Given that Jayne was only thirteen, he knew she would be suffering, too. Her body, under the blankets, held no shape, no womanly form, as though her teenage growth had been stunted by her congenital defect. But there was colour in her cheeks and a glassy sheen in her eyes, and even her fingernails seemed to have a rosy pinkness to them that hadn't been there before Christmas. Caleb had to agree with Mrs Goddard. It was a miracle.

Dr Hughes arrived with Jayne's pills laid out on a red velvet cushion, and the available nurses of the ward gathered in the doorway. Hughes gave his speech about rainbows, and by the time he'd finished, everyone was singing along. Jayne hid her face with the blankets and pretended she wasn't cringing. Caleb didn't have such a fan fair when he was in her position, and he could tell how embarrassed she was.

"Okay, everyone. Back to your stations," Abigail said.

Dr Hughes shook Mr Goddard's hand and Mrs Goddard hugged him, and when it was just the four of them in the room, Jayne said to her parents, "I don't need an audience. Just Caleb."

Mrs Goddard said, "Sweetheart, it's your first time taking so many pills at once."

"I've taken enough before the surgery. I know how to swallow."

Caleb said, "Wouldn't you rather they stayed, so you can get them off your back later on?"

"No."

"Honey," Mrs Goddard said with a comforting hand on her shoulder.

Her husband said, "She's a young woman now, Maisie. Let her do her thing."

To Caleb, she said, "Make sure she swallows them all."

"I know."

"If she needs more water, we'll be right outside."

"You bet."

"And if you—"

"Mum. I'm fine. Go."

Caleb gave them an apologetic look as he closed the door behind them. Jayne shimmied up in bed and scratched her collarbone right next to the stitches that appeared above the collar of her pyjamas. Her chest tubes that carried away the accumulation of fluids had been removed two days ago, Abigail had told him, and she'd been brought back to the ward from the cardiothoracic unit just two days after her surgery.

"I can't wait to have a shower," she said.

Under her shirt, Caleb knew, would be a pacemaker and a line of wires going in through the flesh to her heart. They'd be monitoring her heart rate for the first couple of weeks.

"I can smell you from here," he laughed.

She still had an IV line in her neck, which would top up her fluids when required, but she looked as though she was recovering well.

"I've had a sponge bath, dingus."

"Dingus? Do you kiss your mother with that mouth?"

He took out his pills and spread them on the table in front of her. When they counted, she had two more pills than he did, but Dr Hughes would be perfecting her regime before she was discharged, and her dosage would change over time.

"Gotta take the disgusting grey ones first," he told her.

"Do they taste bad?"

"Only if you burst them open in your mouth. And trust me, you don't want to do that."

He poured two glasses of water and then lowered his mask, maintaining a safe distance from her. "Ready?"

He matched her pace, encouraging her to keep going when she stalled after her sixth pill, and he had to top up her glass because she wasn't used to swallowing so many. She was taking bigger gulps of water than she needed.

When she was finished, he said, "And you get to do the

same thing all over again this evening."

"And every day for the rest of my life."

"You get used to it. So. What's it like having a second-hand heart?"

"It feels weird. Like the heart is running faster than it should be."

"That's normal. For me, it was running slow for the first couple of days, then for about four weeks my base rate was elevated." He pulled a chair up and sat at the foot of her bed. "You can feel it, can't you? Your body knows it's not yours."

"No one has ever told me about that," Jayne said. "It's like I know it's a foreign object and my body is—I don't know. It's doing this thing, like it wants to get rid of it. Why didn't you tell me?"

"The doctors think it's our imagination. Our bodies know the heart is foreign, but we aren't supposed to feel it. And there's a difference between our brains knowing it's there and the sensation of it being wrong."

"You didn't tell me."

"It's not something you can explain. How could I tell you that it feels wrong?"

"Does it go away?"

"No. Every day, I know my heart isn't mine. The blood pumps through it and I wake up alive every morning, so it's doing its job. But it's Alice's heart, not mine. It's like I've got it on loan."

"But the person you've borrowed it from isn't around to give it back to."

"Exactly," Caleb said. "It's a permanent loan. But it's still just a loan."

Jayne yawned. Her energy would come in bursts over the next few months as she readjusted to life with a functioning heart, and under his sweater, Caleb's scar flamed hot. Alice knew he was talking about her.

Speaking of Alice, he said, "Who's your donor? Have you named it?"

Caleb knew the heart came from a road traffic accident, but Abigail had told him no more, and he wasn't sure if Jayne knew the heart's origins. But like him, she was adamant in creating her donor's backstory.

"Alonso Garcia."

"Mexican?"

"Spanish," Jayne said. She shuffled down the bed, her eyelids drawing closed in languid blinks. "He was fourteen. We would have been married one day and have six children. He was on his way from Spain when his plane was hit by Russian cosmonauts on their way back from the International Space Station. Sadly, no one survived, except Alonso's dog, Paco. Paco limped away from the wreckage to get help, and a team of doctors with sled dogs found the bodies in the middle of a field of tulips. And because Dr Hughes knew how much Alonso was in love with me, he gave me his heart to keep safe. Some boys give girls a locket to wear around their neck. Alonso gave me his heart."

Caleb said nothing, and in a few minutes, she was asleep.

When he went into the corridor, her parents were also asleep in a couple of chairs outside her door. That's another thing nobody tells you. After heart surgery, everyone is tired, not just the recipient. Caleb's parents walked around in a daze for the first couple of weeks, doing everything they could to make him comfortable, and taking turns to sit up through the night to keep watch. The tightness in Caleb's chest from the pulling of his scar was enough to disturb his sleep, so that when he woke, he'd startle at the vision of Mum or Dad leaning over him.

"Are you okay?" they'd ask.

"I'm still alive," he'd say, pulling the covers up around his chin.

Invariably, Mum would say, "Thank God," while Dad's response would always be, "Are you sure?"

Once, a week after he got home, he woke up with a heavy feeling on his chest and for a minute he thought his sternum had cracked open and Alice's heart had escaped. But when he reached for his chest, it was Mum's head he felt, pressed against him.

His T-shirt was wet from her tears.

"Mum?"

"Sorry."

"What're you doing?"

"Listening."

He sat up, pulling away from her. "Why?"

"It doesn't sound like you."

"Mum, you're not getting enough sleep," he said, but he knew what she meant. Alice was keeping her own rhythm. She was banging her own drum.

"When you were born, I would press my ear against your tiny chest and listen to the sound of you. I don't know why I did it. It was like one day I knew I'd have to listen again."

"I'm still me," he said.

"I know, baby. I just need to relearn your new beat."

He took her hand and pushed it under his T-shirt where the stitches were dissolving. "We both do."

She switched off his bedside lamp. "I'm sorry I woke you."

As she left, he said, "Mum?"

"Yes?"

"That thing Charlie said, about not loving him because I have a new heart? It's not true. I love you all."

"I know."

And maybe it was the ghost of light from his lamp that shadowed her face, or the dull yellow glow from the landing behind her, but he didn't see a smile on her lips, didn't hear it in her voice. For the rest of that night, he couldn't sleep, worried that she didn't love him as much as she said she did. If he no longer had the heart that she gave him at birth, he was no longer worthy of her love.

The feeling came back to him now, standing in the corridor outside Jayne's room, looking down on Mr and Mrs Goddard. He didn't wake them. Right now, everyone needed their sleep. Including him.

He went outside. The January air was southern ice. And his cheeks were flushed.

And his chest was tight.

He tried to zip his coat up, but it wouldn't catch.

The carpark was huge and packed. And his breath caught in his throat.

Alice was forcing blood through his veins like she was angry.

Mum didn't love him. And Dad hated him. And Charlie

couldn't look at him. And Jayne had to suffer the same fate.

He couldn't breathe.

His fucking zip wouldn't work.

And an ambulance siren blared nearby.

The electronic doors slid open and closed behind him, and his vision blurred. He reached for his phone. But Mum didn't answer.

So he called Kai.

And he pressed the phone to his ear even as he fell to his knees.

23.
KAI

"Caleb?"

"I—can't—breathe."

"Calm down. Where are you? What has happened?" Kai stepped out of the lounge where his mother was busy scrolling through her tablet, and he walked through the kitchen where Dad was sitting at the table. They both had some level of English—Mum more than Dad—but Kai wasn't going to take any chances. He hurried up to his bedroom and closed the door.

He heard Caleb's voice struggling and he wished he was still in Ireland to protect him from whatever was going on.

"Mum. Heart. Jayne."

"Caleb, you're not making sense. Is Jayne all right?"

"Uh-huh."

"You're panicking. Do you understand? I want you to breathe. Breathe with me. Okay?" He took a deep breath, loud enough for Caleb to hear him, and he listened as Caleb laboured to inhale. "Hold it," he said. "Four seconds. Then let it out. Slowly. Slower. And again."

He heard the catch in Caleb's throat, the rattle of his pain.

Downstairs, Dad cursed in Kabyle, probably at the piece of wood in his hands. Kai heard Mum tell him off.

And in Ireland, Caleb took another breath. "I—" he tried. Then said, "Fuck." He exhaled, and Kai's deep breathing made him feel dizzy. He sat on the chair at his desk.

When he was certain Caleb was all right, he said, "You fuck what?"

"Huh?"

"You said, 'I—fuck.'"

"Shut up," Caleb said, but he was laughing. His voice was still weak.

"Where are you?"

"At the hospital. I've just been to see Jayne. She's okay, but it brought up some old memories. I just got in a panic."

"Isn't that my job?"

"You don't have exclusive rights to panicking."

Kai said, "If I lie on my back, we can talk about it."

"I'm okay. Where are your parents?"

"Downstairs."

"Are you okay to talk?"

Kai checked to make sure no one was hovering outside his door, and he said, "I've got a few minutes."

"What are you wearing?"

"Very funny. Is Jayne really okay?"

"She's just taken her first cocktail of pills by mouth. That's a big step. She seems to be doing well."

Their conversation held nothing of importance, but Kai felt more at home the longer he heard Caleb's voice. He leaned back in his chair and closed his eyes, and it was as though he hadn't left Ireland.

When Caleb stopped talking, Kai cleared his throat.

"Are you there?"

"Yes," he said. "I was just thinking."

"About what?"

He lowered his voice. "About how much I miss you."

"Only five more days."

"Good."

"I should go. But Kai?"

"Yes?"

"Thank you. For talking me through my panic attack."

Kai thought he was going to say something else, to express an emotion that he thought they both felt but were too reticent to say. But this ache in his chest couldn't be that thing he wanted it to be; they'd only known each other for four months. And only children fall in love so fast.

But the more he talked to Caleb, the tighter his chest got. The thing with love is that it feels so much like pain that it's difficult to distinguish between the two.

He hung up, but he sat at his desk for a while longer, staring at his phone. He shouldn't have come home. Secrets can't be kept forever, and the more time he spent around his parents, the harder it was to keep his mouth shut.

When Mum knocked on his bedroom door, she opened it without waiting for an answer. "Are you ready?"

He was going to accompany her into town while she picked up the ingredients to make a *quatre quart*, what Caleb would have called a pound cake. Before Sunday, she would make four or five of them for her after-church gathering, where the older parishioners would congregate in the church hall for coffee and cake, and they'd discuss the life of whichever old friend had passed away most recently. Old people only ever talk about the dead, and young people about the living. There is no crossover.

His phone buzzed.

"Sure," he said. "I'll be right down."

"Is that Emily? Tell her I said hello."

Kai looked at his phone. The message was from *Benoît*.

"No. It's just someone from school."

"Don't be long."

When Mum went downstairs, Kai opened the message. When he decoded it, it read, *Got news. Can't talk. Need to speak alone. 8 P.M. your time.*

Benoît knew that their mother would be at church on a Friday evening, and Kai just had to get away from his father so that they could talk in private.

In the car, Kai rubbed his hands together and held them to the air vent. He wore the blue scarf Mum had knitted for him and still he was freezing.

Mum said, "Do you remember when we used to bake together? You, me and Fatima. You would always argue over who got to lick the spatula."

"I'm surprised we didn't get salmonella."

"Things were different then."

"It wasn't that long ago."

"*I* was different then."

They all were. But he didn't need to say it. He cupped his hands over the warm vent and wondered what the point of conversation was. People don't ever say what's on their minds. Lovers say love with flowers. Enemies make arguments with guns. And all they need to say is "I love you" or "I hate you" and the world would be right. Mum wasn't talking about baking. She was thinking about Fatima.

To help her, Kai said, "Remember the time we tried to bake brioche for your birthday?"

Mum laughed. "You made an absolute mess of the kitchen. I didn't know what had happened when I came down that morning." She touched his arm and then returned her hand to the steering wheel. "And you were covered in eggs and flour from head to toe. Twice I had to march you back into the shower."

"And you had to throw the baking tray out."

"And your sister swore they were perfectly edible."

"Isn't that when she chipped her front tooth?"

"It cost a fortune to fix that tooth," Mum said. And then she sighed. As memories go, it wasn't painful. She made a sign of the Cross.

Kai said, "Dad was hysterical when he got home from work that night."

"We were scraping dried flour off the countertops for weeks."

"It wasn't that bad."

"Wasn't it? Your father had to work three extra shifts that

month to cover the cost of Fatima's tooth and you couldn't sit down for a week because he'd smacked you so hard," Mum said, but she was smiling. As she indicated into a parking bay on the road outside a local supermarket, she said, "I'll tell you a secret. Your father never liked smacking either of you, but especially you."

"Why me?"

She turned off the engine and they sat in silence for a moment. "You were always so small for your age. And I told him not to touch either of you, but you know what he's like. He doesn't have a temper, but he does command respect." Her smile was lopsided as she looked at him. "He never hit you hard. Not really. Not you. He was afraid you were—different."

Kai felt the heat rising in his cheeks. He dared not say it. "Different?"

"Never mind," Mum said. "All is well. And Emily is such a lucky girl."

She got out of the car, and he joined her in the warmth of the supermarket as she pushed a small trolley around in search of flour, sugar, vanilla extract, and the other ingredients she needed for her *quatre quart*.

Kai dragged his feet behind her. Different? He couldn't believe they were discussing his sexuality back then. He'd been eight years old when he and Fatima tried making brioche for their mother. He didn't think it was possible that anyone could have spotted his nature at such an age. He wasn't sure he'd known it himself. Not at eight years old. At least not until he met Louis Chastain a few years later.

But he couldn't ask her now. He wondered if they'd spotted

Fatima's difference at an early age, too, or if her relationship with Avery was as much of a shock as he was led to believe.

He remembered sneaking into her room when he was small and brushing the hair on her dolls. And there were the times she dressed him in their mother's heels and paraded him down the street to her friends. But Fatima never gave off any signals that he could pick up on. Is it true that a mother always knows? He didn't think so.

"What did you mean by saying I was different?" he asked her at the checkout. He didn't mean to say it, but the question had been wedged in his throat since they got out of the car.

"Quiet, Kaiser," Mum said. She was packing her ingredients into a bag and the young guy at the register was far from interested.

But he couldn't be quiet.

"When did you first think I was different?"

"Enough," she said in Kabyle. It was one of the few words he knew. Dad had said it often. She handed him the bag and packed the remaining purchases into a second one.

"Thirty-seven Euros and ninety-two cents," the kid at the till said.

"I have a coupon."

He scanned the clipped paper and Kai's cheeks were burning.

"Mum," he said.

"Go to the car, Kaiser. I will be right out."

He stood at the car and watched her through the tall windows of the supermarket. She paid the young man and waited for her change, and then she raised her head, composed herself, and walked towards the exit.

"Mum."

"Get in the car."

"It's locked."

She fumbled with the key fob.

Kai put the bag on the backseat and then got in the front. His hands were no longer frozen, but his fingers were tingling as much as his cheeks. He clipped his seatbelt on and waited.

Mum paced away from the car, stopped, came back.

She got in.

"Mum."

She shook her head. "Don't."

"Don't what?"

"Don't speak. I don't want to hear it." She started the car but didn't put it into gear.

Kai's voice was a whisper. "Why did you think I was different?"

"You know why."

"I don't."

"You don't remember?"

"Remember what?" He had no clue.

"Your father caught you in the bathroom with Matthieu Babin when you were six."

"That?" he said. "That was nothing. It was innocent. There was nothing sexual about that."

"Your father thought so."

"And you?"

"What do I know of such things?"

Kai shook his head and tears blurred his vision. "You thought I was gay since I was six?"

"But you're not. So it's fine."

"What if I am?"

She slammed the car horn until the sound of it made his ears ache and the people on the street stopped to stare.

When she let go of it, the silence was louder.

"You are not."

"Is this what you do?" he asked. "You deny it until it either goes away or I kill myself just like Fatima did?"

She stared at him, and he flinched, waiting for her slap. But she didn't reach out to him. Her voice was level. "You have said enough. When we get home, you will go straight to your room. You will stay there until this evening, and you will come with me to Mass. And after that, you will have a chat with Father Pierre. And Kaiser? You will not say a word about this to your father. Do you hear me?"

He did not speak.

"Do you hear me?"

He nodded. And on the way home, Mum's driving was slow and controlled. He folded his arms across his chest and sank his chin into his scarf to hide his face. And although he didn't want to cry, his cheeks were wet. He couldn't look at her. And he knew she couldn't look at him.

When they pulled up outside their home, she said, "Go to your room."

"But the groceries."

"Leave them."

"Mum. It isn't your fault. It isn't anything you or Dad have done."

She turned her face from him. "I know damn well it isn't

my fault. But I am not going to let you be the death of me the way Fatima has. You will change your ways." He opened the car door, and she stopped him. "Tomorrow, you will call the university in Dublin. You will complete your education in Paris. Whatever belongings you have there can be shipped back."

"No."

"It is not up for discussion."

"Mum, you can't do that."

"You are my son. I will do everything I can to protect your soul."

"I do not need protection."

"Give me your phone," she said.

"Mum, no."

"Your phone."

Kai slipped his phone out of his pocket, pressing the off switch until he felt the power-down vibration. He handed it over. She didn't have his PIN and she wouldn't think to use his thumbprint, he hoped.

"And your wallet."

"What?"

"Now."

His life was in his phone and any means of escape were in the billfold of his wallet.

"Go to your room."

Kai slammed the car door and stomped through the house to his bedroom. He reached under the bed for his iPad where he'd stored it the night before. He wanted to call Caleb, but he needed time to calm down. He didn't want Caleb to hear the pain in his voice, not after their last call when Caleb had been the one in pain.

The iPad was dead. He plugged it in and waited, shaking the tension out of his hands and pacing his room. And when the screen finally sparked alive, he sent a message to Benoît. *Call me. Urgent.*

The iPad rang a few minutes later. He answered it before the sound carried beyond his room. Fatima said, "Where are they?"

"Downstairs. I don't have long. She knows I'm gay. I told her. I shouldn't have told her. I'm such an idiot. She knows."

"Kai. Calm down. Does Dad know?"

"Not yet. Will she tell him?"

"I don't know. But listen, Kai. Listen to me."

He forced his panic into a box. His thoughts raced from faking his death the same way that Fatima did—that'd show them—to leaving a note and running off into the night.

"Are you listening?"

"What?" he asked.

"We're going to Ireland."

"What?"

"There's a place there."

"What do you mean?"

Her words didn't come at once. But when they did, her voice carried the weight of excitement. "There's a place in Ireland. Somewhere we can belong. It's a place for people like us."

24.

CALEB

Dad's car horn sounded outside and Caleb rolled over in bed. When his alarm had pulled him out of an intensely erotic dream about Kai, he had forgotten he promised to spend the day at Dad's with Charlie. Never mind that it was already more than two weeks since Christmas and any gift from Dad now would just be an afterthought.

Mum knocked on his door and when he didn't answer her, she knocked again.

"I'm up," he said.

But Mum came in anyway. "You didn't have to promise to spend the day with him, but now that you have, you'd better get up. Charlie's waiting downstairs for you. He's refusing to go out to the car until you do."

Charlie was still annoyed with Dad over Christmas, and

Caleb couldn't blame him. He hadn't been the most reliable parent when he and Mum had been together, and now that Joanne had moved in with him, they saw even less of him than before.

Mum sat on the edge of his bed. "What's she like?"

"You met her a few months ago."

"She was in your father's car, and she managed to say hello. That's hardly meeting her."

"She's nothing like you. Now can you get out so I can get dressed?"

Caleb's phone vibrated on the nightstand. It was Dad.

Mum said, "I don't know what I'm going to do without you until tomorrow."

"You'll enjoy the peace and quiet," he said, answering the phone. "Dad, we'll be out in two minutes."

"Pack your pills," Mum said. "And make sure Charlie has his toothbrush." She opened his underwear drawer and sorted through it for the boxers she'd bought him at Christmas, and she left them on top of the chest of drawers so he'd remember to pack them. Forget Diesel or Calvins. These were Dunnes Stores' finest.

He waited until she'd closed the door before groaning and rolling out of bed. He sniffed his armpits. When they got to Dad's, he'd go for a run and shower in the ensuite. It was one of the perks of visiting the enormous house; he'd have the second floor all to himself.

Downstairs, Charlie sat at the kitchen table, He had his coat zipped up and his backpack was on the table in front of him, with his chin resting on it and a forlorn look on his face.

"Cheer up, Squirt. It's only for one night."

"He doesn't even have a PlayStation."

"Just use the Xbox he bought you last year."

"As if."

Caleb couldn't understand the difference, and Charlie wasn't in the mood to explain it.

Mum hovered. "Have you got your pills?"

"Of course."

"Has Charlie got his toothbrush?"

"I don't know. Charlie, have you got your toothbrush?"

"Yes."

"He does."

"Good," Mum said. "Is your watch charged? You don't want your blood pressure to rise, and your watch battery to die so you don't know about it."

"Oh my God, can we get in the car already?"

"I'm just trying to look after you."

"I know, Mum," he said, kissing her cheek. It was all she ever did, and it was murder.

Charlie said, "Bye, Mum," and he stomped out of the door.

In the car, Dad said, "What kept you?"

They didn't respond. Charlie hadn't even shouted "shotgun". He folded himself into the cramped backseat of the sports car and when Caleb got in the front and asked if he had enough room back there, Charlie just grunted.

It was going to be a long day. But Caleb was trying to keep his spirits up. Only four more days until Kai was back from France. He pulled his phone from his pocket, sent him a text full of kissing emojis, and before putting the phone away, he noticed his message from last night was still unread. It was unusual, but perhaps Kai's parents were being just as clingy as Caleb's Mum, and he couldn't get away from them long enough to reply.

He couldn't imagine how much he was going to miss Kai until they had to spend this time apart. Two nights ago, he'd even wanted to crawl into Kai's bed just to feel near him, but he knew Mum would have asked questions. He was surprised she hadn't said anything already.

Kai gave him a feeling in his chest that wasn't entirely unlike a palpitation. Love is measured in the quiet between heartbeats.

Love. Alice had admitted it even before Caleb was ready. And he wasn't sure that was how he felt until Kai got on that plane and went home. And the longer they were forced to remain apart, the more he missed him. The more Alice beat for him.

Four more days. It wasn't long.

It was an eternity.

And then his phone buzzed. He looked. But the message was from Charlie. *Tell Dad to slow down.*

Caleb looked over his shoulder. "Really?"

And Charlie stared out the window.

When they hit the carriageway, Dad had flipped the turbo switch and they were breaking the speed limit. The engine purred as though it was asking a question. Faster? Do you want to go faster?

Caleb said, "Are you in a hurry?"

"The thing about these cars is that you have to open the throttle every once in a while or they forget how to drive."

"Remember that excuse. I'm sure it'll work well when we get pulled over."

Dad relaxed his foot a little—just enough to bring them back under the speed limit.

Happy now? Caleb texted Charlie.

Charlie replied with a thumbs-up emoji.

Caleb wasn't sure why Charlie was giving Dad the cold shoulder, but if it continued, there'd be bloodshed by night-fall. It's not like Dad forgot about Christmas. He just wanted to have his own Christmas celebrations with them in person. Caleb understood that. And Mum had tried to explain it. But Charlie still took great pains to show how annoyed he was.

When they got to Dad's house, he dragged his feet over the gravel and, inside, he kicked his shoes off by the door and dropped his bag in the hallway.

Dad's home was like a showhouse. The lawns were man-icured, and the water feature gurgled. Ivy hugged the outer brickwork, and the front door was almost twice the height of a normal entryway, and twice as wide. Inside, the sitting room was all white leather and grey herringbone. And the occasional tables—even the legs—were made of glass. The open fire was lit, and the orange flames were the only welcoming aspect of the room. But no one ever sits in Dad's sitting room. It was a showpiece for clients on their way from the front door to his office in the rear.

Charlie slipped into his bedroom, one of two guest rooms on the ground floor, and Dad said, "Come and say hello to Joanne. She's prepping dinner."

"It's only nine-thirty," Charlie said.

Caleb checked his phone. For all the wealth of the area—Dad's house was by no means the biggest—the phone signal was spotty at best.

In the kitchen, Joanne raised her hands. They were coated in breadcrumbs. "I'm making coconut shrimp. You boys both eat seafood, don't you? Your dad couldn't remember."

"Yuck," Charlie said. "Have you changed the Wi-Fi code?"

Caleb said, "I'll eat anything as long as it isn't tripe." When Charlie stepped out of the kitchen in search of the router, Caleb added, "He'll not even try cod. Sorry."

Joanne shook her head. "I think there might be some chicken nuggets at the back of the freezer."

Dad grabbed two beers from the fridge. "Here."

"Dad, it's not even ten o'clock."

He put one of the beers away. "Who wants to kick a ball around outside?" he said, loud enough for Charlie to hear him.

Charlie grunted from the front hallway.

"You ask him that every time and you know the answer."

Dad made a game controller motion with his hands. "The only muscles in that kid's body must be in his thumbs."

"It's keeping him off the streets. Come on. You're in goal."

The air was crisp, and the backyard was as preened as the front. The grass was bright green and neat which, for January, meant it was either fake or sprayed. Caleb couldn't tell. It looked like the real thing.

They didn't so much have a full-sized football pitch as a long flat lawn with a metal goalpost at one end. The net was pristine and intact.

Dad hopped around in front of the net, his beer in one hand,

and Caleb tried to take it easy on him, but he was five shots up when they swapped positions.

Dad kicked and Caleb deflected. "Put some effort into it."

"I'm just warming up," Dad said. He kicked again. Missed. "Anyway. Have you given it any more thought? About moving in."

Caleb didn't break his stride. He knew the question would come, but he hadn't expected it so early in the day.

"I told you Mum wouldn't cope without me."

"She'd learn."

"And who'd be there to look after Charlie?" For some reason, his little brother hadn't factored into Dad's equation.

"Just dial into his PlayStation games once a week. He'll be fine."

"And anyway, the airfield isn't that much closer from here and I'm nearly ready for my final test." He knew Kai wouldn't be living at Mum's house forever, and Dad's place was further from the university, which meant fewer opportunities to spend time together.

"But you have the whole second floor to yourself here."

"If you want a lodger, you should put an ad online."

"I want my son, not a lodger."

Caleb caught the ball. Dad had yet to score. He trapped it under his arm. "You have two sons, Dad."

"You know what I mean."

"I really don't."

Dad drained his beer bottle. And although he could never explain it in words, Caleb knew exactly what he meant. He meant the son who inherited the heart disease, the one he felt responsible for. Most kids inherit male pattern baldness or their dad's eye colour, not HCM. Caleb was convinced Dad cared more about his own guilt than he did about him.

Dad muttered something that Caleb didn't catch.

"Save it, Dad. Let's just get through the next twenty-four hours without Charlie feeling like an outcast or an orphan, shall we? I'm going for a run." He kicked the ball back to Dad and went inside.

As he changed into his sweats, he escaped into thoughts of Kai. Only there did he find hope. Dad was smothering him with guilt, and Mum was choking him with her fears. They both wanted him to live with them, but they were acting through their own perverse needs. Dad needed to be forgiven and Mum needed to feel loved.

And right now, all he wanted to do was fall into Kai's arms and stay there forever. He had no phone signal in his bedroom, but he texted Kai anyway. He'd pick up reception while he was running.

Hurry back. I miss you.

He put an aggressive death metal soundtrack on his ear pods because it helped him run faster, and in thirty minutes he was about five kilometres from Dad's, and he didn't want to go back. But his watch was beeping at him, and he turned around to jog his way home at a slower pace. It took longer for his heart rate to come back down than it did to go up, but he enjoyed the feeling of the forceful thumping in his chest and the flush of oxygen. His cheeks were burning, and his neck was slick with sweat.

And he was smiling.

Only when Alice was working hard at keeping him alive did he actually feel it. If there was a heaven, if he ever met his donor, she'd slap him instead of hugging him.

And before he got back to his dad's house, he had decided he didn't want to live with either of his parents. When Kai returned from Paris, he'd suggest moving into a place together, just the two of them.

A love nest.

Because he knew it now. He did love Kai. It was the one word that Alice had been pumping through his veins for days.

At home, Dad was sulking in his office. Charlie was slumped into the window seat in his bedroom, playing a game on his phone, the Xbox in the corner ignored. And Joanne was grating coconut by hand in the kitchen.

Caleb checked his phone. He still didn't have a message from Kai. Upstairs, he showered and, knowing nobody could come up to the second floor without him hearing them, he didn't get dressed immediately. He stood on the balcony outside the bedroom in his boxers, feeling the chill air of mid-January washing over his pale skin, and he didn't want to feel warm again until he was wrapped in Kai's arms.

His scar glowed hot white.

The rest of the day dragged as much as he knew it was going to. Charlie kept to himself for the most part and, when Dad made them sit in the dining room for dinner, Charlie pumped chicken nuggets into his mouth as fast as he could, and then asked if he could be excused.

"Of course you can," Joanne said.

But Dad said, "Sit there until we're finished." Joanne

frowned her sympathy at Charlie, and he slouched in the chair until Dad sighed, got another beer, and said, "Go, then."

They could hear Charlie's door slam from the dining room.

Caleb said, "I'll go."

"Leave him."

Caleb went anyway.

He knocked on Charlie's door but got no answer. He knocked a second time and then tried the handle.

As the door swung open, he felt a cold breeze. The sash window was open, and Charlie was a brooding figure outside in the darkness by the unlit firepit.

Caleb climbed through the window and approached, grateful that Charlie's room had been on the ground floor.

Charlie had pulled his arms inside his T-shirt sleeves for warmth, and as Caleb sat on the bench beside him, he pulled his hoodie off and offered it to his brother. When he drew it over his head, the sleeves were too big, and the soft fabric crumpled around his thin body. The hood swallowed his head.

He said, "There's a button to turn the fire on but I can't find it."

Caleb said, "Sometimes it's nice to be cold."

"Cold like Daddy?"

"You know he doesn't mean to be. He's just never been any good with words."

Charlie scuffed the toe of his shoe in the grass. "He doesn't even like me."

"Of course he does."

"He doesn't like me because I'm not into sports like you."

"Have you seen Dad kick a ball? He's worse than a

one-legged granny strapped to a kangaroo."

Charlie didn't laugh. Instead, he said, "If I had HCM, he'd notice me."

The words stung Caleb in the chest. "Dad doesn't hate you because I took HCM from his genes and you didn't. If anything, he hates himself. It's his fault I got sick. Or that's how he sees it."

"Don't you see it that way?"

Caleb shrugged. "I drew the short straw. Besides, if one of us had to have it, I'm glad it was me and not you."

"But Dad treats you better because of it."

"No. He treats me different. Not better."

"But it's always you he wants to see. You're the one he's always asking about when he calls."

"Not because he loves me more. It's because he feels guilty and doesn't know how to deal with that." He shuffled closer on the bench. "When people grow up, they don't know what to do with all the emotions they had as a kid. So they stamp it down and then it gets harder to let out. But you know what I think? I think we need to scream sometimes. Do you want to scream?"

"I'm not one of your friends doing that truth game."

"I know."

Charlie looked at him. And Caleb howled at the moon.

"Stop it. I'm not playing."

Caleb howled louder.

And like a little wolf cub following the pack leader, Charlie gave in. He flipped the hood back and filled his lungs. And he howled into the night.

And when their laughter meant that they had no breath left,

Caleb put his arm around Charlie's shoulders.

"Feel better?"

"No."

"A little bit?"

"Maybe."

Caleb crouched by the fire and found the starter button. The flames were blue and warm.

"Caleb?"

"Yes?"

"Are you and Kai a couple?"

"Is that okay?"

"I like him."

"So do I."

"If he hurts you, I'll punch him in the nose."

"If he hurts me, you can punch him twice," Caleb said. He pulled Charlie into a hug. "We look out for each other, me and you. We always will."

"Brothers from the same mother," Charlie grinned.

"I think that's just called brothers."

They laughed. And despite the circumstances, regardless of Dad's inability to profess his love for his two sons, Caleb was happy.

Happier than he had a right to be.

25.
KAI

The collage of photos on his bedroom wall was a lie. Every smile, every face captured mid-laughter—there was no truth in them. Kai pulled a pin out of the wall and took down one of the lies. It was an image of him at seven, clinging to Fatima's neck as Mum and Dad stood behind their children with a formal air, as though they didn't know how to stand in front of a camera.

Eleven-year-old Fatima had her tongue out and Kai's mouth was formed into a word. He remembered that day. It had been Mum's birthday and Fatima put her phone on the back of the couch to capture the moment. Kai had been counting down the numbers with the timer and was still saying, "One," when the flash popped.

Mum had insisted Fatima upload the images to the family

computer so that she could order prints. In the photo, Mum was smiling. And Dad was staring at something off to the side of the camera, his attention elsewhere.

There were four lies in that picture, none of which had voices back then.

Kai crumpled the photo and dropped it at his feet. And then he tore the others from the wall.

It was five A.M. and he hadn't slept.

Mum didn't come to him last night to force him to church. He didn't sit in a pew and listen to the words of an unforgiving God, or suffer the lies of Father Pierre. Mum hadn't gone to Mass at all. He heard her say, "Ibrahim, I have a migraine," and then her bedroom door closed. And a little after midnight, Kai heard his father's heavy footsteps on the stairs, the bathroom door open and close, open again, and then their bedroom door dragging over the carpet.

Dad was snoring within twenty minutes.

She would tell him. She couldn't help herself. And when she did, Kai's life would be over.

He'd crawled into bed before his father came upstairs last night, fully clothed, the blankets pulled tight around his neck in case Dad came in, and he lay there, listening, waiting for the explosion that never came.

But it would.

By one in the morning, Kai was staring out of his window, and by two, he was forming a text to Caleb on the iPad. He wrote, *I'm trapped*. And then he deleted it. He typed, *Mum knows I'm gay. My life is over.* And he deleted it. Then he wrote, *I love you. I'm sorry.*

And he deleted it.

He didn't know what to say. But he needed to say something. Caleb would see that he'd read his messages, the string of kissing emojis and the *I miss you* text.

He typed, *I miss you too*. And he sent it.

At three A.M. he heard Dad get out of bed and use the bathroom. And then he heard Mum whisper something as the bedroom door closed again.

The night dragged.

At five, tearing photographs from the wall, Kai wasn't certain if the sun would ever rise. The moon would gloat over him forever.

When the wall was bare and the floor was littered with crumpled photos of a liar's past, he opened the window and let in the frozen January night. The air chilled his burning cheeks.

Mum would tell Dad.

And if she didn't, Kai would.

Waiting was the worst part. The pain was not in the execution but in the stay. The time in between lie and truth, that was where the agony crouched. He opened his door, walked across the landing, and raised his hand to knock.

And then he retreated.

Mum would tell Dad. He could not say the words himself.

He closed his door. And he closed the window. And he closed his eyes.

And in the pre-dawn darkness, he stilled his breathing and when he wanted to cry, when he needed to, he could not.

There were no tears left.

He sat on the floor, at the foot of his bed, and he faced the door, knowing that the next time it opened, his truth would be free. And his pain would end—one way or another.

When he heard his father's alarm going off, an old-fashioned clock radio whose glowing red numbers would be the only light in their room at six-thirty on a dark January morning, Kai sat up straight.

She would tell him now. She'd had all night to worry about it. She'd have let Dad sleep so that his fists were well rested. All the better to hit you with.

But Dad shuffled downstairs.

This was torture.

Kai opened his bedroom door. He stood at the top of the stairs. He put his hand on the banister, his foot on the top step. He was reminded of standing outside Caleb's room on Christmas morning, watching as Charlie itched to dash downstairs. But today there was no joy.

He went down three stairs, in the dark, and he listened as Dad opened the fridge and lumbered across the kitchen.

And then he heard his iPad ping.

It would still be five-thirty in Ireland so it couldn't be Caleb. He crept back to his room and closed the door.

Fatima said, *You awake?*

Yes, he replied.

He turned down the volume, knowing that she'd call him.

"What's happening?" she asked.

"Nothing. She went to bed. She didn't even go to Mass. Dad's awake. He's downstairs."

"Why hasn't she told him?"

"I don't know," he said. "Maybe she won't?"

"She will. Do you have any money?"

"Mum has my wallet. And my phone. But I turned it off before she took it. I'll never get it back."

"You can get a new one," Fatima said.

"Tima? What if she never says anything?"

"She will."

"I mean, what if she never says another word to me? Ever."

"You can't live a lie, Kai. I won't let you."

"I could just pretend she misheard me. She hasn't told Dad yet. That's got to mean something, right?"

"Her silence bought you a night. But it won't last. You know what she's like. And worse: you know what Dad's like."

"He's going to kill me."

"I won't let him."

"You're a million kilometres away, Tima. How can you stop him?"

"I'll think of something. Just stay out of his way until I do. Can you go somewhere?"

"Where?"

"Anywhere."

"No. I don't know anyone to go to."

"Stay in your room. Is there a lock on your door?"

"He's going to kill me, isn't he?"

"Keep your door locked. I'll call you soon."

She disconnected the call. And Kai plugged the iPad in to make sure it was fully charged.

He turned the lock on his bedroom door, but a good shove from Dad would break it.

He waited.

And he sweated.

And Death rapped at his open window with her icy scythe so that he pulled it closed and drew the curtains against a blood dawn.

And forty minutes later, when Mum rose and went to the bathroom, and Dad was still downstairs, Kai threw his clothes back into his small suitcase. He would run. He had no other choice.

But he didn't know where to go. He had no money, no phone, and away from Wi-Fi, he wouldn't be able to call Fatima on his iPad. He was trapped.

He was already dead.

He heard Mum go downstairs.

It was now or never. Run. Run before it's too late.

He looked at his bedroom door, and then he looked at the window.

And downstairs, something smashed. Dad shouted.

It was too late.

Dad's footsteps were on the stairs. Kai heard the pull of the banister where Dad always gripped it on his way up, and the screw was loose, the bracket grating against it. And he heard the creak of the third stair from the top. Dad had fixed it twice in the last four years but whatever ghost lived beneath it screamed every time they stood on it. It was Fatima, Mum said.

Kai's bedroom doorhandle twisted.

And then Dad thumped his fist against the door.

"Open up," he shouted. "Open the door."

Kai backed away. He reached for his iPad.

Dad hammered again.

Kai dialled Fatima's number.

"Kaiser Ibrahim Kateb," Mum said. She'd joined Dad on the landing. "Open this door at once."

Kai put the tablet on speaker and listened as it rang. He dropped it onto his mattress and gripped the bedframe. He dragged it across the door as a barrier.

"Kaiser," Dad shouted. He thumped the door.

Fatima answered. "What's going on?"

Dad shouted, "Open this door."

Mum said, "Kaiser. Open up."

And Kai said, "Shit."

"I'll kill him," Dad said.

"Tima, help."

"Get out. Go now."

"I can't."

Mum said, "Break it down."

Dad shouldered the door. The frame was splitting.

"Tima, help."

"Out the window," she said. "Head for Rue Brocharde. Get to the corner. Now."

"I can't."

"Do it. Go now."

He thumbed the latch on the window. Dad smacked against the door.

The lock gave, but the bed stopped the door from swinging wide.

Kai pushed the window open. He threw his suitcase out.

Dad shoved the door. The bed moved. He shoved again.

Kai grabbed the iPad and rolled out of the window onto the balcony. It was a short hop over the railing to the garage roof.

On the iPad, Fatima said, "Are you out?"

Dad pushed his way in and stumbled over the end of the bed.

On the landing outside the door, Mum said, "Stop him."

Fatima said, "Go, Kai. Go."

And Mum's eyes were wet. "Fatima?"

Kai jumped.

He slipped across the wet garage roof, rolled off the edge, and landed on the plant pots beside his suitcase.

When he got to his feet, Dad was standing on the balcony and Mum was framed by the window. The iPad's screen was fractured, but the call was still active.

"Kai? Kai? Are you out?"

He grabbed his suitcase and ran. He didn't know where he was going, but he was free. He turned the corner and crossed the road. And he was laughing. Not because he was happy but because he was crazy.

He laughed.

And he looked at the iPad. He was out of range from the Wi-Fi. And the call had dropped.

Rue Brocharde, she'd told him. Or Rue Brochant? He couldn't remember.

He dragged his suitcase behind him.

He didn't know if they were chasing him.

And then a car horn blared. He turned the corner.

He ran.

And the car came alongside him. It honked again.

He didn't want to look.

He kept running.

And then the car stopped. The driver's door opened.

Someone said, "Are you Kai?"

Kai turned.

"Fatima sent me. I'm Avery's brother."

He heard Fatima's voice. "Kai? Kai, are you there?" It was coming from inside the car.

He ran to it, but when he pulled the door open, the car was empty. Avery's brother got back in the driver's seat. "Get in."

The car stereo said, "Kai?"

The phone on the dash was lit up with Avery's name.

Kai got in. "I'm here."

"Thank God," Fatima said. And he heard Avery in the background, shouting her delight.

"I'm Théo," the driver said.

From the speakers, Fatima said, "Introductions later. Just get to the airport. Kai, do you have your passport?"

"It's in my suitcase," he said. "But I don't have any money for a plane ticket."

"I've bought you a ticket. It'll be at the desk."

"Where am I going?"

"Dublin. You have someone there you can stay with, right?"

"Yes. But what about you?"

"We'll be there tomorrow," she said.

And Théo said, "Nothing like an escape plan to get the blood pumping, eh? This is my second one."

It took Kai a second to realise he meant he'd been involved in Fatima's disappearance.

And when Kai imagined hugging his sister again, he didn't think he'd ever let her go.

26.
CALEB

C aleb stood in the middle of the busy airport concourse and watched the Arrivals door. He wasn't sure what was going on, but Kai was on his way back to Ireland a few days early.

This morning, he'd had breakfast with Joanne in the bright kitchen while Dad spoke to a client in his office and Charlie stayed in bed. The coffee was fresh, and the cream cheese bagels were delicious.

"Have you got a picture?" Joanne had asked. He'd told her about the French boy who'd invaded his home and his dreams. Joanne wasn't all that bad. She wasn't the ogre Mum or Charlie made her out to be and, although Caleb had an issue with her age—she wasn't that much older than him—he figured she must be a good person to put up with Dad.

He showed her Kai's Instagram profile and she whistled.

And then Charlie slouched into the kitchen with his hair sticking up at the back and he opened half a dozen cupboards until he found the cereal boxes. He didn't say a word and Caleb and Joanne watched him in silence until he poured the cereal into a bowl, grabbed a spoon, and left the room.

"No milk?" Caleb called after him.

There was no answer.

"Ignore him," Caleb told Joanne. "He might not be a teenager yet, but he's certainly acting like one."

"I have three younger brothers," she said. "I don't hurt easily. One's a year younger than—' She didn't finish her sentence.

"Me?"

"Yeah. That's weird, isn't it?"

"I don't hurt easily, either."

"Are you sure?" she asked.

"I mean, it's a little weird that you're—what?—eight years older than me?"

"Eleven."

"But at least you're not trying to tuck me into bed at night and read bedtime stories."

"Damn it, I've just ordered a copy of *The Very Hungry Caterpillar*."

Caleb lowered his eyes and busied himself with a bagel, spreading more cream cheese over it.

"Oh my God, that was creepy, wasn't it?"

He laughed. "No creepier than my mum picking out my boxers for today."

"Really?"

"Really."

"And you're certain you don't want to live with your dad and me?"

"Honestly, I'd rather have my own place. I'm not a kid anymore."

"I'll talk to your dad."

"There's no need. I can say everything I need to, don't worry."

"I'm sure you can."

Later, when Dad had finished his meeting, he rounded them up and they got back in his car. He drove them home and Mum was standing in the driveway when they pulled up as though she'd been watching for them from the windows. She hugged them both, and Charlie pulled out from her embrace and dashed inside. Tall enough for her to wrap her arms around his neck and cling to him, Caleb wasn't so lucky. He stood on the drive, his arms hanging at his sides, and Dad waved, pumped the horn, and drove away.

"How was it?"

"Good."

"Just good?"

"What do you want me to say, Mum?"

"I don't know. Tell me it was a nightmare, and you never want to stay there again."

She followed him into the house, and he was grateful when his phone vibrated. The text was from Jayne. *Are you ignoring me now that I'm out of hospital?*

He called her without excusing himself from Mum, and when she answered, he said, "Hey, Jayne."

Mum leaned against his shoulder. "Hi, Jayne," she called. "How are you?"

"She says she's fine." He went upstairs and closed his door. "How are you really, though?"

"I thought you'd forgotten about me."

"It's Jenny, isn't it? Or Janice? Judy?"

"You're a riot."

"You should come to my open mic nights. How're you feeling?"

He heard her sigh. "They've got me under lock and key. It's like they think I'm going to drop dead at any minute."

"Try not to do that, eh?"

"It's not on my to-do list. You should come over and rescue me. And bring ice cream. They won't let me have any."

"Such cruelty," he said. "Don't they know ice cream is the best medicine in the world?"

"Mint choc chip."

"Rocky road."

"Agree to disagree," Jayne said. He heard a rattle of fabric over the phone, and he imagined she'd be sitting up in bed or on the couch where her parents could watch her. "Is it supposed to hurt this much?"

"Your chest?"

"It's like someone's driving a stake through my heart but nobody's told them I'm not a vampire."

"Your surgeons literally cut through your breastbone and ripped your ribs apart, tore your old heart out and stitched a new one in before yanking your bones back together and super-gluing you shut. Of course it's going to hurt. Are you still on tramadol?"

"Yeah."

"Capsules or injection?"

"Capsules. I'm sick of needles."

"Maybe call Dr Hughes if you're worried. But I'm sure it's nothing."

"Will you come and visit me sometime?"

"Of course I will. I owe you a dance, remember?"

They talked about her desire to go back to school as soon as possible and he asked her if there were any boys in her class that she liked, but she refused to answer. And when his phone beeped, he checked the screen. It was an incoming voice call on his Facebook Messenger account, something he hadn't used in a long time. He rejected it.

"What was that?" Jayne asked.

"Nothing. Go on, you were telling me about Pythagoras' theorem."

"Was I boring you?"

"Not even."

When he hung up from Jayne, he had half a dozen texts in his Messenger account from someone called Félice Kessner.

Hi, Caleb. I hope you're the right person. My name is Fatima and I am Kaiser's sister.

This might be a surprise. I don't know if he told you about me.

Anyway. I need your help. Please.

It's urgent.

I've tried calling you. Please pick up.

He looked at the name again. Félice Kessner. She had the same initials as Fatima Kateb. Could it be? Wary, but panicking, he hit the call button.

She answered before the first ring ended. "Caleb?"

"Yes."

"Where are you?"

"I'm at home. What's going on?"

"I can't explain. But Kai's on his way back to Ireland. He lands at Dublin on the two-forty flight. Can you meet him?"

"Are you really his sister?"

"I am. I know he probably told you I was dead but, please, Caleb. This is important. Can you meet him?"

"Is he okay?"

"He's fine."

"How can I trust you?"

"Why would I lie?"

"I don't know. You could be his mum trying to trick me."

"*Tête de noeud*. What does he see in you? Meet him at the airport. He's counting on you. Will you do it?"

He didn't know what she'd said in French, but it didn't sound like something a mother would say. "Is he in danger?"

"Twenty to three," she said. "Please. I beg you."

"I'll be there."

She hung up.

It was after eleven and it'd take him over an hour to get to the airport. He tried not to panic, but Fatima—if it was really her—hadn't put his mind at ease. He checked her Facebook profile, but it was locked down tight and she didn't have a profile photo. Not that he'd recognise her anyway.

He sent Kai a message. *You okay?* But it remained unread.

And when he'd paced his room enough times to feel dizzy, he checked the time, and then went downstairs.

"I'm going out."

"Where are you going?" Mum asked.

"Out."

"I'm making lunch soon. Don't go far."

He closed the garage door behind him, pinned a second helmet to the hook below the steering column, and rode to the airport with all the speed of a snail with a cold. It was the first time he wished he'd learned to drive a car.

And when he stood on the concourse, watching the Arrivals door, knowing he was an hour early, he checked his phone again. His text to Kai was still unread.

He messaged Fatima. *I'm here.*

Thank you, she replied. *I'm glad he has you.*

Is he in danger?

He watched her typing, pause, type again. *If he gets off that plane, he won't be. Not any longer.*

If?

She didn't reply.

An hour later, when the Arrivals board said that Kai's flight had landed, Caleb moved closer to the door. He could see the customs officers inside. It was twenty minutes later when the first trickle of people emerged through the doors.

Caleb stood on his toes to see over the milling crowd. Kai wasn't there.

"Come on," he whispered. "Where are you?"

He doubted the validity of his mystery caller and worried that he'd been sent on a wild goose chase, but then he spotted Kai's black hair, his brown skin, and those perfect freckles on his cheeks and across his nose.

"Kai!"

Kai's face crumbled as he ran to him. His eyes were red, and his lips were dry. But Caleb kissed him and held him tight.

"I didn't think you'd be here."

"Fatima called me. I didn't believe it was her at first. Are you okay?"

Kai locked his arms around Caleb's neck and wouldn't let go. "I can't go back," he said.

"You don't have to. You can stay here."

"I love you."

Caleb pulled back from him so that he could see his face. His cheeks were burning, and his heart was racing. Alice was singing. "I love you, too."

As the crowd dispersed when most of the passengers had come through the gate, Caleb took Kai's hand.

"Come on."

"Where are we going?"

"Anywhere you want."

"I don't want to go home yet."

"Are you hungry?"

"Starving."

In the car park, he realised he didn't have enough room for Kai's suitcase. It wasn't a very big one, but he didn't have a rack on the back. "We can get some of your clothes in the storage box under the seat, but we probably won't fit everything in."

"Most of my things are still at your house," Kai said, unzipping the suitcase and pulling out a few shirts and sweaters that he wanted to keep. "What should I do with the rest?"

"You can't leave it lying here; they'll think it's a bomb and evacuate the airport before blowing the case up."

"I'll be right back," Kai said. He went into the airport and returned a few minutes later without the case.

"Where is it?"

"I emptied the remaining clothes into a bin and slipped the case into the corner of the Luggage Store when no one was watching. It's still in good condition; it shouldn't go to waste."

"They'll have a laugh when someone wants to buy it and they can't locate it in the system," Caleb said and kissed him. They rode into town where he parked outside a café.

He waited until Kai had eaten half of his sandwich before saying, "What happened? Why did you move your flight up?"

"Mum found out I was gay. And she told Dad. And I'm not sure, but I think they heard Fatima on the phone. It's a mess."

"How did she find out? Shit, was it my messages?"

"No. She took my phone from me. That's why I couldn't call you. But it's switched off. The battery on my iPad is dead, but as soon as I can charge it I'm going to locate the phone and wipe it."

They ordered another coffee when Kai had finished eating, and they sat beside each other in silence. Caleb didn't know what thoughts were running through Kai's head, but he knew he was processing something. He'd never see his parents again. Never go back to Paris. It's the kind of break from his family that Caleb often wished for, but knew that if it happened, he'd be miserable.

He nudged Kai's leg under the table with his knee. When Kai looked at him, his eyes were sad.

"I'm here for you. Whatever you need."

"I need sleep. And a hug."

"I can make sure you get both. Are you ready to go home now?"

When they got back to his Mum's house, Caleb walked the moped into the garage and slipped the interconnecting door open. He'd wanted to sneak Kai in unnoticed. Kai followed him in a daze, his head bowed, and he looked exhausted.

But when they got to the end of the hallway and Caleb put one foot on the stairs, he heard Mum's voice from the lounge.

"Where have you been? You missed lunch. Kai? I didn't think you'd be back for another few days."

Kai tried to smile. "Hi, Mrs Burke."

Caleb said, "He's tired. We're going to bed."

Mum got off the couch and stood in the doorway. "We?"

He pushed Kai up the stairs ahead of him. "Yes, Mum. Good night."

Guiding Kai across the landing and into his room, he drew the curtains, pulled back the blankets, and Kai got in. He climbed in behind him, fully dressed, and flipped the blankets up.

"Are you warm enough?"

Kai nodded and Caleb spooned him, his arm across his waist, the hand tucked against his warm stomach.

With sand in his voice, Kai said, "I haven't told you the best part."

"There's a best bit?"

"Fatima's coming to Ireland."

"I can thank her for sending you back to me. When is she coming?"

"Tomorrow."

"Are you happy?"

Kai nodded once. And he was asleep before he could lift his head again.

27.

KAI

Visions of his angry father swamped his dreams, and when he woke it was with a start. He couldn't breathe. Dad's calloused hands had been wrapped around his throat, and he could feel them still, tight on the flesh of his neck. For a moment, the weight of Caleb's arm over his waist was the impossible reach of his father, pulling him back to France for retribution.

He sat up. Breathed. In the dream, he had tried to jump out of the window, but Dad had caught him. He pulled his hair, twisting his head back, and threw him across the room. Kai had smacked his head against the cabinet. It felt hot and wet and, awake, he reached up to feel the back of his head. Dad stomped his heavy foot into Kai's chest, crouched, pulled him to his feet, and punched him.

And behind Dad, Mum had stood with her hands on her hips, and one word was forced from her lips. "Queer."

Dad gripped his neck and tightened his fingers. Kai was choking. He couldn't breathe. His throat was constricted. The air was heavy. His vision blurred. And Dad was grinning. Mum kept saying, "Queer."

Kai opened his mouth, but he couldn't fill his lungs. He was dying. Dad was killing him, squeezing, his hands so tight they were curling into fists. And Kai didn't have the strength to lift his arm in defence. He couldn't stop him. And just before he woke, he gave in. He blinked the hot tears from his eyes, and he looked at Dad, and he saw Mum over his shoulder.

He let go. He felt Dad's fingers tighten further.

And then he was awake.

He breathed for the first time in his life. The air was clean. And as he shuffled up in bed, with his back against the pillows, he cried. He didn't move. He covered his face with his hands and wept. He was homeless now. An orphan, bereaved of his parents.

Even if he wanted to go home, he couldn't. Dad would never accept him now, and Mum wouldn't forgive him. His life was fractured. There was Before. And there was After. And even though he had no in between, he was stuck in it, in this empty void, waiting for what comes next. It was a dark gorge with no means of crossing. Only Caleb's voice—his light—was Kai's reference point in the grim darkness.

He looked at Caleb's sleeping face, his damp hair spread across his forehead, plastered in a sheen of sweat that shimmered in the half-light of night. He wanted to lean down and kiss those lips, to feel the burning of his skin against him. But he had his mother's voice in his head, taunting him.

If she felt what he felt, she could not deny this emotion. Love is never dirty. It is compassionate. Kai saw in Caleb the same thing that Nabila Kateb saw in her husband. And why should he not? Kindness is eternal. And love is beautiful.

Caleb moaned in his sleep and turned onto his back. And even the soft snores that thrummed from the back of his throat was the sound of love.

Kai didn't deserve his kindness, but it was offered to him freely and he clawed at it with a ferocious hunger. He might not have a family, but he would always have love at Caleb's side. He knew that. That was now his truth.

On the floor, Caleb had plugged Kai's iPad in to charge when they got home. It would be three A.M. in Paris and if Mum hadn't already given his phone to the police, Kai could erase it now. He pictured her and his father sitting at the kitchen table, the coffee pot stewing on the stove, holding hands and wondering what they ever did wrong. They would never know. It was not in their nature to ask the correct questions.

Kai eased across the bed and leaned out. He paused, making sure he didn't wake Caleb, and then he settled back against the pillows and waited for the iPad to start up. He launched the Find My app, despite the crack across the screen from his fall off the garage roof outside his parents' house, and he located his phone from its last known location. When he told the app to erase it, it asked him if he was sure.

He hesitated. Of course he was sure, but killing his phone felt like murdering his past. As soon as he pressed the button, he would reset his life. He would be Kai Kateb, zero days old.

Caleb's quiet voice said, "You can do it." He shuffled up the bed with a yawn.

"I know I can. I just needed a minute." He looked at the screen, and then tapped the button to confirm. A minute later, it told him the action was complete.

"How do you feel?" Caleb asked.

"Free."

They stared at the screen until it dimmed and turned off.

In the renewed darkness, Caleb said, "When does your sister arrive?"

"I don't know the details yet." In Théo's car as they drove out of Paris to Charles de Gaulle airport, Fatima remained on the phone until they parked near the terminal.

She'd said, "Your ticket will be at the desk. Pick it up and get through security as quickly as you can. If Mum calls the police, I don't know how fast they can alert the airports. Your ticket will tell you what gate your flight leaves from. Get to the gate but keep out of view. And Kai?"

"Yes?"

"Don't cry."

"I'm not crying."

"He's not," Théo agreed.

He heard Fatima's sigh as it came from the car's speakers. "But you'll want to, as soon as Théo leaves you and you're alone. I'm your sister. I know you. But don't cry. Okay? You can't draw that kind of attention."

He didn't cry. But as soon as he was alone, after Théo stood with him at the ticket desk and then waved at him as he went through security, he walked to his gate, found a seat in the corner, and he kept his head low. He remembered how much he hated flying.

"I thought of you," he told Caleb now. "When I was waiting to get on the plane. I was terrified of flying, but I said to myself, 'Caleb is not afraid.' And I willed myself to stop feeling that fear. I clenched my fists and my jaw, and I said, 'Stop it.'"

"Did it work?"

"No. Not exactly. I was still afraid. But I was also determined. When I got on the plane, I took my seat, and I fastened my seatbelt and then closed my eyes, and I didn't open them again until we landed. I'm still scared to fly, but I know now that I can do it. I have that in me."

"You can do anything you want if you believe."

"I believe you can kiss me now."

"Your wish is my command."

They settled into each other's arms again, Kai's head on Caleb's chest, listening to the beat of his life. It was a comforting sound, his personal lullaby.

He slept. And he did not dream.

In the morning, he woke before Caleb and went downstairs. Mrs Burke was in the kitchen and Charlie was twisting his school tie into a fat knot at his neck while his cereal was soaking up the milk in his bowl.

"Welcome home," Charlie said, and Kai wanted to hug him. "I've got a new game we can play after school."

"Sounds good."

Mrs Burke said, "Hurry up, Charlie, or you'll be late for the bus."

He kissed her only after she reminded him to, and on his way out of the kitchen he offered Kai a high five. It was so out of the ordinary that Kai obliged.

"He likes you," Mrs Burke said when they were alone. "And he's not the only one, I see."

"Sorry."

"Don't apologise. I knew Caleb would like you from the minute you arrived. I could see it."

"I will move out."

"Hold your tongue. I'm not suggesting you should move out. But you remember the rule I gave you when you came here? No bedroom guests."

"I'm sorry."

"Stop apologising. I know I treat him like my baby sometimes, but I understand that he's an adult. I don't want him to grow up, but kids have a way of doing that regardless. Just be cautious. You boys are not the only people in this house, okay?"

Kai hugged her. And she must have felt from the tightness of his arms how much he needed it, so she hugged him back.

"Is there something wrong?"

Kai sat at the table and picked up one of the coasters so that he had something to occupy his hands. "My parents. They don't agree with my lifestyle."

She took the seat opposite him. "Don't call it a lifestyle. I said this to Caleb a couple of years ago. Saying 'lifestyle' makes it sound like a choice, and it isn't. You can choose to live a hedonistic lifestyle, or a frugal one. You can't choose who you are. I don't know your parents or your circumstances, but while you are in this house, you are free to be you." She tapped the table.

"Just be discreet. Charlie's old enough to be consciously aware, but I don't want him thinking about sex before he's old enough to make an informed decision about it."

"There is something else," Kai said. "The reason I returned early. My parents found out that I am gay, and I left. I'm worried that they may try to find me. Here."

Mrs Burke nodded as she contemplated his words. Then she asked, "What is the age of majority in France?"

"Consent is fifteen. But you are an adult from the age of eighteen."

"It's awful, having to walk away from your parents. But the law is on your side. You're an adult. You have a right to do as you see fit."

"Mrs Burke?"

"Charlotte."

"Thank you. For everything."

"You can repay me by putting the bins out."

"Deal."

It was that simple. In exchange for taking the bins to the kerb, Mrs Burke accepted him for who he was. There was no greater kindness.

When he showered and returned to his bedroom, Caleb was awake, browsing his phone in bed.

"Fatima will call soon."

"We should get you a new phone today. You can't carry around a massive tablet every time you want to make a call. Do you want to be alone when she rings?"

"No."

Caleb showered and dressed and when Mrs Burke went to

work, they sat on the couch with Kai's body pressed into Caleb's side, and the iPad sat on the coffee table. He leaned forward and lit up the screen every few minutes to make sure it was still switched on.

"You haven't seen her in six years? Not even a video call?"

"No."

"Are you excited or nervous?"

"Both, I think." When the tablet rang and the name Benoît appeared on screen, Kai swiped to answer it.

On speaker, Fatima said, "Kai? Are you safe?"

"Yes. I'm here with Caleb."

Caleb said, "Hi, Fatima. He's safe. I've got him."

"Are you in Ireland yet?" Kai asked.

"No, we're still in Sweden. Avery is still packing. Our flight is this afternoon. We arrive in Cork at seven thirty-five."

"Why Cork?" Caleb asked. "We're in Dublin."

"Cork isn't our final destination. We're heading north."

"I thought you were coming to see me."

"Can you get to Cork?"

"What's in Cork?" Caleb asked. "Where are you going?"

Fatima said, "Kai. Do you remember I said there's a place for us? Somewhere we can belong?"

"Yes, but I don't understand."

"It's outside Limerick. It's a place called Runaway Bay."

"What is it?" Kai asked.

"It's home. Will you come? At least come and see us. I miss you."

"We'll be there. Cork Airport?"

"It's tiny," Caleb said. Blink and you'll miss it."

Fatima said, "Try not to miss it. We'll wait for you."

When she hung up, Kai took Caleb's hands. "Will you come with me?"

"I wouldn't miss it."

"Do you know where Cork is?"

"We can follow the signs. Or I can get onto the airfield and take Colin's Cessna. We could be there in two hours or so."

"No way. I'm not strapping into a tin can with you. And you don't have your licence yet, anyway."

"Where's your sense of adventure?"

"On the ground where it belongs."

They stood up.

"Fine," Caleb said. "We'll take the Vespa like boring people do."

28.
CALEB

They stopped at a roadside café called Ma tha's. Caleb could just about see the dirty outline of the missing R. The blue glow of the bug zapper above the door made the café look inviting only to insects, but Caleb and Kai were hungry. They'd been on the road for over two hours.

Getting out of Dublin hadn't been easy. It took them more than forty minutes to weave through town and another twenty as they sat in a line of traffic that had slowed down to rubberneck at an accident. As they passed the overturned car, Caleb felt Kai's arms pull tighter around his waist. An ambulance hugged the side of the road, its lights off and its siren silent. Caleb couldn't tell if that was good news or bad.

Another hour and Kai tapped him on the arm and shouted, "Can we stop for food?"

Martha's was the only place they'd seen in the last eight kilometres. It was a squat brick building with three picnic benches outside and, inside, the patrons eyed them with suspicion. For a place so run down, it was busier than the ladies' toilet in a gay bar.

They took their food outside and sat at one of the tables with their coats zipped up against the freezing air, listening to the hum of the bug killer and the whine of traffic on the road.

Kai unfurled the greaseproof paper around his burger and inspected the contents. He pulled out the pickle slice and ate it.

"Disgusting," Caleb said.

"You don't like pickles?"

"I'd rather eat snails. Oh, wait. You do that too, don't you?"

Kai laughed. "Every day for breakfast. No. We just sell them to tourists, and you guys buy into the elitist hype."

"Stop ruining my opinion of you, Monsieur Kateb."

Kai bit into his burger and looked away.

"Did I say something wrong?"

"No. My father is Monsieur Kateb."

"Maybe you need a new name."

"Maybe I do." He dipped his fries in a small pot of mayonnaise and Caleb shuddered. He'd forgotten Kai put mayo on his chips instead of ketchup. Caleb had tried it once. He'd never do it again.

He pulled up a map on his phone. "According to this, if we were in a car, we'd have another three hours to go. But the moped struggles to hit fifty kilometres an hour, so I'm going to guess maybe five hours. If we're lucky."

"I didn't think Ireland was that big," Kai said.

"Four hundred and eighty-six kilometres from top to bottom. We learned that in school. How big is France?"

"I have no clue. Bigger?"

"Everything's bigger than Ireland." He looked in the direction they'd been travelling before they stopped for lunch. The horizon was blurred by rain and the clouds were swollen and bruised. Caleb didn't believe in omens, but he said, "We should get back on the road. We'll make it to Cork in time to meet your sister, but we'll never make it back home before midnight. We'll have to find a cheap hotel to stay in."

"One room?" Kai asked, wrapping up the end of his burger to discard.

"I promise not to pounce on you in the night. I'll even keep my gloves on."

"I think we should staple them to your sleeves."

Caleb smiled and tossed his rubbish in the nearby bin. "That might be a good idea."

He couldn't wait to share a bed with Kai again.

They got back on the road once Caleb texted his mum to say they'd gone on a road trip and would be back in a day or two. He shut his phone off before she tried calling him. He didn't need to hear the worry in her voice. But to ease her mind, he ended his text with, *Yes, I've got my meds*, and he added a couple of heart emojis.

Then he sent another text. *And my watch is fully charged.*

When the rain hit, it came hard and cold. His jeans were soaked but he was glad he'd worn a waterproof coat and the leather gloves his mum bought him for his birthday. They'd dry out in the hotel.

When the storm finished its tantrum, he felt as if they were chasing the splintered sun as they rode southeast. And as the miserable January afternoon floundered towards evening and the sun ricocheted off the wet tarmac to blind him, he slowed the moped to compensate. When he blinked, he remembered the upturned car just outside Dublin, and he wasn't prepared to risk Kai's life that way.

Twilight stole the colour out of everything and his headlight on the tertiary road ahead was a spit in the dark. When they arrived at a junction, Kai tapped his shoulder and pointed. The sign said they were eighteen kilometres from Cork. If they could skirt the eastern roads, they could circle around to the airport in thirty or forty minutes.

"What time is it?" he called over his shoulder.

"Twenty past six."

"We're in good time," he said. He pulled his visor back down and turned onto the N-road into Cork. He'd be glad of the brighter nights now that they'd got Christmas and the new year out of the way, though it'd be a few months before they'd notice the difference.

They slipped into a bay in the short-stay car park and while Kai got a ticket from the machine, Caleb searched for a local hotel. Without knowing where Fatima was staying, or how long they intended to be in Ireland, he was reluctant to book anything until speaking to her.

He watched Kai as he walked back towards the moped, and Caleb wasn't sure how this reunion would go. They had a lot in common, Kai and his sister. But she'd abandoned him six years ago. It didn't matter that she had her reasons; she'd left him behind.

"Are you ready?" he asked.

Kai handed him the parking ticket and nodded.

Inside, the terminal was warm. They stood at Arrivals, just as Caleb had done in a different airport the day before, and they waited. Kai paced, and Caleb saw the nervous tension in his jawline, his muscles clenching.

"You'll wear a hole in the floor."

Kai hugged him and buried his face against his neck. "I can't stare at the Arrivals board anymore. Tell me when they land."

Caleb wrapped his arms around him and said, "It won't be long." But five minutes before the plane was due to land, the board updated. *Expc'd. 19:55.*

Kai resumed pacing.

Caleb switched his phone back on and ignored the four messages from his mum. He'd deal with them later. He texted Jayne. *On a scale of* ☺ *to* ☹, *how are you?*

She replied with a single emoji. ☺.

By eight fifteen when the Arrivals' door opened, Kai couldn't contain his anticipation. He looked as nervous as Charlie did when he was seven years old and terrified to go downstairs on Christmas morning in case Santa hadn't arrived.

He covered his face with his hands. "Is she there?"

Caleb saw her at once. Her dark skin and unruly curls stood out against the other passengers. She had an enormous rucksack on her back, and she carried the air of a woman on a mission. A smaller, blonde woman came through the door behind her and took her hand. Caleb couldn't remember her girlfriend's name.

He leaned in and pressed his lips to Kai's shoulder. "She

looks just like you."

Kai removed his hands from his eyes and sucked his lips into his mouth so that they disappeared.

Fatima Kateb said, "*Oh mon Dieu*," and ran to him. She drew him into her arms and smothered him in kisses. At first, he was rigid, his hands at his sides, but the longer she held him, the more he sank into her. His fingers gripped the rear straps of her rucksack as he tried to hug her.

The blonde girl reached her hand out. "You must be Caleb. I'm Avery."

And when Caleb took her hand, she pulled him into an embrace. They parted quickly and watched the reunited brother and sister who held each other forever.

"You would think they haven't seen each other in six years," Avery said.

"Sorry," Fatima said, pulling away from her brother. She hugged Caleb but returned to Kai's side a second later. She said something in French, and he responded.

Avery nudged Caleb. "She says you are cute."

Fatima said, "I can see why he likes you."

"Well, we can't stand around here all night. Maybe we should leave before my head gets any bigger."

"Where are you staying?" Kai asked.

Caleb said, "We haven't booked anywhere yet, so hopefully wherever you're staying will have a room available."

"There is no need. We have booked a suite. You can stay with us. And tomorrow we go to Limerick." Fatima hugged Kai again. "I cannot believe how big you've become."

"You must be shrinking," he said.

Caleb couldn't leave the moped behind, and Avery suggested she travel on the back of it with him so that brother and sister could catch up.

"Do you mind?" Kai asked Caleb.

"Of course not. I'll put the address in my phone, and we'll meet you there." They kissed, and Fatima made a cooing sound as she fluttered her eyelids.

"Adorable," she said.

Kai punched her shoulder and laughed. It looked, to Caleb, as though they hadn't been separated for more than a quarter of their lives. But as he and Avery followed them out of the terminal, he saw that they were walking a few feet apart, as if the instant familiarity gave way when they turned, and now they remembered that they'd been estranged for so long.

Caleb and Avery couldn't have much of a conversation as they followed Fatima's rental car into Cork. Avery's hands clung to his waist with just enough effort to support herself, the way Kai had done in the early days until their time on the bike became a hug. But when they got to the hotel, Avery gave her bag to Fatima and said, "We'll go into the bar. You two come down when you're ready for dinner." She took Caleb's sleeve and dragged him towards the bar.

"Shouldn't we find out what room you're in?"

"Calm down. Just give them some time to catch up. Let's get a drink so I can quiz you about Ireland." She winked.

When they got a table in the corner, she said, "You and I don't matter tonight. Tomorrow, maybe. But for now, the only thing that matters is that they can talk."

Caleb looked at the door from the bar to reception as if he

could see them from their table. "Kai has told me as much as I think he can about what happened."

"You cannot ask me," Avery said. "Fatima's story is hers to tell."

"Aren't you part of her story?"

"Fatima and I are one story. She and Kai are another."

Caleb raised his glass. "I'm beginning to think everyone from France speaks like Yoda."

She clinked. "You do not study the ways of the Jedi in high school?"

"I'll raise it at the next PTA. Why don't you tell me your story, then? Who is Avery and why is she here?"

"That's a very big question. 'Who' is a mystery even to me. As for 'why', isn't it obvious?" she took the saltshaker from its tray at the edge of the table and spread some of its contents on the dark table. In it, she wrote *Adorer*.

"I recognise that word, but it seems to me that I'm going to have to start learning French."

"It's the language of love, after all," she said.

Caleb looked at the salt. "Ah-door-ay," he said, sounding it out.

She laughed. "Close enough." And then she took his hand and studied his palm, tracing the creases with her finger.

"What do you see?"

"The letter K—for Kai, I hope." She leaned closer. "But what is this? The letter A?"

He looked. He hadn't noticed before. From the base of his fingers towards the pad of his thumb, the jagged creases spelled KA, although the crossbar of the A wasn't as pronounced. Caleb smiled and made a fist as though he was capturing the letters. "Alice."

"Who?"

He tapped his fist to his heart. "A long story."

"Will she come between you and Kai?"

"No. She loves him as much as I do."

"Perhaps not *as* much?"

"Precisely as much."

"Now I am intrigued."

Caleb glanced at the door, knowing that Kai and Fatima would need some time to talk, but feeling lost without him at his side. And then he told Avery about Alice.

When he was done, she said, "Now I see. Without Alice, there can be no Kai and Caleb."

"Kaileb," Caleb said, trying out a couple's name.

She shook her head. "I did not realise you were twelve years old."

When he was done laughing, Caleb said, "Sometimes, he does make me feel like a lovestruck twelve-year-old."

"I am glad to hear it. When you go to bed in love, you wake up younger. This is why love never dies—because it does not age."

"Thank you, Master Kenobi." He finished his drink and ordered another round, and he was glad now that Kai and Fatima had left them alone. If they were to be the sphere that contained brother and sister, they would have to get along. When he came back to the table, he said, "This place you are visiting tomorrow. What is it?"

"Runaway Bay? It is a community, I suppose. Fatima spoke

to the man who established it, so she knows more. But she says it is a utopia."

"Does such a place exist?"

She shrugged. "Tomorrow, we will find out, no?"

And they clinked their glasses again. Caleb wasn't sure if a utopia was real, in any sense, but he was keen to find out.

29.

KAI

xcept for the dusty shard of daylight that woke him, the room was dark and sombre.

Next to him on the pull-out bed, Caleb had turned onto his side, facing away from him, and when Kai woke, he'd been huddled against Caleb's back for warmth. He slipped his hand out from under Caleb's hip and crawled out of bed. They hadn't thought to pack any clothes before jumping on the moped and journeying half the length of Ireland, so he pulled on yesterday's jeans and sweater. He took one of the two door keys and let the door ease closed behind him.

Fatima's suite was made up of a living area with a dresser, desk and chair, side table and a wall-hanging TV. A small couch turned into a comfortable pull-out bed. Beyond the living area was a functional bathroom with a separate shower room, and then Fatima and Avery's bedroom. He had sat cross-legged on the bed last night when Caleb and Avery stayed downstairs in the bar, and he'd listened to her as she gave him the CliffsNotes version of her life since she disappeared.

Kai took a small table in the dining room and hugged a cup of fresh coffee. He tuned out the noise of the diners who were enjoying their full Irish breakfasts, and he stared through the large window at the evergreens that lined the neat garden and shielded the hotel from the main road.

Last night, Fatima said, "You understand why I had to leave, don't you?"

"We've been through that already. I just can't believe you're here now."

"Do you really think they heard my voice on the phone?"

He recalled his escape from their Paris home. Dad had been shoving his shoulder against the bedroom door and, as he pushed it open wider, Kai was certain he'd heard Mum say, "Fatima?"

"If she did, surely she wouldn't believe it was you."

Fatima had stretched out across the bed, with her head in his lap. "They've declared me legally dead. I don't think there's a judge that would take her seriously anymore."

Kai stroked her hair like he used to when he was younger, before she left and broke his world. Sitting with her now, he felt as though he was thirteen again, holding Fatima's confidence and sharing secrets. A lifetime had passed, but it went in a blink. He sighed.

"Why do you sigh so hard?" She sat up and touched his sad face.

"They're our parents."

"You think of them as Mum and Dad, but they will not think of you as Son. Why should they be your parents if you cannot be their child?"

"They raised me. They raised us."

"They gave birth to straight children. And that isn't us."

"They could have come around to the idea. Lots of parents do."

"And many don't, Kai. The world is filled with strays, men and women who are forced to leave home to escape bigoted parents. Many are beaten. Some are murdered. And every single one of them is just a statistic. And for each one that makes it— for every kid that escapes—two more never speak up. They're living in quiet fear that one day their parents will find out the truth and that will be their end. Be thankful you don't have to suffer that."

"But they're Mum and Dad. Everyone needs a Mum and Dad."

"Why?"

"Because."

Fatima shook her head and took his hands. She held them tight. "You haven't started grieving yet. But you will. They are not the parents you need to have. You're free now. Whatever you do from this moment on is your choice to make. Yours and no one else's."

"I can't just forget about them."

"I'm not asking you to. You'll always have whatever good memories you've already made. I'm just thankful you've had more good ones than bad."

Kai had swung his legs off the edge of the bed to sit up and she joined him.

"Was it really that bad for you?" he asked.

She didn't answer at once. She reached into her rucksack and pulled out a small wooden keepsake box. She gave it to him.

"What is it?"

"Just open it."

When he unhooked the clasp and lifted the lid, he saw a photograph of a very young but unmistakable Fatima grinning at the camera. In her arms was a baby with the fullest head of black hair he'd ever seen.

"Me?"

She nodded.

He turned the photo over but there was nothing written on the back, no names or loving sentiment.

In the box beneath the photo, there was a handwritten note, as well as a thin silver chain with a pendant that said F+A.

"Read it," Fatima said.

"But it's private."

"Read it."

He unfolded the square of paper.

Renounce the devil and pray that you return to the Kingdom of Heaven. You are no daughter of mine. You are Sin. And Sin is evil. If you do not return to the Lord's arms, you will burn in Hell, and I will not mourn you.

—N

The page blurred as Kai let the tears come. "When did she give you this?"

"She pushed it under my bedroom door that morning. This was the last straw. This is why I left."

"She signed it *N*?"

"Nabila. She couldn't even call herself my mother. We were already strangers."

He hugged her. "Why did you keep it?"

As she took the letter from him and folded it, she said, "Because I needed the reminder. Every time I wanted to call her and ask her forgiveness, I would look at her note and it would stop me. She didn't want me to apologise for being gay. She wanted me to be straight. And I couldn't do that."

This morning, sitting in the dining hall and staring at the evergreens, he understood her logic. He wanted to call home, to say he was sorry and beg for Mum's forgiveness.

But she wasn't that kind of woman. And he couldn't live a lie.

He finished his coffee and got another from the self-service counter.

When the others joined him, Caleb slipped into the chair at his side and kissed him. His hair was wet from the shower, and his eyes were bright. Fatima and Avery sat opposite.

Fatima said, "Did you sleep well?"

He shrugged. He didn't remember falling asleep. He recalled hugging her for half the evening, crying against her hair. And then he woke this morning.

"Who's ready for a road trip?" she asked.

Avery lowered her forehead to the table and groaned. "Why

are you shouting?"

Fatima rubbed her back. "Finally, we have met somebody who can outdrink Avery."

"We didn't even have that much," Caleb said.

Kai laughed. "That reminds me, I should probably message Emily soon."

"Who?" Fatima asked.

"Just a friend from college. Another one who likes to drink."

Caleb said, "The Irish aren't all alcoholics, you know."

"No, pumpkin. Just the cute ones."

"Pumpkin?"

"Oh my God," Avery said, perking up. She propped her elbows on the table and rested her chin on her hands. "This is too cute. You haven't firmed up your pet names yet?"

"Can I take Pumpkin off the table?" Caleb asked.

"No way," Fatima said. "Because from now on, I think I'm going to call you Pumpkin, too. Is that okay, Pumpkin?"

Avery said, "Yeah, Pumpkin. Is that okay?"

"Sorry, Pumpkin," Kai said.

"Cut it out."

They laughed, and Kai threw his arm around Caleb's neck. He didn't know how the four of them could feel so comfortable this fast. They had come together with a weight hanging over them. But now that weight bound them.

"What is a runaway bay, anyway?" Kai asked.

Fatima said, "I hope it's the end of the road."

They took Fatima's rental car north to Limerick, and from there they crossed into County Clare, passed Ennis, and then out towards the coast. The sun was burning through the clouds two and a half hours later as they pulled up at a small road sign that read, *Lahaine Beach 5km.*

Fatima pulled the car into the side of the road. She wanted to pose for a photograph by the sign, as though Lahaine Beach meant something to anyone.

"Is it famous?" Kai asked.

"Maybe it was in a movie or something?" Caleb said.

Fatima handed Kai her phone to take some pictures of them. "It's the secret location of Runaway Bay."

Caleb said, "It's not so secret if you know the location."

They got back in the car and continued their journey, and Kai could feel the excitement between Fatima and Avery in the front seats. In the back, Caleb linked his fingers with Kai's and tried to look enthusiastic.

And then they crested a hill with a wooden sign that said, *Runaway Bay. Private Property.*

As they drove down the sandy road, they saw the dark ocean ahead of them that stretched out from the V-shaped coast towards a hazy horizon. The waves tortured the beach with foamy spray.

"Look," Caleb pointed.

Out in the ocean, a dark speck bobbed among the waves.

"Who the hell goes surfing in January?"

Kai squeezed Caleb's hand. "Aren't you exactly the kind of person who goes surfing in January?"

"Honestly, if I had a wetsuit, I'd be straight in there with him."

"Wow," Fatima said. She'd turned the car to follow the narrow road and, as they veered away from the beach into a valley, they looked around.

At the end of the road, a wide turning circle gave way to a grassy area that served as a focal point in the valley. Eight detached cottages surrounded it, giving it the feel of a close-knit community. The shared garden was bordered by red and yellow tail flower blooms as well as winter honeysuckle and, along the outer edges, a row of drooping snowdrops.

Two picnic tables stood on either side of a tall oak tree, and a tire swing hung from one of its sturdy branches.

As Fatima brought the car around the turning circle, the door of one of the cottages opened and a tall man in a pale blue tracksuit came out to greet them. In his hands, he carried a bottle of champagne and two glasses.

"Welcome," he said, as they got out of the car, and when he saw the four of them standing in the chill January air, he said, "I didn't realise there'd be four of you. Let me get more glasses." He handed the bottle to Kai and the two glasses to Caleb. "Crack it open," he said. "This is a celebration."

When he returned from his home, he gave Fatima and Avery a champagne flute each and then looked at Kai.

"Haven't you opened it yet?"

Kai looked at the bottle in his hands. The situation was surreal. He wasn't sure what was going on or why they were there. But he smiled and tore the foil off the neck of the bottle, pulling the cork free with a pop. It fizzed but didn't spill.

As Kai poured the champagne into everyone's flute, the man said, "Forgive me, I always get so excited that I forget to speak. I'm Oliver. You can call me Ollie."

"No way," Caleb said, and Kai stared at him.

Oliver winked.

"You're Oliver Lloyd."

"I used to be, yeah."

"Oliver Lloyd?" Avery asked.

Ollie said, "Long story. This young man can bore you with it later. Come on, let's take a look around."

Caleb said, "You're not having a glass?"

"I'm good, thank you." He turned. "I take it you must be Miss Kessner."

Fatima said, "Call me Félice. And this is my partner Léna, my brother Kai, and that's Caleb."

Oliver repeated their names as though he was trying to memorise them. His smile was warm and genuine.

"We have space for all four of you, but Number 8 isn't furnished yet. If you guys are planning on staying too, you'll have to share with Félice and Léna for a few months, if that's okay?"

Kai glanced at Caleb, who looked as confused as Kai felt.

Caleb said, "I don't understand. Is this some kind of holiday home thing?"

Oliver looked at Fatima. "You didn't tell them?"

"Tell us what, Tima?" Kai studied her face and waited as she swallowed her drink.

Fatima put her arm around Avery, and they leaned their heads together. "Surprise," they said.

"What's going on?"

From behind them, a voice said, "I can field this question."

When Kai turned, he saw a man around his age coming up the hill towards them. He carried a longboard, and his wetsuit was unzipped and pulled down around his waist. He wore a black hoodie that engulfed his upper body, and his short dark hair was wet and brushed forward over his forehead.

He placed his board on the grass and then kissed Oliver Lloyd.

"You're just in time," Oliver said. "This is Denis. Denis, this is everyone."

"Hi, everyone."

Oliver said, "Girls, why don't you come with me, and I'll show you to your new home."

Denis pointed at one of the picnic tables and when the three of them sat, Kai remembered sitting in Caleb's backyard on a similar bench, crying more often than not, wishing he had a way out. Two months ago, he'd never guessed that he'd have got the guy, and now—now what?

Denis smiled and brushed some wet sand off his cheek.

"That was you out on the waves?" Caleb asked.

"You surf?"

"I haven't been on a board since I was about thirteen."

"You should paddle out with me sometime. You'll love it." He let the silence draw out before saying, "Seems to me like you guys need an explanation."

Kai reached down and clasped Caleb's hand. "My sister told me this is a place for people that need somewhere to be alone?"

"That's a good way of putting it. I hate the word 'community' but that's pretty much what we are. Ollie bought our home just over a year ago and we've built the other cottages around us. We have planning permission for another six homes and we're aiming for more. And just over that hill, we have a few all-purpose buildings, a garage and so on."

Caleb said, "So, this isn't Airbnb?"

He laughed. "No. You won't find us on a map. We're not a tourist hotspot. We're just a bunch of people who couldn't fit in out there. So we came together here." To Kai, he said, "I think it was your sister who first reached out, am I right?"

"She hasn't told us very much, but yes, she seems to be the reason we're all here."

"If Ollie believes in her, that's the only reason you found this place. I don't get involved in the politics of who lives where. I trust his judgement."

Caleb said, "Are all the houses occupied?"

"Six of them are. Number 7 is where Félice and Léna will live, but I get the feeling those are pseudonyms."

Kai swallowed his words before he said anything.

Denis shook his head. "We all have our reasons, don't worry. This is a private community, and that's the way it will stay. Everyone here respects that." He pointed. "Number 8 is yours if you want it, but only when the interior is finished."

"What's the catch?"

"Honestly? Don't be a dick. That's about it. Don't get me wrong, it's not rent-free. We're not a charity, as much as Ollie wishes we were. But you'll find the rent is reasonable, and the people are amazing."

"Are they all gay?" Kai asked. It still felt new saying the word out loud.

"If you have to label it, most of them are. That cottage there, next to ours, is Annabelle and her father. She's Ollie's wingman. This place wouldn't exist without her hard work. If you need anything, she's the one to ask." He stood up and stuffed his fists into his hoodie. "Anyway. There's no pressure. Talk to your sister. Have a look around. We're having a get-together this evening, so you'll meet everyone then. I'll catch you later." He held out his fist and they bumped it. "If you do decide to stick around, I expect to see you out in the water one day soon. I've got a couple of spare boards, so you've no excuse."

He walked away.

Kai watched him go, and then he turned to Caleb, who was staring towards the ocean.

"Is this for real?" Kai asked, folding his arms around Caleb's shoulders.

Caleb twisted so that his back was against Kai's chest, and he leaned into him. "Are we dead? Is this heaven?"

"Why wouldn't Fatima have told me this last night? Do you really think we can stay here?"

He felt Caleb sigh. "I'd love to, but we have lives."

"Do we?"

Caleb turned and looked into his eyes. "I," he said, but closed his mouth. He kissed Kai. And then he said, "My parents would flip. Which, to be honest, isn't enough to stop me. Could you live with me? For real?"

Kai looked at the small cottages, and the winter flowers that bordered the grass. And he inhaled the sea air. "If you promise not to wake me at five every morning to go surfing."

"Spoilsport." Caleb's phone rang, but he didn't pull it from his jeans pocket. "What about you? As soon as I finish my flying lessons, I can walk away. Mum will just have to get used to it. But you have university."

The phone stopped.

Started again.

"I don't want to go back to college. Maybe I can get a job. Or find a local university here where I can study something different. Are you going to answer that?"

"I probably should, shouldn't I?" He leaned in and kissed Kai again, and then pulled the phone from his pocket.

Kai said, "It would be good to be near Fatima again."

Caleb answered his phone with a smile. "Hey, Abigail. How's it going? I thought you were my mum calling to spoil my fun."

The call wasn't on speaker, but Kai heard some of Abigail's words. "Jayne," she said. "Heart," she said.

Caleb's eyes blinked. They were wet.

When he hung up, he stared at the screen until Kai said, "What's wrong?"

"It's Jayne," Caleb said. "Her transplant has failed."

30.

CALEB

aleb stood up. "We should go. I should go. I need to get back." He tapped his pockets and remembered that his keys to the Vespa were back in Fatima's hotel room. "How am I supposed to get home?"

Kai held him. His cheeks were burning as though he'd been slapped. But he didn't have time to stand around.

And yet his brain wasn't working. "I don't know how to get home."

Abigail had said Jayne's transplant was unsuccessful. "She's in a lot of pain. She doesn't have long. Can you come?"

"Yes," he'd said before hanging up. But his throat was already tight, and his voice was dry.

"It's okay," Kai said now. "Come on. I'll sort it." He took Caleb by the hand and led him towards Fatima's new home.

Inside, Caleb didn't take notice of the room or its furnishings. He didn't even know who was there.

Kai said something in French and Fatima responded. Avery put her arms around Caleb's neck.

"I'm sorry," she said.

He looked at her. For a moment, he couldn't recall her name. "I have to go," he said.

Fatima handed him her car keys. "Take the car. You can bring it back whenever."

"No," Kai said. "He doesn't have a license for a car, and I don't think he's capable of driving."

"I can drive."

"No, you can't."

Fatima said something to Avery, then she said, "I'm sorry, Oliver. I should drive him back to Dublin."

The smile on Oliver's confused face set into resolve. "I understand, but if it's urgent, I can have a car here in a minute." He pulled his phone from his pocket and dialled. "Scott, are you in the garage? I need a favour."

Caleb looked at him, this tall man in a blue tracksuit who exuded the confidence of a guy whose demands were never refused.

When Oliver Lloyd ended the call, he said, "Scott will take him. If you want to go with him, you can, but Scott will get him there faster."

Caleb felt Kai's fingers slip into his and give his hand a squeeze. "Fatima can drive us. We don't mean to put you out."

"It's no trouble. Scott has been itching to take the bird out for weeks."

"The bird?"

Caleb said, "I need to go. I'm sorry."

A car pulled up outside a minute later. "This is Scott," Oliver said. "He's been my driver for years. He'll get you there in no time."

The black Subaru SUV idled outside the cottage. The only thing Caleb could think about was Jayne and getting back to Dublin before it was too late. Somebody slipped into the back-seat beside him and it took him a second to realise it was Kai.

Outside the car, Fatima said, "Are you sure you don't want us to come with you?"

"We'll be fine," Kai said. "We'll see you soon, okay?"

"Godspeed." To the driver, Oliver said, "I'll call ahead and let them know you're coming."

Caleb hadn't told Oliver Lloyd the name of the hospital, so how was he going to call them? But as they pulled away from Runaway Bay, he noticed that he turned north instead of south. A couple of miles later, they pulled into an airfield.

Scott left them in the backseat of the car for a few minutes while he went inside.

Kai took Caleb's hand and said, "Are you okay?"

Caleb studied his face. He had already mapped those freckles in his mind, and he knew where the larger clusters were and how dark they should be against Kai's brown skin. But what he didn't understand was what he'd just said.

"What?"

"Are you all right?"

He shook his head. Jayne was dying. How could he be all right?

Scott came back and opened the rear door. "This way," he said, and Kai ushered Caleb out of the car.

Behind one of the hangars, Scott led them to a small helicopter. He pulled a baseball cap over his head. "We can be in Dublin in under an hour."

"Oh," Kai said.

Caleb looked at him. And in that instant, he remembered every touch, every word Kai had ever uttered. Every glance and smile and tortured breath.

"Kai," he said. He held his hands, pulled him close. "We need to go. Can you do this? For me?"

Kai stared at the helicopter. Caleb could feel the fear emanating from his pores.

"For Jayne," Kai said. And he climbed into the helicopter.

The blades whirred to life. Scott radioed the tower. And when the landing gear lifted off the concrete, Kai's body tensed.

And grateful for the interruption to his thoughts, Caleb put his arm around Kai's shoulders. "We're okay. Trust me."

Kai nodded. He refused to look out of the windows.

The helicopter banked to the right. And under different circumstances, Caleb would have glued his eyes to the horizon. But he kept his focus on Kai.

"Are you okay?"

Kai smiled, but it was brief, and it disappeared as Scott tilted the body before raising her altitude.

Green fields and tiny houses stole beneath them.

As they approached Dublin from the skies, Scott handed Caleb a headset. He pulled the cans on and heard Scott say, "I'll not be able to drop you on the hospital helipad; not without getting Oliver in trouble. How close do you need me to get?"

"As close as possible," he said. He pointed. "But I need to go home first. Head north. Do you see those fields? Can you set her down? I'll be five minutes, tops."

"Kid, are you going to get me shot by a farmer?"

"Just five minutes. That's all."

Scott veered towards the row of fields.

"What are you doing?" Kai shouted above the noise of the motor and the thump of the blades above them.

Caleb pressed his lips against Kai's ear. "I need to make a stop. Can you trust me?"

When the helicopter set down on the winter-browned grass, Scott said, "Five minutes. But if a farmer comes over that hill with a shotgun, I'm taking off. Got it?"

"Five minutes," Caleb agreed.

He took off at a sprint and he'd jumped the fence onto the main road before he realised Kai was coming along behind him.

They ran. Caleb almost went over on his ankle as he came around the corner at the end of his street, but he rolled with it and carried on running. He burst through the front door.

"Caleb? I've been worried sick. Where on earth have you been?"

"Can't stop. Going out again."

He dashed upstairs, and Kai didn't follow. He heard him saying something to his mum, but he wasn't paying attention. He went to his room, grabbed a backpack and put a few things in it. And then he went into his mum's bedroom, searching through her wardrobe.

Downstairs, he said, "Sorry, Mum. It's Jayne."

"Go," she said. "Give her my love."

Caleb hugged her and she kissed his cheek.

He said, "I don't have time to talk, but me and Kai—we're a couple now."

"I know, sweetheart. Now go."

"You sure?"

"Go."

They left. Kai took the bag from him. "What's all this?"

"I'll tell you on the way. Come on."

When they got back to the field, Scott saw them running and started the engine. "That was the longest five minutes of my life," he said.

They took to the air. "That way," Caleb said, pointing out the direction to the hospital.

"How close can I get without dying?" Scott asked.

"All the way."

"I can't land on a hospital's helipad."

"Squawk an emergency. 7700. You land, we jump, you go."

"Look, kid, as much as I understand your urgency, I can't do it. I can't fake an emergency and put the entire hospital at risk."

Caleb sulked. But he knew it was true. And when Scott set the helicopter down at the side of a disused railway line half a mile from the hospital, Caleb shook his hand.

"I owe you one."

"It's not me you owe, kid. It's Ollie."

They watched as the helicopter lifted off the ground and disappeared back towards Limerick.

"What time is it?" Caleb asked, hefting the backpack over his shoulder.

"Just after three," Kai said.

"Come on."

By the time they got to the hospital, he was sweating, and the sun was low in the sky.

"Woah," the security guard said as they stumbled through the automatic doors. "Slow down."

"It's Jayne," Caleb said, steadying his breathing and looking at the guard in his black suit.

"Oh, shit. Go on then."

"Wait," Caleb said. "Can I borrow your jacket?"

"What?"

"I don't have time to explain, Darren. I'll bring it back, I swear."

Upstairs, Abigail raised her arms to stop them from going any further. "You can't go in."

Caleb cursed. "Are you serious? You told me to be here."

"I asked you to come. I didn't say you could see her."

"But it's Jayne."

"I know. Lower your voice. Can't you feel it? Can't you see what's going on?"

Caleb looked around. The family area which was usually a hive of activity was sombre and quiet. It was Death. He knew it. He'd experienced it before.

When a patient is close to the end, the other kids gather in the family room, and they sit in a semicircle. They don't talk. They don't move. They sit there until it is over.

Caleb caught the eye of one of the young patients, a girl no older than Jayne, but he didn't know her name. She was new. But even she understood what was going on.

He pressed his lips together. "I'm sorry," he said to Abigail.

He was aware of Kai's hand on his back, a lifeline that grounded him.

"It's all right," a voice said. "Let them through."

Caleb looked up. Mr Goddard was wearing a disposable apron and surgical gloves, and his face mask was pulled down under his chin.

Abigail said, "Connor, I must advise you. Your daughter's safety is paramount."

"She's dying," Mr Goddard said, and his voice fractured on the word. "She'd want him there."

Abigail shook her head. "It's hospital policy."

"Fuck policy," Connor Goddard said, and the swear word sounded harsh and violent on his lips. He led them through to Jayne's room.

Caleb stopped outside the door. He closed his eyes.

And Kai was there, pulling him into his arms. "Shush," he said, his lips pressed against Caleb's cheek. "You can do this."

"I don't think I can."

"You know you can. She's counting on you."

Caleb nodded. He was strengthened by Kai's presence. "We've been through a lot, haven't we?" He couldn't bring himself to enter Jayne's room.

"Everything we've faced has brought us here. Every stumble, and every fall. There isn't anything you've been through in your life that hasn't contributed to you being here right now. This is what your life is about, Caleb. It's Jayne. And all the other Jaynes that will ever be. You love them. And you will always be there for them."

Caleb looked at him. And Kai touched his chest, his fingers resting over the shirt where the scar of his transplant surgery was.

"Not everyone has a heart, Caleb. But you? Yours is big enough to encompass us all."

Caleb nodded and kissed him. And they stepped into Jayne's room.

She was tiny. Her body was thin, and her skin was grey. The first few weeks after a transplant were the hardest. Her new heart was a foreign object, and the rest of her organs would have set up a picket line. Organs don't like intruders. They would have done everything they could to tell the new heart to piss off. The sole point of immunosuppressants was to trick the body into accepting the new organ. "I'm one of you," it said. "I belong here."

But Jayne's regime hadn't worked.

"Hey, champ," Caleb said, looking down at her.

Mrs Goddard cried, and Mr Goddard put his hand on her shoulder.

Jayne's eyes rolled in her head until she could focus on him. "Dude." Her lips were cracked, and her neck was hollow. "I look as grey as Mr Michaels now, don't I?"

He looked at Mr Goddard, who nodded. Caleb and Kai hadn't scrubbed up. And Mr Goddard hadn't pulled his mask back over his face. Contamination was no longer an issue.

Caleb took her hand. She was cold.

"You will never look like Mr Michaels. He was far prettier than you."

She laughed. Or rather, the sound that came from her throat

was a weak approximation of laughter. Her sticky grey spittle sprayed on her grey chin.

He held her sunken eyes. "On a scale of happy to sad, how do you feel?"

"Frowny face," she coughed. "I want to go to sleep."

"Don't go to sleep." He tightened his fingers around her hand. Over his shoulder, he said, "Mr Goddard. Can I have a word?"

She was reluctant to let go of him, but he brought her hand to his lips and kissed it. And then she closed her eyes. He stepped outside with Mr Goddard and told him his plan.

And Mr Goddard said, "She's my baby girl."

"I know."

Mr Goddard shook his hand.

Caleb took some things out of his backpack and handed the bag to Kai. "Give me five minutes. You know where to meet me."

Kai hugged him. "Are you sure?"

"I promised her."

He walked away, and as he did, he pulled the security guard's jacket on over his shirt.

On the roof, he strung some Christmas lights across the walls. He pushed the button on the battery packs to light them up. He connected his phone to a Bluetooth speaker, and he pulled a couple of blankets out from the service hatch to spread on the ground. The last time he'd been up here was with Kai, the day they'd first kissed.

He stood by the wall, and he looked out across Dublin as the sun set on the western horizon. Fatima and Avery were out there somewhere. And Mum and Charlie. And Dad. Joanne. People he knew, and people he'd never know.

He'd taken Charlie's clip-on bowtie from their house, and he was attaching it to his shirt collar when the door opened. Kai came through, pushing a wheelchair. In it, Jayne was wearing one of Caleb's Mum's dresses, a silvery, shimmery backless dress that was far too big for her. And although her head hung low so that her chin hugged her breastbone, she was smiling. Her stitches were visible at her collarbone. They didn't even have a chance to dissolve. Her drip bag attached to the pole above the chair was half empty.

Behind them, Mr and Mrs Goddard stepped onto the roof. Caleb had brought Jayne up here before. But that was strictly patients only. Her mum and dad had no clue about this place. They looked across the roof with caution.

Caleb pressed play on his phone and soft music drifted from the Bluetooth speaker. He was wearing jeans and a shirt, a bright blue bowtie and the security guard's jacket, and the Christmas lights sparkled behind him. In his hands, he carried a small box.

He said, "May I have this dance?"

Her fingers flapped when she tried to clap, but she didn't have the energy to connect them.

Her father stood before her. He kissed her forehead, and then lifted her out of the chair. And as he turned, Caleb caught Kai's eye.

Kai smiled and nodded.

Mr Goddard faced Caleb with his daughter in his arms. And Mrs Goddard unhooked the drip bag from the chair and sat it in Jayne's lap as Caleb opened the box he was holding.

"It was Mum's," he said. He slipped the corsage over her fist. The silk sweetheart roses were pale pink and he had to tighten the elastic strap under her thin wrist.

Mr Goddard gave his daughter to him. And the music swelled.

A heavy wind tousled Jayne's thin hair. Her eyelids drooped.

Caleb held her close. He stared out across Dublin. And he danced.

Her smile was electric.

She was light. She weighed so little.

And yet his heart was heavy.

Alice was quiet.

The music moved them.

And in that moment, they were the world. They were everything.

They were life.

Jayne touched his cheek. "Caleb?"

"Look at the sunset. Isn't it beautiful?" Orange light burned through the black evening clouds.

Her fingers fell from his skin.

Caleb moved. The music told him to. His hands held her tight, one behind her back, the other under her knees. She did not have the energy to stand, and so he moved for them both.

She put her arms around his neck.

"I'm scared," she said. Her voice was faint.

He nodded. "I know."

And Dublin stretched out below them. An aeroplane left a vapour trail overhead. And the music from his speaker hugged them.

He felt her breathe.

And he pressed his lips to her temple.

She sighed.

And her spirit left them.

He felt her body slacken. But he couldn't stop dancing with her. He didn't want to. He turned. And he turned.

And he turned.

And when the song ended, he held his breath. In the silence, he could hear her laughter. Her presence engulfed him. He could feel her warmth as it slipped away. And he kissed her forehead.

"Truth," he whispered. "There is only truth."

He cradled her. And he turned to Mr Goddard. He held her out to her father.

And Mr Goddard opened his arms for her.

"She is gone," Caleb said.

And Mrs Goddard fell to her knees.

Caleb unhooked his bowtie, and he dropped it to the blankets under his feet. He went to the wall at the edge of the roof.

Kai came to him. He stood behind him and slipped his arms around his waist.

And below them, Dublin darkened into night.

Caleb leaned into him.

And he cried.

31.

KAI & CALEB

K ai stood on the tarmac outside the hangar and stared at the sky. He heard the little engine, but it took him a moment to spot it as it came into view. Caleb's Cessna held a steady line. This was it—his final skills test.

He watched the aircraft as it flew towards the west, and when the propellor stopped turning mid-flight, the nose dipped.

"That's the required stall," Colin Moore said, shielding his eyes from the sun with his hand. "Come on, kid. Fire her up again."

Kai crossed his fingers. The examiner who met them on the tarmac when they arrived looked stuffy and angry, as though the scowl on his face was a permanent feature.

"You've got Mick O'Sullivan," Colin told Caleb before he took off. "He's a hard bastard, but he's fair. Just don't mess up."

The plane had been out of view for thirty minutes before coming back. And as Colin Moore prayed that Caleb would restart the engine in time, Kai held his breath.

They waited.

And the propellor turned alive.

"Good boy," Colin said.

They watched from the ground as Caleb performed manoeuvres in the sky, and when the plane came in to land, Caleb pulled it off the runway and taxied across the concourse. Kai was about to run towards them when Colin gripped his arm. "Just wait. Watch his face."

Caleb's face through the glass was reserved. Mick O'Sullivan was saying something, and then he handed him a slip of paper. He opened the door and dropped to the ground.

As he walked past them, he nodded and said, "Colin."

"Mick."

Caleb was still in the Cessna.

"Did he pass?" Kai asked, but Mick had already gone. He repeated his question to Colin.

"I can't tell."

Kai couldn't wait any longer. He ran to the side of the small plane and, as he came around the back, he traced the letters of the call sign. They were dirty, and he wiped his fingertips on his jeans.

"Well? How did you do?"

Caleb looked at the paper in his hands, and then he said, "Get in. Do you want to go for a spin?"

"Not even."

Caleb laughed. He jumped out and kissed Kai.

"So, you passed?"

"Yeah."

Kai threw his arms around him with an ecstatic shout. And as they approached Colin, the flight instructor held his hand out.

"I knew you could do it. Congratulations."

"You're not going to ruin another shirt with scissors, are you?"

Colin laughed. "Not this time. But we still have to do a pancake fly-in sometime. So you'd better not be a stranger now that you've passed."

Kai asked, "What's a pancake fly-in?"

"It's where you fly into another city for a pancake breakfast. It's right there in the name."

Caleb shook his hand again. "We're actually leaving tomorrow. We're moving to County Clare. But I promise, the next time I'm in town, I'll be hammering at your hangar for pancakes."

They left Colin Moore after they'd pulled the Cessna into the hangar and tied it down. And then they walked out to the car park and Kai got behind the wheel of his car. The day after Jayne's passing, Oliver Lloyd had Caleb's Vespa sent home on the back of a trailer. And Kai said, "I'll learn to drive a car. Getting across the country will be quicker that way."

He completed his lessons in just over three months and passed his driving test two days ago. It wasn't even weird, driving on the wrong side of the road.

In the passenger seat, Caleb studied his pass sheet. "We can hang it next to your driving certificate."

"You'll have to buy a plane now. Maybe Oliver will let you

keep it at his airfield."

"Do you know how much those things cost? I'd have a better chance of shitting a baby."

Kai said, "Do you want a shitting baby?"

"That's not what I meant."

Kai started the engine. "I know." He drove them back to Caleb's mum's house, and on the way, Caleb was silent. He rested his temple on the side window and watched the traffic roll by. It wasn't an energy slump after passing his test, Kai knew.

"She'd be proud of you."

Caleb nodded. Before his final flight, he'd said, "This isn't for me anymore. I'm doing it for Jayne."

Abigail, the ward manager, had told them off for taking Jayne onto the roof, but then she hugged Mr and Mrs Goddard and squeezed Caleb until they'd both stopped crying. She was declared officially dead at 16:46 on January twelfth.

By the time they'd performed whatever tests or autopsies they needed to do and release her to her family, it was almost two weeks before she was cremated.

Kai helped Caleb twist his tie into a suitable knot when Caleb's trembling fingers weren't working right, and then he held him. He wasn't crying, but Kai could think of nothing else to do other than wrap his arms around him until Caleb felt comfortable with walking.

As they came downstairs that morning, Mrs Burke and Charlie were standing in the front hall. A taxi was waiting for them outside.

Mrs Burke ran her fingers over Caleb's hair, pushing it flat at the side, and Kai expected him to pull away or tell her off.

But he let her do it.

Charlie said, "Her heart wasn't strong. But yours is." He wrapped his arms around Caleb's waist for a moment, and then he was gone.

Kai led Caleb to the taxi, and when they arrived at the crematorium, Mr and Mrs Goddard welcomed them with hugs. They gathered in a small chapel, and Kai held Caleb's hand throughout. Caleb had been racked with guilt since taking her onto the hospital roof for the dance he'd promised her months before.

"It wasn't your fault," Kai told him.

"If she stayed in her bed, they could have saved her."

"There was no saving her. You should be proud that you gave her a beautiful dream."

"She didn't have to die." He'd told Kai that they could have put her on life support and found a replacement heart. But that was impossible, her doctor had said later.

When her small white coffin was taken out of the chapel to be cremated in private, Caleb stood up. His leg had been restless the whole time.

Kai followed him, and when Caleb approached Mr Goddard, he said, "Sir. I'm sorry."

Mr Goddard turned. His eyes were swollen in grief. But he shook his head. "I told you, Caleb, it wasn't your fault."

"I can't help thinking that if I didn't take her to the roof, she'd still be here."

Mrs Goddard brushed the tears from her face and pushed her hand under Mr Goddard's arm for support. "You gave her hope."

"I killed her."

"No," she said. "You saved her. I see that now. Caleb, you are an angel. My baby got to go to prom. If only just for one dance. You are not to blame. Put it out of your mind. She adored you. And because of that, you will be in my heart forever."

That night, in the last week of a cold January, Caleb sat at the picnic table in his mum's backyard, and Kai sat beside him. They were staring into the darkness of night, their backs to the house, and Kai wanted to reach out and touch him, just to let him know he was there. But they sat in silence, untouching.

Caleb had loosened his tie earlier that evening, and now he pulled it from his neck. He said, "Let's go."

Kai nodded. "Go where?"

Caleb didn't look at him. "Runaway Bay."

"Are you sure?"

"Yes. Your sister's there. We can make a life."

"Okay."

It took a few months, but when Kai had passed his driving test and Caleb officially had a pilot's license, the time had come.

Kai wasn't involved in Caleb's discussions with his mum or dad about leaving, but once it was out in the open, Mrs Burke sat with Kai at the kitchen table.

"Do you love him?"

"With all my heart."

She nodded. "When his own heart—Alice—when she gives out one day, years from now, would you give him yours?"

"He already has it. But yes. I would offer him my heart if it means he will live."

"May it never happen," she said. "Though I am glad to hear

you say it. But don't take my baby from me. I will worry. Promise me. Promise you'll bring him back every month."

"I promise to bring him back as often as he likes."

That had been three weeks ago, and every time Mrs Burke came into a room where Caleb was, she touched him, as though she was trying to imprint his skin upon her fingers.

Charlie knocked on Kai's door one evening while Caleb was having a flight lesson. He gave Kai the last cookie from a packet and said, "Can I come and visit you at your new house sometime?"

"Of course. You can stay over whenever you want."

"Will you have a PlayStation?"

"Maybe."

"Good."

And that was that. Kai sat on the edge of his bed and heard Charlie go back downstairs. Children don't need heartfelt goodbyes. They just want to know if they can play games when they see you next.

Kai started packing in those final weeks, though he didn't own a lot. He got a box from the garage and put some of his smaller things in it. And when he opened the bottom drawer of the nightstand, he saw the sky-blue scarf that his mum had knit for their fake Christmas.

He brought it to his nose and inhaled the scent of her. Fatima had been right. They would never think of him as their son, so he shouldn't think of them as his parents. But it was hard to let go. French police had called Mrs Burke two days after he escaped Paris. He hadn't asked her to lie for him, but she said, "I haven't seen him since he went home. If he comes back here,

I'll let you know." When she hung up, she said, "Fuckers." And then she laughed. She put her hand on Kai's shoulder and said, "Lies—even white lies—are bad. There is only one exception: to save a life."

"Thank you," he said.

They shared a bottle of prosecco to celebrate Caleb's pilot status, and Mrs Burke cried. She hugged them both.

"We're only going to Clare, Mum. It's not like we're jetting off to the moon."

"It might as well be," she sobbed.

Charlie said, "Can I have Caleb's room now?"

"No," Mrs Burke said.

"Of course he can," Caleb said.

That night, Kai crawled into bed beside Caleb and Caleb's arms slipped around his waist. Mrs Burke had relented on her rule about overnight visits when Caleb had a word with her one day. Kai wasn't sure she liked it, but she didn't stop it. They were adults.

In the morning, they packed their things into the back of the car and said goodbye to Dublin.

"I already miss you," Mrs Burke said before they got in the car.

As they drove away, Caleb smiled. Maybe he felt as free as Kai did.

And when they got to Runaway Bay, Fatima and Avery were standing on the grass, with Denis and Oliver, and the rest of the residents. Between them, they held up a banner that read, Welcome home, Kai and Caleb.

Their cottage had been finished before they arrived, and

there was a large bow taped to the front door.

"Your keys," Denis said, handing them two sets.

"This is still surreal," Kai said.

And when they had finished partying, Caleb put his arms around him. "Let's go home."

For a second, Kai panicked. He thought he meant Dublin. But Caleb saw his confusion and dangled his keys in front of his face.

They said good night to everyone, and Oliver shook their hands. He gave something to Caleb. When he opened his fist, Kai saw that it was another key.

"What's it for?" Caleb asked.

"You're a pilot now, right? You can take the helicopter up any time you want."

"Wow," Caleb said. "I'd love to, but I trained in a Cessna, not a chopper."

Oliver shrugged. "I guess you'll need more lessons then, won't you?"

Caleb hugged him. And then they went home.

The open fire was lit. Although it was late spring, the sea air was cold. Kai settled down in front of the flames and patted the rug beside him.

When Caleb sat, he kissed him.

"I know what I want to do now," Caleb said. "With my life, I mean." He looked at the helicopter key, turning it over in his hand. Until now, learning to fly wasn't about being a pilot. It was about achieving something, some arbitrary goal. Now, he said, "Live organ transportation. With a helicopter, I can get from one side of Ireland to the other in no time."

"And we can take weekend trips to Dublin."

"We just left Dublin, why do you want to go back?"

"I don't, but your mum made me promise."

Caleb kissed him. "I don't want to think about Dublin tonight, Mr Homeowner."

"Okay, Pumpkin," Kai said.

"I thought I took Pumpkin off the table?"

"How about I put you on the table?"

"I like the sound of that."

They lay on the rug, and the warmth of the flames blushed their skin. Kai felt Caleb's heart beating. And when he kissed the scar that streaked down his chest like a shock of lightning, he knew that the spark was his.

Caleb's heart belonged to him.

Are you a donor?

Over 100,000 transplants are performed every year across the globe.

Being on the organ donor register means that people like Caleb and Jayne can have a fighting chance at a future.

The International Registry in Organ Donation and Transplantation (IRODaT) includes a page of links to international organisations that can provide you with further information: https://www.irodat.org/?p=links.

Save a life! Become a donor.

About Simon Doyle

Simon Doyle (he/him) was born and raised in Ireland. He discovered that he could travel the world on a shoestring by reading books at a very young age. When he won a local poetry competition at the age of nine, it sparked a lifetime love of words. But he swears never to write poetry again.

His first novel release was *Runaway Train*, followed by *Runaway Skies*, in the Runaway Bay series.

He lives with three cats, two dogs, and Lucas, his human soulmate. They met in kindergarten. Where all good stories begin.

Find Simon online at www.simondoylebooks.com.

Printed in Great Britain
by Amazon